ONE KISS FROM RUIN

HARROW'S FINEST FIVE SERIES

NANCY YEAGER

To Devra —
I hope you love Daniel & Emma's
2nd-Chance romance!

All my best,
Nancy Yeager —

Published by Nyb Publishing, Inc., Boston, MA

ISBN: 978-1-946574-03-9

For my first love. You know who you are...

AUTHOR NEWSLETTER

For sample book chapters, hero introductions, and an
exclusive author Q&A, sign up for Nancy's News at
nancyyeagerbooks.com/newsletter
to receive your free copy of
Harrow's Finest Five Sneak Peeks.

15 February, in the Year of our Lord 1870

To Mr. Daniel Hallsworth, son of the late Marquess of Edensbridge:

Upon the death of Lord Hamilton Hallsworth, challenger to the title of Marquess of Edensbridge, the challenge to the title remained unsubstantiated. Therefore, the esteemed Committee for Privileges of the House of Lords invites you to solicit for reinstatement of the Marquessate of Edensbridge, with all the rights and privileges accorded thereof. We request your presence at a Committee hearing in the House of Lords on 18 March 1870 to present your case for recognition as the rightful heir to the title of Marquess of Edensbridge.

Respectfully yours,

The Hon. Mr. Charles Alby
Clerk of the Committee for Privileges
House of Lords
London, England

CHAPTER 1

Spain, March 1870

aniel Hallsworth, the once and future Marquess of Edensbridge, hung from a sail rigging and debated whether death in the Bay of Biscay was preferable to life in England. Thus far, the bay was winning.

"It won't do you any good." From the deck, Percival Carlyle, Earl of Granston and captain of the SS *Lizette,* shaded his eyes from the sun and squinted up at Daniel. "You'd survive the fall."

"Bloody bastard," Daniel muttered.

Granston was right. The most damage a plunge into the water might do would be a few broken bones, which, when healed, would no doubt ache like a son-of-a-bitch during the long, dreary English winters.

"What the hell are you doing up there, anyway? You *do* know we pay a crew to check the lines, don't you?"

Daniel uttered a few choice oaths, took in a deep drag of the crisp, salty air, then lowered himself hand-over-hand down the reef line. A few feet from the deck, he let go and dropped to his feet, which were bare, drawing Granston's scowl.

Daniel spotted a bottle of American whiskey and two glasses on the deck beside Granston. "I see you've brought sustenance."

Granston moved his gaze from Daniel's feet to his rolled-up trousers, then up to his sweat-soaked work shirt. "How does your current state contribute to restoring your reputation? We agreed you'd practice the role of a gentleman with our passengers." Granston pressed his thumb to each finger as he ticked through the passenger roster. "There will be a viscount with his wife and small children, an elderly couple, a widow and her traveling companion, a government official and his secretary. Who amongst them will want to be greeted by the future marquess in his current state?"

"There was no discussion of greeting them," Daniel said. "Only some talk of boring dinners at the captain's table." He pointed to the whiskey bottle. "Are you going to pour that swill or shall I?"

Granston snatched up the bottle and glasses before Daniel could reach them. "Just one drink, then you'll go make yourself presentable."

"Is that an order, Captain?"

Granston pulled himself up to his full height, half a head taller than Daniel, and stared down at him. "On land, we're partners in this venture. But on the water, I'm in charge."

In the five years since they'd started their shipping line, Granston had spent as much time as possible on the water, while Daniel had managed the business details and contracts from the company's offices near Bilbao. Other than occasional visits to Spain to sign paperwork and carouse with Daniel, the only time Granston spent on land was to oversee their business affairs in England, where Daniel had vowed never again to set foot. Until now.

Laughing, Daniel took the glass Granston poured and lifted it in a mock toast. For all his height and deep voice, Granston's light hair and freckled nose gave him the look of an eternal child. "Aye, aye, Captain."

Granston lifted his glass. "To the health of the marquess."

Daniel took a swig of his drink and grimaced. "I'd rather keep that last bit between us, at least until all the legal formalities are out of the way."

"Your uncle did his damnedest to wrest that title away from you and failed. You can't be worried there's anything else he can do from the grave."

Daniel worried about exactly that. While legally his uncle had never been able to prove Daniel's illegitimacy, factually it was true, and he might never be able to rest easy because of it. Perhaps if the marchioness, the only mother he'd ever known, hadn't told him the truth about his parentage on her deathbed, he would have stayed in England and fought harder to maintain marquessate and, more importantly, to remove the blight from the Hallsworth name. But there was no changing the past five years. Nor the carefree, naïve years of youth, for that matter.

"Best to be cautious for the time being, especially among our guests." Daniel took a long, slow pull of whiskey, draining the glass. "Society life will be a shock to the system after all these years."

"To hell with society, Hallsy. Once we've set foot back in England, we'll focus on pursuits of a much baser nature. Being a marquess again will add to your appeal immensely, and the fairer sex did always respond well to the look of you—something I never understood, by the way—so we'll be the toast of the town in no time."

"More likely the bane of it. And you've conveniently forgotten that if I'm to convince the Committee for Privileges of my fitness to inherit the title, I'll need to be a paragon of virtue once we're... home."

Daniel had to force out that last word. It had been so long since he'd used it to describe anything for himself. If England had truly been his home, would his uncle's supporters and gossip-mongers have been able to drive him away so easily? Would the months of canceled invitations, society mothers' snubs, even being turned away at his late father's own club have been enough to send him into exile? The summer he'd fallen in love and decided to marry had changed all meaning of belonging for him. It had no longer been about the place or the properties or even the title he was to inherit, but about making a life with *her*.

Then she'd given in to the pressure of her family. The day she'd turned him away was the day England had stopped feeling like home.

Daniel held out his glass for another steadying drink.

Granston shook his head. "Not a drop until you're fit for company. Consider it my contribution to your status as a paragon of virtue. Once you've secured the title, it will be a different story."

"And a different set of rules." Daniel scowled at the irony of being required to play the part of saint to inherit a title, often the only thing that stood between some of the worst men Daniel had ever known and Newgate prison. But he needn't play the part of the saint just yet. "You'd withhold a drink from one of your oldest friends? Even that nearly undrinkable swill?"

Granston crossed his arms over his chest.

"I just need one more day to get used to being on my best behavior, then I'll do your bidding."

"Yes, there is a certain freedom to being an outcast, isn't there?" Granston splashed another finger of spirits into Daniel's glass. "One more drink and one more day, but the least you can do is stop insulting my spirits. I'll have you know, I won this off a Yank in Kathmandu, and—"

"And you were bamboozled. You did him a favor taking it off his hands. In fact, he might have played you, after all."

Granston raised his eyebrows in feigned insult. "Now you've really crossed a line! Insulting my whiskey is one thing, but insulting my card skills is quite another."

Granston carried on with his complaints, but Daniel was only half listening. Something had caught his eye. Or rather, someone. Two Englishwomen—an elderly lady and a much younger one—had just alighted from a carriage, while their servants oversaw the transfer of their luggage to the docks. Nothing remarkable about that. The bread and butter of his and Granston's shipping line was carrying cargo, but all of their ships were equipped to ferry a small number of England's finest citizens and their servants to and from their sojourns on the Continent.

Daniel pondered what had drawn his attention. Not the plump, gray-haired woman with the cherubically round face. Perhaps her companion, then, although he couldn't even see the younger woman's face, which was blocked by her large parasol. As he watched, she tossed her head, and reddish-brown curls caught in the breeze.

When the realization hit him, he sucked in his breath. Still gasping, he tossed back his drink and savored the burn that raced down his throat. Anything to stop himself from doing what he'd done far too often over the past five years. He'd see a woman with some slight similarity to the girl he had once believed he'd loved, and he'd convince himself she was there.

She never was. And he'd never quite gotten used to the disappointment of it.

"What is it, Hallsy?" Granston asked. "You look like you've seen a ghost."

"Not a ghost. Just two Englishwomen. I suppose it's time to make myself presentable after all."

"Damn it, the lady and her traveling companion!" Granston snatched up his captain's coat from the deck rail and slid it over his shoulders. "I should have been on the dock five minutes ago. Our man in the office promised the old girl I'd personally look after them."

"*You*, look after two ladies? Surely they have no idea of your reputation."

"You will recall that I, too, have a title and the manners to go with it, when the situation requires it. Besides, I was told the lady is nigh on seventy." Granston glanced at the dock and grimaced. "But her traveling companion looks to be an entirely different matter."

Daniel clapped him on the back and took the whiskey bottle out of his hand. "Steady as she goes, Captain. Duty calls."

"Of course. But I can't be held responsible if the young woman happens to be attracted to my irresistible charms on one of those long nights out at sea, under the moon and the stars."

Daniel chuckled as his incorrigible friend left to collect the women, but his humor was short-lived. The young woman did it again, moved in a hauntingly familiar way. After five years, he shouldn't remember such things so well. His mind was playing tricks on him, but he'd steer clear of the young woman anyway. It wasn't the poor girl's fault, but damn it all if she didn't remind him far too much of Emmeline.

He gripped Granston's bottle more tightly and headed toward his stateroom at the opposite end of the ship. He doubted the remaining whiskey would be enough to drive memories of Emmeline from his mind, but he was willing to spend the rest of the afternoon trying to prove himself wrong.

*I*f she'd thought she could actually make it, Lady Emmeline Radcliffe would have dived into the Bay of Biscay and swum to France. She'd rather go anywhere than the place the vessel in front of her was headed. Home. Or so it was supposed to be, though she hadn't missed England one bit.

A gust of wind blew off the water, bringing with it the smell of rotten fish and the threat of falling into the waves, despite her decision to remain on the quay. The wind eddied under her lace-edged, cream-colored parasol and tugged it upward. Emme wrestled to bring it to heel.

"Ridiculously oversized thing."

"The only thing wrong with the parasol, Emmeline, is your distaste for holding it." Aunt Juliana, holding her own reasonably-sized parasol above her, laid a steadying hand on Emme's shoulder. "And we both know it's not the poor parasol's fault."

Aunt Juliana vigorously waved her fan as another gust of fish-filled sea air wafted over them. "Where on earth is the captain? He's to escort us personally. How long does he suppose he can keep us waiting? And what kind of ship is this odd contraption, anyway?"

Emme pressed her lips together to keep from smiling. Aunt Juliana hated travel. If the doctor hadn't ordered a trip abroad for her health, the old woman would have spent the past year in her drafty old house in Cambridge, and Emme would have spent it in London on the marriage mart, living in fear that she'd be married off to a man who wouldn't forgive her past indiscretions.

Emme snapped her parasol shut and propped it like a cane at her side. "I don't see why Father can't give us one more year abroad."

"They miss you, darling."

That was the devil of it. Emme missed them, too, especially Mother. And Edward. She did quite look forward to seeing her older brother's smile, so much like their dear Eleanor's, the one she'd never see again. And going home now had other advantages. She'd be able to set to work on the plan that had been borne out of her passion for helping other women. If Eleanor were here, she'd squeeze Emme's hand and remind her she couldn't single-handedly save the world; then she'd warn Emme not to broach the subject with Father, as he'd never approve.

However, Eleanor couldn't be here, and now it was Emme who squeezed her aunt's hand when she spotted the captain walking down the gangplank toward them. "There's our wayward captain now."

As he approached, Emme tightened her grip on her aunt's hand, like a small child clinging to her mother. She knew this man. Or she had, once upon a time.

The last time she'd seen him, he'd been visiting her family's country estate with her brother during a school break. Back then, Lord Percival Carlyle had the same ginger-blond hair and mischievous glint in his gray eyes, was just as tall, and was about to take his commission in the Royal Navy. With his uniform and broad shoulders, he was even more handsome now than he'd been in his school days. Still, his looks had not held a candle to those of Edward's other friend, with his wavy black hair and wild blue eyes.

Holding her breath and pushing down that memory, she dropped her gaze to the wharf under her feet and said a silent prayer of thanks to Eleanor, or whatever angel had been looking out for her when she'd insisted her aunt not list Emme's name on her ticket. "Aunt Juliana, please don't introduce me as Lady Emmeline. Call me Miss Emme Trent."

Her aunt shot her a worried gaze. "To what end?"

She curled her toes inside her soft, worn calfskin boots, the most comfortable shoes she'd ever owned, which her father would probably make her burn, as they were far from elegant. She wore thin stockings that came up only to her ankles and one thin petticoat under her simple gray travel gown. By the time they reached England's shores, all of that would change. She'd have to dress and speak and play the part of a lady every minute of every day, and the thought of it made it difficult to breathe.

"If I'm Lady Emmeline, daughter of the Earl of Limely, there will be obligations, even onboard ship. I'm just not ready. I'd like to take some time to myself. Rest. Write my letters to the ladies of the Spinsters' Club." That would be the best use of her last days of freedom, focusing on the letters to the members of the club she hoped to join, as their mission to help women in need was the same as her own.

Aunt Juliana sighed in a way that sounded much like Emme's mother when Emme vexed her, but she still nodded her acquiescence just as the captain reached them.

"Ladies, Captain Lord Granston, at your service."

Emme ventured a glance at his face as he flashed a smile at her aunt. He maneuvered between them and offered an arm to each of them.

"Lady Kendall, I trust your journey from Barcelona was uneventful," he said as they stepped toward the gangplank.

"If you mean boring, young man, it was indeed."

As he raised his eyebrows, Emme stifled a laugh.

"And you, Miss...?" The captain glanced in Emme's direction.

"Miss Trent," her aunt said.

"Ah, Miss Trent. Did you find the journey as dreary

as my lady?" If he had recognized her as Edward's sister, he was doing a fine job of concealing the fact.

"Yes," she murmured.

The captain kept up the conversation. "We're to have calm weather for the duration of our voyage. If it's too calm and the wind fails us, we'll turn to the most modern of coal-powered steam engines to deliver us safely to England's bonny shores."

As he recited what Emme assumed were impressive facts about the ship he referred to as a screw schooner, a movement to her right caught her eye. Two of the crew stood talking on the far side of the deck. At such a distance, she could hardly make out their faces, but one had dark, wavy hair. Fear caught her breath in her throat. She forced herself to exhale, and shook her head to clear the troubling thoughts.

It wasn't Daniel. His bare feet and dirty clothes were proof of that. Seeing one of Edward's friends had simply made her see her old beau where he wasn't, where he could not be. After all, what was the last thing she'd heard about him? That he was exploring the silk trail in China. Or was it smuggling harem girls out of Constantinople? Or perhaps it was the story about trading in illegal ancient artifacts in South America. So many scandals had been attached to his name, she could hardly keep track of them.

"And, of course, you shall dine with me," the captain was now saying. "Will dinner at the captain's table suit you, Miss Trent?"

She had no intention of dining with him or anyone

else on board. She and her aunt would come up with some excuse—seasickness, perhaps—to keep Emme out of his purview and diminish the likelihood of him recognizing her as Edward's sister. But manners dictated politeness. She managed a smile. "Of course, Captain."

Still, Emme was relieved when the captain saw them below decks and deposited them safely at the door of her aunt's stateroom, pointing out Emme's room beside it. As soon as he was out of sight, Aunt Juliana crossed her arms in front of her.

"The captain hardly seems inclined to let you stay out of sight. And it's obvious you know him. He's bound to recognize you sooner or later, and you'll have been caught out lying to a perfectly nice young gentleman."

Emme hoped her aunt was wrong. "I didn't know him that well. He was one of Edward's school friends, and I was still a child, really, the last time he saw me."

"You're no longer a child, and don't think he didn't take notice. He might see you as easy prey, without the protection of your father's title."

Emme hadn't considered that potential pitfall, but she still remembered a thing or two Edward had taught her about throwing a jab and an undercut before she'd set sail for Spain. "I promise you, I won't allow the captain or any other man to take liberties with me." Not again.

And if any man thought otherwise, he would regret it, as she would prove herself a skilled boxer.

CHAPTER 2

*A*fter nearly a week of uneventful seas, during which he'd had far too much time to resume the role of a gentleman and ponder the life awaiting him back in England, Daniel had an unrelenting headache. He sat at the simple wooden table affixed to the wall of the captain's cabin and sipped cognac, while Granston whistled some abominable tune as he unbuttoned his cuffs and collar. The blasted noise reverberated against the wood and metal surfaces of the captain's quarters and exacerbated the pain in Daniel's temples.

"What has you in such an unbearably jovial mood?" he asked when he couldn't stand another second of Granston's off-key chirruping.

"Tomorrow night will be a fine one, Hallsy. There will be a full moon and the stars will appear near enough to the earth to touch. The ocean will roll gently beneath us—"

"And Lady Kendall's traveling companion will finally join us for dinner?"

"Oh, aye. When the doctor saw her earlier today, he found her amongst a stack of papers, lesson plans or some such. It appears she's a governess when not serving as a lady's traveling companion. He said she looked quite recovered."

"You've had McReedy spying on one of our passengers?" Daniel rubbed his aching temples.

"Just keeping me apprised of her health." Granston threw back the rest of his drink. "From what I understand, the fetching creature finally has her sea legs and is set to make an appearance at my table tomorrow night."

Daniel smirked. "You always did have a flair for the dramatic. I'd wager her appearance has nothing to do with you."

"Then you would lose a bet. After a few hours in my company, I'll have her helpless in my arms."

Daniel raised his glass. "I'll take that wager. Your finest bottle of cognac against an even better one in our next port. And I do mean your finest bottle, not this barely passable swill you've been pawning off on me."

"Swill? Hardly." Granston sniffed his empty glass and grimaced. "Perhaps you have a point. I'd expected more from this bottle. I won it off a chap in Portugal."

"Enough of your gambling spoils. Next time, you'll open the good stuff."

"Yes, I can't take your wager in good conscience, with the odds so profoundly in my favor."

"That poor young woman."

"Nonsense," Granston said. "She took a shine to me immediately. It was a mutual attraction. And before you assume the obvious interest in her delightful curves, I'll tell you she has an air of breeding about her."

"So that's what you're about. Looking for a wife, are you, Granston?"

"Not on your life. Let's just say that I, too, need to become accustomed to refined English company again."

"From governess to mistress for her, then."

Granston took a seat across from Daniel at the small table by the window that overlooked the main deck. "Why not? Her pay would improve. But you know, that's not a half-bad idea, marriage. For you of course, not for me."

Daniel choked on a sip of the swill. "What?"

"You have the fortune to support a wife from any of the finest families. And think of how a merger with a fine, upstanding family would impress the Committee for Privileges, not to mention the society mavens who dragged your family's name through the muck. And then you could finally forgive yourself for breaking the promise you made to the marchioness."

Daniel cursed the night he'd been entertaining Granston and Swimmer at his chateau in Spain, and had been drunk enough to tell them about his mother's confession. How she'd begged him to fight for the title and the marquessate to keep the late marquess's line alive in spirit, if not by blood, and to cleanse the stain of hinted illegitimacy from the family name. It wasn't that Daniel distrusted his old friends with his secret. Quite the contrary, he believed they'd take it to their graves. It was what Granston would do in the meantime, in the name of helping his cause, that worried Daniel.

"You forget, my last association with one of England's finest families didn't end well."

Edward Radcliffe, Viscount Meriden, had been one of his closest friends. Meriden's sister Emmeline had been...could have been...Daniel couldn't bear to remember it. They'd rejected him outright at the first whisper of a scandal. Hells bells, what must they think of him now, after so much more about him and his family had been whispered and said outright?

"I think I'll enjoy the life of a bachelor, as I'm sure you'll understand."

Granston shook his head. "Sorry Hallsy, but you know the quickest route to redemption in London will be making a good match. And I know who can help you. Swimmer's mother."

"The duchess?"

"She's earned quite the reputation as a matchmaker since her widowhood," Granston said. "I've always suspected she had something to do with James Alcott's untimely passage into the world of married men."

His friend continued, but Daniel was distracted by a

shadowy figure that appeared on the deck and walked the length of it, the same as she had every night since they'd left port. For one so assailed by seasickness, Miss Trent certainly did take to midnight constitutionals. Daniel wondered if Granston had been kept apprised of *that* strange behavior.

"Sometimes I think you're hardly listening, Hallsy," Granston said. "I try not to take it personally. One can hardly expect you'd find the likes of me interesting after your escapades across three continents."

Daniel scowled at his friend. "You could have warned me about just how many ridiculous scandals you'd concocted about me. Last night at dinner, I thought Lady Kendall might faint when one of the gentlemen brought up the matter of harem girls. What exactly is it I'm to have done with them?"

Granston grinned. "Not nearly as much as I would have done, or as much as I'll do with the governess. I'm so looking forward to our strolls under the moonlight. Then perhaps I can place her."

Daniel set his cognac glass on the table, his hand shaking. "Place her? What does that mean?"

"Hm." Granston shrugged. "There's something familiar about her. She reminds me of someone... Perhaps the eyes. I'm not sure."

The eyes. Emmeline's eyes had been quite like her brother's.

It couldn't be her, of course. Limely would never allow his daughter to travel abroad, let alone to hold employment as a governess. The disquiet in Daniel's belly eased as he talked himself out his illogical fears.

"I'm sure you'll figure it out eventually," he told Granston. "With your proclivities, odds are you've seduced at least one of her female relatives."

"I'll choose to take no offense at that remark," Granston said. "Not to mention, it's possibly true. Sadly, though, your rudeness leaves me no choice." He pointed to the cabin door. "Out with you."

Daniel laughed as he stood. "I was just going to excuse myself."

"Be sure to ask forgiveness for your insolence when you say your night's prayers."

"I'll consider it."

"Hallsy." Granston glanced at Daniel, who stood with his hand on the doorknob. "Remember, I saw her first."

Daniel held up his free hand. "I have no plans to cross paths with the governess."

"I'll hold you to your word."

Daniel stepped onto the deck and soundlessly closed Granston's door behind him. He had every intention of keeping his word. He had neither a reason nor a desire to meet the woman. He did, however, intend to see her face, once and for all. Surely, he wouldn't know the woman, so what harm would it do to confirm it with a glance? Then he could hie to bed and get the first decent night's sleep since his glimpse of the woman on the wharf had inspired haunted dreams of his beautiful, green-eyed, would-have-been lover.

A salt-soaked wind stung Emme's face the moment she stepped on deck. In the six days they'd been traveling, her nighttime constitutional had become her favorite part of the long, monotonous days. She pulled a lungful of air deep into her chest, determined to enjoy the freshness that was so unlike the stale mustiness of her cabin. This was her last night of freedom, having made the mistake of opening her cabin door to take in an afternoon breeze, which had allowed the doctor to find her hale and hearty and presiding over her completed stack of correspondence to the members of the London Spinsters' Club.

But it was just as well. Feigning illness and squirreling herself away in her room had become tiresome, and she'd longed to walk on deck in the sunlight for days now. But tonight, the stars were exceptionally beautiful, there was no one about to bother her, and she would enjoy the solitude one last time.

The headwind made her shiver and she pulled her cloak more tightly around her gray frock. The simple cut and mourning colors of her dresses did much to disguise her station. Besides, she was hardly ready to move beyond them. Perhaps she'd continue to wear them once she officially joined the spinsters. Then when she met the unwed mothers and their young children the spinsters helped, they wouldn't wonder why a young, well-bred woman chose spinsterhood. They'd assume her mourning was for a husband cut down in the prime of life. Not a sister, drowned long before reaching her prime.

Emme hesitated when she neared the captain's cabin. Light spilled from the window. Typically, by the time she took her walk, everyone but a few crew members who steered the ship were long since abed. She moved as far as she could from the window, hugging the railing at the edge of the deck. She made the mistake of glancing down, just once, at the roiling ocean out beyond the railing. Her stomach lurched and she was overcome by the illness that, up until now, she had only feigned. She closed her eyes and took deep breaths. She had conquered this beast in Spain, taking near-daily swims in the strong ocean currents until she'd lost her fear of swiftly moving water. Or so she'd thought.

Her stomach calmed, but her nerves still sparked. She crossed the deck to the stairwell leading below-decks, toward the safety of her room. Instead of abating, her unease grew as she reached the bottom of the stairs. She could have sworn someone was watching her. She prayed the captain's interest in her had led him to discourage any ruffians on his crew from attempting to take liberties with her.

The prayer died on her lips when, a few steps into the shadowy passageway, she ran into a hulking mass. Instinctively, she balled up her fist. A strong hand encircled hers and held it in place, inches from her intended target—his face.

For a moment, she thought her muddled mind had conjured up her first love. But that couldn't be. He was off to see the world, leaving scandal and no doubt heartbreak in his wake. It had to be this man's cologne, so similar to Daniel's, that made it difficult to catch her breath.

When he whispered in her ear, any hope that her first love was somewhere far, far away evaporated.

CHAPTER 3

"You seem to have made a miraculous recovery, Miss Trent." Daniel was shocked by the solid sound of his own voice, given how his head swam from her lilac scent and her warm skin. He opened her clenched fist with his fingers and stroked her palm with his thumb.

"The medic gave me a tonic." Her voice was reed-hin.

It scraped against his skin and made him burn.

"Now might be a good time to tell me what this is about, Lady Emmeline. Or is it Miss Trent? Tell me what you're playing at, kitten."

She tensed at the use of his endearment for her. He hoped it reminded her of being with him in the garden at her family's country estate. And the swimming pond. And most especially the library, where they'd had their midnight rendezvous. He regretted there wasn't enough light to see whether she blushed from remembering it. How many times had he relived those moments over the past five years? It seemed only fair that she should, as well.

"So, you've found me out." She snatched her hand out of his grasp. "I beg of you not to breathe a word of this to anyone."

Well, this does sound interesting. "First, tell me how you came to be on this ship with an elderly lady and no suitable chaperone."

"She's my great-aunt and a perfectly suitable chaperone."

"Who is conveniently absent at the moment."

"You can't truly be here," she said, shaking her head. "My aunt would have told me if another of Edward's friends were on board."

She seemed hell-bent on convincing herself he was an apparition.

He touched her shoulder to assure her was very real. "Your aunt and I never met, and I daresay neither of us recognized the name of the other having any association with you."

Emmeline glanced over her shoulder. "This is neither the time nor the place for a discussion, Mr. Hallsworth."

The clawed kitten spit his common name at him. Restoring his title and the reputation for his family name was for his mother, but for the first time, he saw the appeal of wielding the power of the marquessate over those who had turned on him, like the Radcliffes.

"Then let's go somewhere more private." Daniel

walked the few feet to her stateroom and opened the door. The lamp on the bedside table cast a golden glow into the passageway, illuminating Emmeline. She was no longer the pretty girl who had smitten him, but a beautiful woman.

She raised her chin and grasped her skirts to swish past him in her unremarkable gray traveling gown. He followed her into the room and closed the door behind them, then propped his back against the door jamb.

She turned on her heel. Oh, how he remembered Lady Emmeline's set-down stare. So much passion flowed beneath the surface of this lovely woman. He couldn't suppress his grin.

"This situation is not laughable. It's unseemly to be here without my chaperone, as you've already stated." Her cheeks bloomed red and she bit her lower lip as though wishing she could take back the words.

He shouldn't take pity on the spiteful creature. After all, her family could have risen to his defense when his uncle had launched his assault on Daniel and his dying mother, claiming Daniel a bastard to bring his title into question. Instead, they had disavowed him. His best friend Meriden had publicly shunned him. And Emmeline, his beloved Emmeline...

When Meriden told Daniel what she'd said about him, how she'd so easily cast him aside, even after he'd poured out his heart in a letter to her, his pity evaporated. What would she think now that the House of Lords was poised to restore his title? Would she swoon at his feet once more? Should he use it to his advantage to...to what? What did he want from her?

The answer flashed through his mind in all its animal ugliness. He wanted *her*. He wanted to possess her, to bend her to the will of his body, to draw out her passion and make her scream his name. And then to leave her, besmirched and undone, to deposit her back into the bosom of her family a ruined woman.

He wouldn't dare make it public. Such a scandal would threaten his ability to regain the title. Besides, he wouldn't stoop so low as the *ton* had in destroying him. He wouldn't threaten her chances at making a decent match in the marriage mart. It would be enough to keep the humiliation between the Radcliffes and him. It would be enough to break their hearts.

For the first time in days, the tension in his neck eased and the throbbing in his temples subsided. He felt strong. Virile. Voracious.

He advanced on her slowly, first one step, then another. She retreated in rhythm. Even in this cat-and-mouse game, their bodies were undeniably in harmony. In the end, he would leave a part of her destroyed, but in the meantime, he would bring her so much pleasure.

She bumped against the edge of her narrow bed, skittered sideways and pressed against the wall of her small room, breaking their dance.

Daniel laughed. "Surely you don't fear me, Lady Emmeline. I remember a time when you would have run into my arms had I looked at you the way I just did."

That enticing blush stained her cheeks once again. "We knew each other well then. I daresay we're strangers now."

"Fair enough. But for my part, I'm ever so anxious to make your acquaintance again. Surely you won't deny me the pleasure."

He lingered on the last word and was rewarded by the visible shake of her shoulders.

She cleared her throat. "Is that the price of your silence about my identity?"

He narrowed his eyes and appraised her from the top of her auburn curls to the tips of her kidskin boots. "If my silence is worth so much to you, perhaps I've set the price too low."

She worked her throat, and when she finally managed to speak, her voice again rasped and scraped so divinely against his skin. "If you must know, I'm avoiding the obligations of playing the part of the earl's daughter. My days on this ship are the last days of freedom I'll have."

Her echo of his exact sentiments gave him pause. But he refused to let her dissuade him from his agenda. "In that case, Lady Emmeline, yes, the price of my silence is your cooperation in our reacquaintance."

She gave him one curt nod. "Then we'll meet under more respectable conditions and speak as old friends. If that's all..."

He shook his head. "Not so quickly, kitten. It's a start, but just a start."

She stared past him, over his shoulder, and seemed

not to have heard him, although he knew she had. "But you must remember to call me Miss Trent."

"Even in private?"

She glanced at him, then looked away again. "In those cases, Lady Emme. It's what I prefer to be called now."

Her words were like a bucket of cold seawater poured over him. Only her sister used to call her that. "I was sorry to hear of Eleanor's passing," he said quietly. "I sent a condolence letter to the family through my solicitor."

"Yes, Edward told me." She looked directly at Daniel. Her eyes shone with unshed tears. "He said he didn't know whether it would comfort or cut me."

When she didn't offer any more, he took one small step away from her. "So, which was it? A comfort or a cut?"

"A comfort, of course. Not only the condolences, but knowing you were alive and well somewhere in the world."

She'd been as anxious as her brother to see Daniel leave England. When had she become so skilled a liar? He ignored her feigned concern.

"Let me take this opportunity to offer you my condolences personally. It would have been difficult for any family, but for yours..."

Her younger siblings, twins, had died of scarlet fever when Meriden was twelve and Emme was nine. Each of them had spoken of it to Daniel—separately—

exactly once, but it had been easy enough to see the pain it caused them.

Emme crossed her arms in front of herself. It made her look smaller, younger. "Mother never recovered from the twins, not really. And then Eleanor...she was the brightest light of the whole family."

He clenched his fists at his sides as a familiar anger swept through him. He remembered far too well how their parents had doted on Eleanor. At least Meriden, for all his faults, had loved his younger sisters equally. It was one of the things Daniel had liked most about his best friend, in the days when they *had* been friends.

She squeezed her eyes shut for a moment. When she opened them again, she looked more like herself. He remembered that look as well. She no longer needed comfort and she wouldn't accept it if he offered it.

"Thank you for your condolences, Mr. Hallsworth. You were always kind."

He wasn't. He hadn't been for a long time. But she had always been a bit more naïve than she'd cared to admit. After all the world had taken from her, she still trusted it was more good than evil. As was she. Her love for him might have been fickle, but she'd been under no obligation to him. They'd taken no vows. He'd made no proposals, and she'd made no promises.

"Goodnight, Lady Emme. I'll call on you tomorrow to discuss the terms of my silence."

He left her room and made his way to the railing above decks. Staring at the white caps peaking on the black depths of the ocean, his head admitted what his heart had known all along.

He wouldn't hurt Emme. He couldn't. He'd been kidding himself to think for even a moment that he'd wanted to do so. Face to face with the goodness of the woman he'd painted as evil for the past five years, he could no longer carry his grudge against her. Her family deserved his vengeance for cutting him out of their lives, but he wouldn't ruin and abandon her to exact it. There were other ways to make them pay. What had Granston said about the path to redemption? A good match would be the quickest route to it.

"Emme will be mine," he said aloud.

After all these years, he still wanted her. And damn it, he would have her. She probably wouldn't agree to a marriage proposal to an as-yet-untitled man, as she'd never loved him and perhaps never would. But she had desired him and perhaps would again.

Beginning the very next day, he would set out to seduce her. And then the arrogant earl and his pompous son would have no choice but to allow Daniel —nay, *beg* him—to marry Emme.

Regardless of what the Committee for Privileges decreed.

"I'm beginning to worry sea travel doesn't agree with you after all," Aunt Juliana told Emme the next afternoon.

They stood on the main deck enjoying the calm seas and warm sun from under their parasols. Emme would have loved to toss hers into the ocean, but Aunt Juliana was insistent the freckles must fade from Emme's face before her father caught a glimpse of them. Her aunt had also insisted Emme change out of her dull gray frock and into something cheerier. Their opinions of cheery diverged, judging by the look her aunt had given the prim forest-green skirt and blouse Emme had chosen, but it did feel good to wear something different.

"It's a headache, not the sea," Emme said.

Being near the water no longer brought her physical discomfort, and today, unlike last night, she'd tamed the fear of it again. The source of her distress was something else entirely. The lovely weather had brought forth from their cabins everyone on the ship. Everyone except the one person Emme feared seeing. And yet his absence unnerved her.

"Let's sit on the deck chairs." Her aunt led the way and waited for Emme to take the seat beside her. "I've been thinking about your dilemma."

Emme startled at her aunt's words, wondering how she'd found out about Daniel and his price. Then it occurred to her that her dear aunt, who'd been her only confidante for the past year, was pondering Emme's other crisis. "My father's plan to display me like a prized cow to attract a husband. And what are your thoughts?"

"Tell him the truth. Tell him why you want to join

the Spinsters' Club. Tell him about the work they do for widows and deserted mothers with no prospects for themselves or their children. Under his gruff exterior, I believe he loves you. Perhaps he'll listen."

Emme could never tell him the truth, not all of it. She could never tell the whole truth to anyone, not even her beloved aunt.

She shrugged her shoulders. "I wish I could be as sure of his sentiments as you are. Since Eleanor's passing, he's hardened. Maybe if I convince Mother how important this work is to me, I'll draw her over to my side. Between her and Edward, we'll have to be able to convince him."

Her aunt shifted in her seat. It made Emme feel off-kilter. "I don't think you should count on your mother's influence over your father, dear."

"I know they've had their difficulties. There's been a divide. But surely she can help me."

Aunt Juliana patted Emme's hand and silently stared out to sea. Salty spray misted over the deck and moistened Emme's skin. It chilled her to the bone.

"It's a problem for another day," she told her aunt. "Let's not borrow trouble."

There was already trouble enough for this day. Emme clutched the handle of her parasol and kept her gaze fixed on the horizon, dreading yet oddly anticipating, the imminent arrival of the man whose very presence could cause her carefully laid plans to come undone.

*D*aniel knew the moment Emme sensed his approach. She sat up even straighter and let out a sigh, whether out of anger, boredom, or resignation, he couldn't have said. And he damn well didn't care. Just as he didn't care that Granston was scowling down at him from the bridge that very minute, Daniel having just told him he was staking a claim on "the governess" after all. Granston would get over it the minute he set his sights on his next conquest, if not sooner. In the meantime, Daniel had more pressing concerns than his old friend's wounded pride.

He exchanged greetings with Lady Kendall, who had been a lovely dinner companion for the past several nights, then bowed to her niece.

"Mr. Hallsworth, let me introduce—"

"Lady Emme." Daniel took Emme's gloved hand and held it for several heartbeats longer than was respectable. "I'm an old friend of your niece, m'lady."

"I had no idea." The old woman glanced at Emme, who was absent-mindedly rubbing her gloved hand that Daniel had just released. "Then you must join us. Please, both of you, sit on my left side so you don't obstruct my view."

Emme opened her mouth to say something, then shot Daniel a murderous look. "Of course," she told her aunt as she rose and moved to the chair on her aunt's left side.

Daniel took the seat next to her.

"You do realize why she's done this, don't you?" Emme asked.

"Why she's asked me to join you? I assume it's because she has manners."

That nettle seemed to stick as it drew him another murderous glare. "Not that. Why she's seated us to her left."

"To keep a watch out for pirates on our starboard side?"

Emme rolled her eyes. "You can be such a ninny. She's done it because she's deaf in her left ear."

Daniel took a moment to consider her words. "So, our conversation, while chaperoned, is still private."

Emme blushed a lovely color of pink as he emphasized the last word.

Daniel leaned back in his deck chair, stretched out his legs, and crossed them at the ankles. When she graced him with a glance, he shot his most wolfish grin at his prey. But he had no intention of being a merciful hunter, striking with one quick blow.

"So, tell me, Lady Emme, why were you in Spain?"

The confusion reflected in her furrowed brow proved he'd put her off-balance. She told him about her aunt's infirmities and the need for a sunnier clime. She recounted walks along the cold sea in Valencia, and climbs through ruins in Barcelona, having spent half a year in each place. Somehow it stung to learn she'd been so near him. When he'd thought of her, which had been far too often, he'd still pictured her in London drawing rooms, English countryside fields, and especially the library at her family's country estate. Yet for the past year, she'd been in the same country as he had, a few hundred miles away from the new home he'd made for himself. If he'd had any idea, he could have invited them there and shown her the beauty of the place that had earned a piece of his heart.

He told her about his chateau on a hillside in San Sebastian that overlooked the turquoise sea. He'd tried to spend at least a week there each month, watching the clouds turn pink and orange over the lush green hills at sunset, and enjoying wine and *pinxto*—a type of local hors d'oeuvres—on his balcony. He stopped short of telling her how lovely she would look, standing on that veranda, a glass of wine in her hand, the cool evening breeze streaming through her long, loose hair. Or how alluring she would be, flushed with color, wearing a brightly colored *traje*, dancing the flamenco with him at one of the nearby taverns. He told her instead about the time he'd spent along the French Riviera, but he didn't tell her what had drawn him there, didn't mention the man he'd visited, the old family friend who shared Daniel's blood.

Emme smiled prettily when there was a companionable lull in the conversation, then twirled her parasol above her head, reminding Daniel of the flirtatious girl she'd been when he'd met her. He let the memory sink into his bones.

But he was well aware the flirtatious girl was just that—a memory. When he'd known her then, when he'd loved her and believed she'd loved him, he hadn't kept any secrets from her. On the very day the Radcliffes had turned him away, he'd planned to tell her the marquess and marchioness, unable to have children of their own, had taken in their friend's bastard and raised him as an heir. Now that time was past, their trust was broken, and with the marquessate in his sights, his secret would go with him to the grave.

"Whenever did you find time for all the harem girls, I wonder?"

He laughed quite genuinely. She was still a spitfire. He was glad to see grief hadn't taken it out of her. "One can always find time for harem girls. Are there any other bizarre rumors, which might or might not have been propagated by our illustrious captain, we should discuss?"

"Captain Granston attached such elaborate scandals to you? Did you have a falling out at some point? Or perhaps you lost a bet?"

"To Granston? Never. I assume he meant well. He thought muddying the waters might distract from the speculation surrounding my departure from England."

Daniel stared out at the ocean and thought of the last days with his mother, days overshadowed by her guilt about his parentage and his uncle's cruel bid to steal the marquess's title at the dying woman's expense. Despite his promise on her deathbed to fight to regain the title and restore the family's good name, he'd lost heart after he'd lost his best friend and the woman he'd hoped to marry in one fell swoop. A month after burying his mother, he'd collected the sizable portion of his inheritance that wasn't entailed, set up the shipping enterprise with Granston, and set off for France and Spain to parlay his small fortune into a large one. He'd succeeded beyond his wildest dreams, but every day he lived with the knowledge he hadn't fulfilled his mother's dying wish.

Emme reached out one gloved hand and nearly touched his, then withdrew it and set it in her lap. "Your mother was a kind woman. She'd be proud of you."

Not if she had any inkling of his plans for a respectable young lady, she wouldn't. Still, a bit of the tightness around his chest eased. "Thank you. That's kind of you to say." And Emme *was* kind, as his mother had been. "How are your friends?" he asked. "I seem to recall the three of you were thick as thieves."

"Tessa and Luci. It will be such a joy to see them!"

Her face lit up, and Daniel was struck with an urge to trace her cheek with his fingertips. Deep breaths and calming thoughts focused him. He was here to be kind and perhaps mildly flirtatious. Lover's touches, kisses, and so much more would come later.

"They're both well," Emme said of her friends. "Tessa's married. Perhaps you'd heard? Her husband is a friend of yours and Edward's from Harrow days."

"Yes, Alcott. Mr. James Alcott. He wasn't one of the Five, but we did quite like him. He was an older brother figure to our wayward lot."

The corners of her mouth turned up at the mention of the Five. Harrow's Finest Five, as they'd dubbed themselves. Or more precisely, as *Granston* had dubbed them. Swimmer, Steady Eddie, Granston, Harry, and Hallsy. Heirs to a dukedom, two earldoms, a viscountcy, and in Daniel's case, a marquessate, all scandal aside.

"Have you heard any news of Lord Harry?" Emme asked.

"Last I knew, he was in the jungles of Ecuador with a team of research botanists. Granston saw him there a year or so back."

"And did you cross paths with him when you were pillaging in South America?" She flashed her brilliant smile again.

"I've never had the pleasure of setting foot on that continent. Granston's been the world traveler. I've kept up the rather boring side of the business: contracts, licenses, paperwork, other drudgery."

"Have you kept up contact with the Duke of Wrexham?"

"Mostly by correspondence these days, although he was visiting me in San Sebastian when he received the summons from his father to return home to marry. No one knew at the time it was because the old man was sick."

"Still, it hardly seems fair to force a marriage on someone who doesn't want it." Emme pretended to brush something away from her face, masking a tear, if Daniel wasn't mistaken.

Perhaps an arranged marriage was the reason she dreaded returning to England. Knowing her father, it was easy to imagine. Daniel wondered whether the earl had already chosen a husband and made promises on her behalf. Not that such promises would matter by the time they disembarked onto English soil, given Daniel's plans for her.

Was it so different, him making plans for her versus her father? He gripped the arms of his deck chair and stared at the horizon. It was a foolish thought. Her father meant to marry her off by force. Daniel meant to draw her into it through seduction. The new thought didn't do as much as he'd hoped to assuage the tiny bit of guilt that plagued him.

He turned to happier thoughts of the seduction he'd carry out so very, very soon. Perhaps even tonight. He pushed away ungentlemanly images of what lay in store for them, and stepped back into the role of a well-mannered gentleman like shrugging into an old overcoat to find it too short and tight.

"And do you know how the duke's mother is doing?" Emme asked, innocently unaware of his licentious daydreams.

"According to Granston, she made her reappearance in society late last spring. And she still knows absolutely everyone who's anyone in London, and most of their secrets as well."

She smoothed her skirt and didn't meet his gaze. "Yes, she's very well-connected. I'll be sure to visit her and pay my respects when I'm back in London."

Her meaning was hardly opaque. She had something up her sleeve and hoped to enlist the help of the duchess. It must be a desperate case to send her straight to society's most venerable maven. He couldn't imagine how the duchess could help extricate her from an unwanted engagement. So, what else might his kitten be up to? Would he be able to coax it out of her once they were alone?

Thoughts of seduction rushed back to him, and this time, he couldn't dislodge them from his mind. He'd played at this polite game long enough for his taste, anyway.

Guided by the most dignified manners instilled in him by his mother at an early age, he rose to his feet and bowed. "It's been lovely getting reacquainted with you, Lady Emme, but I'm afraid some of that business drudgery I mentioned awaits me." He took her gloved fingertips in his for the briefest second.

"It *has* been lovely." She stood as well and smiled at him.

"Of course, we still have to negotiate the terms of our agreement, but that can wait for another time."

The smile vanished from her face. "Oh, the terms."

He'd set her on notice and on edge, just as he'd hoped. He almost felt sorry for her, thinking their harmless little chat was all he'd require in exchange for his silence. But he would make it up to her. He'd make sure they both enjoyed the seduction immensely.

He bowed toward her aunt and gave Lady Emme one last smile, relishing having caught the kitten in his trap. Now the *real* games would begin.

CHAPTER 4

A crewman had delivered Daniel's missive to Emme barely an hour before the captain's dinner was to begin. A command, more like it. After an afternoon of innocuous chatting and decorous behavior, Daniel had made a decidedly indecorous demand as Emme's next payment for his silence. She was to claim she'd fallen ill again and take to her room for the rest of the evening. That had proven exceedingly easy, as the headache she'd fought all afternoon had lent her a pallor that had concerned Aunt Juliana, who had only left Emme's side after she promised to summon the medic if the pain increased.

A knock on the door made her instinctively check that her hairpins were in place and her dress was in order. She opened the door to a cabin boy with a cloth-covered cart laden with silver-lidded plates. The boy silently wheeled the cart into the room, bowed to

Emme, and took his leave. He was barely out of the room when another figure appeared in the doorway.

Daniel looked striking in his short-jacketed, black silk evening suit and white shirt and bow tie. When she'd seen him last, he'd been in tan pants and striped brown coat of a promenade suit, which had been close-cut and far too well-fitted for her own good. But the memory of that sight paled in comparison to seeing him in his finery. She swallowed a lump in her throat and glanced down at her own attire, glad she'd deigned to "dress for dinner" as his note had requested. She'd retired her dove-gray, princess-cut morning dress for the finest gown she had with her, this one also dark green, but made of silk, with an off-the-shoulder bodice edged with lace, complemented by a matching skirt with a sumptuous bustle in the back. Everyone who had seen her wear it in Barcelona had felt moved to compliment her milky complexion and bright green eyes.

"Lady Emme, you look stunning." Daniel took one of her ungloved hands and fluttered his lips over the back of it.

She found herself wishing he would turn her hand over and lavish attention on her palm as she so vividly remembered him doing in her parents' library. The memory made her blush with embarrassment and something much more base and powerful. She snatched her hand from him.

"You're looking quite well yourself," she said.

She meant to make polite conversation, but found it

difficult to speak as he openly and lasciviously appraised her from the tips of her satin slippers to the top of her simply-coiffed head and back down again.

"Thank you." The low, throaty sound of his voice made her mouth go dry. "Here, let me help you into a seat."

After doing so, he slowly removed two lids from the plates on the cart. The rich, creamy scent of turtle soup wafted up from the tureens. He then uncovered the remaining dishes of fruit, cheese, and cream pastries. And finally, the *pièce de résistance*, a center platter of salmon surrounded by lobster salad and roasted vegetables. Their meal must rival or even surpass anything the captain was serving for the ship's other passengers. Then again, why shouldn't it? This ship was every bit as much Daniel's as it was Captain Percival's. Grayhall. Granston and Hallsworth. That she hadn't realized it immediately vexed her. She could have proceeded much more cautiously if she'd truly believed Daniel might be on board the ship. Now it was much too late.

As he took his seat across from her, she found her voice again. "I hadn't heard you were part owner of a shipping line. The captain didn't see fit to start that rumor, one based on a bit of truth."

He smiled. "Don't be so sure there was no truth in any of the other rumors."

He was baiting her, but Emme wasn't about to fall into the trap of asking a question that might lead to salacious details best left unknown and unsaid.

He poured a glass of claret for each of them and lifted his in a toast. "To our continuing reacquaintance."

"Indeed," was all she managed to mutter before taking a sip.

She barely tasted what was surely delicious food, she was so nervous. But as dinner progressed, Daniel said nothing less proper or innocuous than the things he'd shared that afternoon. Instead, he regaled her with tame but entertaining stories of the adventures he'd had since he'd left England, some of them involving Granston and Swimmer, as the Five affectionately called the duke.

"There, now you know the most interesting things that have happened to me since we were last acquainted. So, Lady Emme, tell me more about what has occupied your time for these past many years."

She saw his smile freeze. The kindness of his concern moved her to touch the back of his hand. "Don't worry Daniel, I won't break at the thought of Eleanor's death. But to get past it, perhaps we should discuss it."

He turned over his hand so they were palm to palm. "I had no intention of making you recount the details."

She shook her head. "I didn't mean to imply you had. But I can only assume Edward never wrote to you about what happened. You were Eleanor's friend once, too. You deserve to know. It happened in early spring, at my parents' estate in the country. You remember. It's where you visited us."

He had done so much more than visit. He'd made her fall in love with him. He'd found her alone every chance he could. He'd given her kisses that she'd happily returned. He'd invited her to a midnight rendezvous where those kisses had led to touches that woke something primal deep inside her. She pressed her eyes closed for a moment to push back the memories.

He gently grasped her fingers. "If it's too much..."

"No." She came back to herself, back to the present moment and the terrible story she needed to share. "It happened there. It was early in the morning. There was a terrible fog. Later it would become such a beautiful day. I remember being angry, furious really, at how beautiful all of nature could be on the day it took my sister's life."

He furrowed his brow. "*It* took her life? You mean nature?"

"Yes. The lake, specifically. You might recall Eleanor didn't swim."

"I do recall that. Quite the opposite of you."

She looked away from him. "Yes, well, she was on an early morning walk around the lake and she lost her footing. She slid into the water so fast." She couldn't say it. She couldn't bring herself to tell him the most awful part. "No one could get to her in time. Edward said between the fog and the frigid water, it was a wonder no one else died trying to rescue her."

"Very good of him. He didn't want her rescuers to feel any worse about not saving her."

"Of course he didn't. He's a very kind man. I think that's why the two of you were such good friends."

He abruptly withdrew his hand and she immediately regretted her words. She didn't know if it was the mention of Edward or the insinuation of Daniel's kindness that had done it, but their closeness had evaporated. Still, she needed to know.

"You must tell me what happened between the two of you."

He clenched his jaw. "Why must *I* tell you anything? Surely you know all you need to know. You and every other member of the gossip-mongering *ton*."

"This is about the scandal? The real one?"

"Yes, Emmeline, the real one. The one that caused you and Meriden to cast me out of your lives."

"Cast you out?" She jumped to her feet, shaking with a rage she hadn't realized she possessed. "You left without a word. You never sent a letter or a note, or even a second-hand message through some mutual acquaintance. And Edward and my father, with their heads bent together, talking in whispers, said not one word every time I entered a room. Even Mother and Eleanor seemed to be part of the conspiracy."

Daniel stood slowly and narrowed his eyes. His voice was low and deadly calm. "Conspiracy to do what, *kitten*?"

Emme shuddered at the way he'd spit out the endearment like a curse. "To keep the truth of your betrayal from me. That's what it was, wasn't it? There was someone else. I know you went through such a difficult time, with your mother's death and your uncle's treachery. I might have even forgiven you seeking solace in someone else's arms, someone more experienced, less naïve. But to just disappear like that."

"Disappear?" He laughed, but not with mirth.

Emme sank back into her seat and waited for him to explain his derision.

"I sent you notes, then a long letter. I begged you to see me, or at least to respond. Then your brother told me what you said, that you wished you'd never allowed me to touch you."

"I said no such thing!" She jumped to her feet again. "Now you're making up stories that make Captain Granston's pale in comparison. Edward told me you'd never be coming back to see us."

Edward. The air forcibly left her lungs and she couldn't seem to catch her breath. Daniel stared at her as he paced like a panther preparing its attack. She turned away from him until she could take a proper breath and speak. She clasped her hands to stop them from shaking. "He didn't say that to you. It's not possible. That's a lie. My brother wouldn't lie."

She turned to face him. Despite the conviction of her words, the stricken look on Daniel's faced caused her belief to waver.

"Daniel, is it true? Did Edward tell you lies about me?"

He ran a hand through his hair and looked past her.

"Daniel, please, I have to know. What happened? Why would he lie?"

"To keep me away from you. To make sure I didn't taint you with my common blood and lurid scandal. And it would seem he lied to us both."

She took a step toward him. "Daniel—"

"No. This was a mistake. I knew it from the beginning."

"No, it wasn't. Please, I didn't know you tried to see me. Of course, I would have spoken to you. Don't leave."

But it was too late. He'd already gone.

Ten minutes later, as Emme paced the room, wondering if she dared go looking for him, the cabin boy came to collect the dinner cart. When he closed the door behind him, her room looked the same as it had before Daniel had ever come to see her. But if he hadn't taken another lover five years ago, if he had been sent away by Edward, or more likely by Edward doing their father's bidding, everything she'd believed about Daniel for years was wrong.

It was past midday the next day when Granston came looking for Daniel in his cabin. Daniel did his best to ignore the infernal knocking, but when the man threatened to break down the door, Daniel conceded. He'd seen Granston do much worse when he'd felt so moved.

He cracked the door. The bright sun filtering

through the thin slit assaulted his eyes and he squinted. "What do you want?"

"Hells bells, what happened to you?"

Daniel gave up on squinting and closed his eyes. "A bottle of rum. Is that it? Are we done here?"

In answer, Granston pushed past him into the room, but at least mercifully closed the door behind him. Granston picked up the empty rum bottle from the floor. "How much was in here before you pilfered it?"

"The seal hadn't been cracked." Daniel tried to make a good show of it by staying on his feet, but when the room started spinning, he gave up and lay on the bed. Being supine didn't stop the spinning, but at least it made the world turn more slowly.

"The seduction went that badly, did it?" Granston's laughter made him grimace, as much from the sting of the insult as from the pain it caused his head.

"That's not what happened."

"The seduction didn't happen, or the failure of it didn't?"

Daniel pushed himself up to a sitting position. "I abandoned my plan."

Granston raised his eyebrows. "And came up with a new plan to sit in your cups, alone in your room. I can see the appeal." He raised his hands like scales. "Gorgeous, nubile woman in your bed, an empty bottle of rum on the floor. That does seem like an easy choice."

He tapped Daniel's forehead. It was enough to make Daniel see stars.

"As I apparently didn't teach you as well as I thought, let me clarify for you. The correct choice was the nubile woman. And did I mention, she should be naked?"

Daniel couldn't tell Granston the reason he'd abandoned the seduction and taken to a bottle of rum had been to obliterate the memory of the pain he'd seen on her face. He'd longed to see the footloose, tomboy of a girl who'd succumbed to his flirtations all those years ago. But Daniel wasn't the only one who'd forever lost the carefree, naïve days of his youth. He never would have wished such a loss on her, not even when he'd hated her most, when he'd left England licking his wounds and nursing his broken heart.

"I didn't intend to change my plan," Daniel said. "Something came up."

"That's quite the idea, lad. And if you're very good and want to make said nubile woman very happy, it will ideally come up over and over again."

Daniel groaned and ran a hand through his hair. "The depth of your ability to disgust is bottomless."

"As is the depth of your ability to disappoint. And what of the young woman? How disappointed must she be? Perhaps she needs my assistance more than you."

"Don't even think it." Daniel tried to show an intimidating glower but only succeeded in intensifying the pounding in his head. "As much as I'm going to live to regret saying this, I'm saying it anyway. I need your assistance."

Granston rubbed his hands together. "That's what I've been waiting to hear. Don't worry Hallsy, Granston to the rescue. I'll have the poor abandoned girl writhing in pleasure within the hour."

Granston's cavalier use of the term "abandoned girl" cut Daniel to the quick. "I'm serious Granston. Something came up in my conversation with Miss Trent last night."

"That was your first mistake. You should never have attempted to converse with her."

"How does any woman tolerate you? Actually, it was something she said earlier in the day. Last night's conversation just solidified my thoughts. Do you suppose the *ton* has moved on from my family's scandal? Might some of them remember my parents kindly?"

Granston grabbed Daniel's shoulders. "Are you an idiot, man? Of course they've moved on. And those who haven't will be silenced quickly enough, once you waltz back into town, title restored and ugly rumors permanently laid to rest. You've been gone so long, and there have been so many ridiculous stories attached to your name, no one worth knowing will consider the charges of illegitimacy."

"About all those scandalous rumors, did you ever consider saying there was no real scandal?"

Granston widened his eyes and looked truly sincere. "But there was! People wouldn't forget that, but the details could become fuzzy over time. I've effectively muddled the whole affair. Now all you have to do is keep it that way. Don't give them a reason to question your honor or your legitimacy again."

"But some of those stories...there are those who could have been hurt by rumors of my sexual improprieties."

"No one was naming names. No young ladies were... Oh, I see. This is about the chit who broke your heart. Meriden's little sister. Let me remind you, she told you she never wanted to see you again. If she couldn't be persuaded to hear your side of the story, to hell with her."

"That's where you're wrong. She never told me. Meriden told me. Do you suppose he would lie about such a thing to keep me away from her?"

Granston shrugged. "He was deadly protective of his sisters. He was never happy about your feelings for her, or hers for you. I remember the thrashing he gave you when he learned she'd sent you a letter at school."

Daniel grinned. "It wasn't even a love letter. It was something she and her friends did on a lark, sending correspondence to boys they knew." Love would come the following summer, so Meriden's unhappiness hadn't been totally misplaced.

"Meriden's not a bad sort. If he lied, he probably thought it was for the best, to protect her. But that's been years. You can't pine over the girl. No doubt she's married and fat, with babes underfoot by now."

Granston still hadn't realized the truth about Emme. It was the only comforting thing that had come out of this conversation. "Regardless of where she is now, what do you suppose it did to her at the time, if she thought I left without saying a word to her?"

Granston patted Daniel's shoulder. "If that's what happened, Hallsy, I'm afraid you probably broke the girl's heart. Tell you what, when we get to England, we'll track her down and you can say you're sorry. Take some flowers to her. Maybe some toys for the children. Lord knows you have the money to get them something nice."

"That is a comfort."

"All right, then my work here is done." Granston jumped to his feet. "As for you, recover from your hangover today. Tomorrow we dock at our last port before Brighton, and you have some fine brandy to buy to get us through the rest of this journey." He set the empty bottle on the bedside table. "Not to mention a bottle of rum."

CHAPTER 5

*E*mme stood on the deck with her arm linked in her aunt's. She was back in her plain gray gown with one thin crinoline beneath it. She no longer wore it to keep up her ruse. While she'd been learning the terrible truth about her brother a few evenings earlier, Aunt Juliana had sussed out that the bachelor on board was engaged, the older couple's sons were married, and none of the other travelers seemed to have unmarried relatives of an appropriate age. As for Captain Percival and Daniel, the former had turned decidedly formal in his dealings with her, and the latter hadn't been able to get away from her fast enough. Still, the gray gown was her lightest and easiest, and she hadn't minded getting the hem dirty while she and Aunt Juliana had gone with a few of the other passengers, a young couple with two small children, to the shops close to the shoreline.

She'd seen the return of every one of the passengers

and crew who had disembarked except one. Daniel had gone off with Captain Percival, but the captain had come back without him. Something akin to panic assailed Emme as she considered he might not return, after all. He could easily find another ship, perhaps even one of his own, to take him the rest of the way to England. Or worse, he could resume his adventurous life in Spain. Their paths might never cross again, and they would never settle what had happened between them.

Gathering her courage, she walked determinedly across the deck to where the captain barked orders at his men. When he turned toward her, his face was set in a stern line. Seeing her, his expression softened and his lips curved into a smile.

He took her hand. "Miss Trent, it's a delight to see you. I would have enjoyed escorting you into town, but my friend had need of my services."

He still referred to her without her title, so either Daniel hadn't told him of her true identity, or the captain was being respectful of her privacy. The way he still held her hand led her to believe it was the former.

"Yes, I saw you leave with Mr. Hallsworth."

"I'm flattered you were looking for me." He frowned at her. "Unless you're going to shatter my heart and my ego in one fell swoop and tell me you were looking for Hallsy."

She bit her lower lip. She saw his gaze drop to her lips. He was a handsome man and charming to boot. Under other circumstances, she might quite enjoy a flirtation with him, knowing she could stop him in his tracks with the truth of her station if he meant to cross a line. But today, she was preoccupied with Daniel. If she were being honest with herself, perhaps she had been preoccupied with him since the day she'd met him.

"I'm sorry, Captain Percival. It's just that Mr. Hallsworth and I have a history."

"Yes, he mentioned the same thing. In fact, I believe he used those exact words. He was rather vague about the details, though."

The thought of those details made Emme blush. He politely glanced at his crew and pretended not to notice.

"I hate to be a bother, but I noticed he didn't return with you."

"Yes, he had one more errand to run. Said I wasn't to set sail without him. But to be honest with you, if I thought I could capture your attention by leaving him behind, I would do so. Just say the word, dear Miss Trent."

She smiled. She did so miss innocent flirtation that had no hope of ending in a marriage proposal. "It might be perceived as unseemly to leave behind one's friend and business partner simply to garner a woman's attention."

"You are not just any woman, and there is nothing simple about it." He bent and kissed her hand, then finally released it. "I'm sure he'll join us any minute."

"Thank you, sir. And if you don't mind, could we keep this exchange between us?"

"Sharing confidences with you. I do like the sound of that. As you wish, Miss Trent."

Emme felt lighter as she crossed the deck to rejoin her aunt.

"Feeling better, dear?"

"I am."

"So, the captain was able to confirm that Mr. Hallsworth will return."

"Who mentioned Mr. Hallwsorth?"

"The glow about you at the mention of his name says it all."

Emme was about to argue the point when some movement to her left caught her eye. Her breath caught in her throat. Something had gone over the railing. Something or someone. Too large to be a doll. Too small to be an adult. One of the young couple's children.

Instinct overtook Emme. She kicked off her shoes and cleared the railing in seconds. She was vaguely aware of screams and shouts as she dove into the bay. Cold water closed over her.

Already, Ann, the oldest child of the family with whom she'd just spent the day, was far away from her, being pulled by the tide. Terror seized Emme and made her swim harder, kick faster. Her thin skirt tangled, but her legs fought against it, propelling her toward the child. She had no idea how far behind her the ship was now, and she didn't care. Her only focus was Ann. She would rather drown herself than watch another girl die because she was too late to save her.

The child somehow managed to keep her head above water until Emme was just inches from her. Then a large wave rose above them, and in an instant Ann disappeared. Kicking wildly and reaching blindly, Emme miraculously grabbed hold of material. The girl's dress. She yanked on it with all her might while treading the waves and praying the fabric wouldn't give way before she could take hold of the child. When the small body bounced against her, she wrapped both arms around the girl.

Ann was flailing in a panic, catching Emme's skirt and tightening it around her legs. Remembering the way Edward had rescued her the day she'd gone into the lake after Eleanor, she wrapped her arm around Ann's neck, resting the girl's chin in the crook of her elbow. With her face to the sun and the ability to breathe, the girl was calmer. But the waves were stronger than they'd looked from the ship, the water was frigid, and Emme was exhausted from her physical exertion.

She spit out a mouthful of salt water and turned to see how far away the ship was from them. Her heart sank. She would never make it.

Before panic could consume her, she saw three figures approaching. Three men were powering through the waves, while at the edge of the ship, sailors had just dropped a dinghy into the water. As Emme's arms went numb and she feared she would lose her grip on the child, one of the men wrapped steel-hard arms around her waist while the other two took hold of the child.

In minutes, Emme was in the dinghy, clinging to the child, who had gone past shock and had begun sobbing. Only when they were nearly back to the ship did she realize the man still held her. Turning to face him, she saw Daniel's intense blue eyes staring back at her.

"Don't you dare scare me like that again." His voice was quiet, but the demand behind his words was unmistakable.

"How did you...you weren't even on the ship."

"I was on the dock when I saw you go over the railing. Do you understand just how close you came to drowning? Christ in heaven, Emmeline, I've never been so terrified by anything in my entire life. I truly thought I might lose you."

The small boat bumped against the wharf, and one of the men who had taken Ann from her arms in the water now took the child from her again and handed her up to a sailor waiting on the dock. Only after he'd taken the child from her did she realize one of their rescuers had been the captain. He heaved himself onto the dock and reached out his hands to take Emme. Daniel helped her stand in the unsteady craft and handed her to his friend on the wharf. He swung up onto the boards beside her, wrapping his arms around her once more.

She made to walk up the gangplank onto the ship,

but her legs, nearly numb, buckled under her. Wordlessly, Daniel scooped her into his arms and carried her on board. Her body sagged and her eyes drifted shut against her will.

"I'm sorry," she managed to say. "I just couldn't let it happen again. I had to save her."

"You did save her, kitten. It was the most foolish thing I've ever seen, but it was also the bravest. Still, I don't think I'll ever let you out of my sight again."

Or out of my arms, she hoped he'd say.

She heard other voices. Her aunt, nearly hysterical with worry. Ann's parents, calling out their undying gratitude to her. Captain Granston, demanding everyone clear the way for them to take her and Ann to the ship's medic. And still Daniel held her. He was the only constant, the only thing keeping her warm and safe.

When there was a soft mattress under her back and a bright lantern over her head, she heard another man's voice tell Daniel to make room for the medic. Daniel stepped a few feet away from the bed, but he kept his hand clasped over hers.

"I'm not leaving your side until I know you're all right, kitten."

"No one asked you to leave." There was so much more she wanted to say to him, but she was fuzzy-headed and nauseated.

"She's swallowed a lot of seawater," the medic said.

Funny, she didn't remember doing so. Then again, she couldn't be sure whether he was talking about her or Ann, and she didn't have the strength to open her eyes to see which of them he was observing.

The medic and Daniel spoke in hushed voices, then Daniel propped her against his body and held a small glass to her lips. "Drink this, kitten. It will warm you from the inside out."

Emme wanted to be warm again. She was so cold. Wet and cold. She could barely swallow the burning liquid, she was shivering so hard.

"I think she'll be fine," the medic said. "We have to get her out of these wet clothes, sir. I've sent for her maid. Perhaps you should take this opportunity to change your own clothes."

"Not a chance, McReedy. Send one of the men to fetch dry clothes for me as well, and stay with the child. I'll keep watch over the lady."

Some distant sense of propriety set in and Emme struggled to open her eyes, to insist he take his leave while her maid saw to her. But she couldn't accomplish either of those tasks. She could sink into a deep sleep while the brandy he'd given her burned warmly in her belly.

A few hours later, in the privacy of his stateroom, Daniel poured Lady Kendall a second glass of scotch. The woman tossed it back with alarming speed. He worried he'd have to deny her a third glass, but she seemed significantly steadied by the second shot.

"As I said, I can't thank you enough for what you did. If you hadn't gone in after her..."

"Lady Emme is the true heroine," he said. "She saved a child's life today."

"But she nearly gave up her own doing it. I've never been so terrified."

He sat in the wing chair beside the elderly woman and glanced across his room to where Emme lay sleeping in his bed. The sight of her there made his heart beat faster. "I said almost those exact words to her."

"I can't believe she took such a chance after what happened to Eleanor. Although, perhaps that's why she felt compelled to save the child."

"I don't understand. Perhaps *what* is why she felt so compelled?"

"Of course, it isn't true, but Emmeline thinks because she saw Eleanor fall into the lake, she should have been able to pull her out of it."

He sat up straight in his chair. "She saw Lady Eleanor fall into the water?"

"Yes. They'd had an argument, as sisters often do. Eleanor left the house and Emmeline followed her. It was a drizzly morning. Eleanor was walking along the lake and lost her footing, and Emmeline went right in after her. But she couldn't save her sister, and Edward nearly didn't save Emmeline."

Daniel poured himself another drink and tossed it

back. Eschewing propriety, he offered Lady Kendall another. She accepted, but at least she sipped this one.

"So Emme nearly drowned that day."

"She would have, if Edward hadn't gotten there in time." Lady Kendall took a long drag of scotch. "Somehow, in her mind, Emmeline has twisted that into the reason Eleanor couldn't be saved, because Edward was too busy saving *her*. She hasn't forgiven herself."

He watched Emme turn over in her sleep. His heart broke for her. "What a terrible burden to bear."

"And an unnecessary one. Edward wasn't the only one who came to their rescue. He was on a morning ride with the stable master and a few of the lads when they heard Emmeline scream. When they got to the lake, they didn't even catch a glimpse of Eleanor. They speculated that with her heavy cloak and skirt and layers of crinoline, she'd been pulled under quickly."

"I had no idea," Daniel said. "I knew Lady Eleanor had died, but I didn't even know how until a few days ago. To think Lady Emme witnessed the whole thing. Yet she boarded a ship to Spain, and on this one to return home. And today she went over that railing after the child without a second thought."

"Not to mention the fact that she swam in the ocean nearly every day during our time in Barcelona. At first, I thought it was to conquer her fear. When I finally asked her about it, she said she needed to be stronger so she wouldn't fail the next time someone needed her. Perhaps now she'll feel vindicated and will be able to sleep without nightmares."

Daniel was rendered temporarily speechless. His carefree tomboy, who'd he'd come to view as a broken girl, proved him wrong again. She was no wounded bird. She was a phoenix, a force of nature. A woman strong enough to take on the ocean itself to save others from nature's cruel punishment. Every cell in his body longed to go to her, to hold her, to replenish some of that depleted strength with his own flesh.

Beside him, Lady Kendall finished her drink, then set down her glass and yawned. Daniel knew the day had been taxing on her.

"I think she'll sleep peacefully this night until morning," he said. "I'll keep watch over her, and the medic is just down the hall if anything goes awry."

"I could hardly impose upon you like that. Perhaps we should move her to my room."

Daniel shook his head. "I appreciate your sense of propriety, but in this case, I must insist you choose reason over modesty. It's best for her health that she not be disturbed." And as he'd told Emme earlier, he wasn't about to let her out of his sight again. At least not any time soon. "A crewman is right outside the door. He'll see you back to your room. Get a good night's sleep, and you can reunite with your niece in the morning, when you're both feeling in tip-top shape again."

The set of the woman's jaw said she wanted to dig in her heels about the matter, but the deep shadows around her eyes proved she didn't have the energy to stand up to him for long. She seemed to realize it, too, and conceded.

Daniel walked her to the door and gave his man instructions, then closed the door and locked it behind them. He moved slowly to his bed, the bed where the first woman he had ever truly desired—not only physically but also emotionally—now sighed and turned toward him. He sat beside her and placed his hand on her cheek. She smiled in her sleep and the beauty of it undid him. He wanted to hold her, just for a moment, so he slid under the quilt and wrapped his arms around her. The heat of her skin radiated through the thin chemise she wore. When he pulled her close, her curves melded perfectly against the planes of his body.

It wasn't terribly late, but it had been an eventful day, and he was so tired. And her warmth and softness enticed him to stay with her just a bit longer. Such a delightful—albeit unspoken—invitation couldn't be ignored. Daniel closed his eyes.

CHAPTER 6

*E*mme woke in a dimly-lit room. Something heavy lay over her, trapping her, and something solid pressed against her back.

Daniel.

His hand was splayed open and pressed against her thin chemise beneath her navel. Her breath quickened as her body remembered the sensation of those hands tracing the curves of her body through her nightgown. Need shot through her so rapidly and unexpectedly, it left her panting. She wriggled to press more tightly against him, inadvertently sliding his hand across the fabric of her chemise. Fire ignited between her legs. She longed to feel his hands on every inch of her skin.

As she remembered their late-night rendezvous in the library at her family's country estate, her breath came in ragged gasps. It was only then she realized something had changed. Behind her, Daniel's breath had stopped for one quick second, then had returned, more rapid and shallow than before.

He was awake.

And judging from his erection pressing against her backside, he knew the erotic memories she'd been reliving. For a moment, they both lay still. Emme wondered if she should feign sleep, leaving them both with the dignity of being able to deny the lust that flared between them. Then he pressed his lips to her neck, just below her ear, and she gasped. There was no deniability left. She turned in his arms to face him.

He ran his fingers over the chemise and gripped her hip. "Tell me what you were thinking, Emme. Tell me what you remembered when you wriggled against me."

Despite the embarrassment that suffused her face with heat, she longed to tell him. She had to know whether he recalled every intimate detail as clearly as she did. "I was remembering when you touched me the night we were alone together."

"Tell me," he whispered, bringing his face within inches of hers. "Tell me the details, kitten. Start with the kisses."

She smiled. He did remember. They'd shared clandestine but chaste walks through the garden for days. And then one afternoon, he'd come across her alone at the swimming pond. It was the first time they'd ever touched. When they'd met in the library later, he'd feigned lost memory, and to remind him had made her describe the details of how, as they'd floated side by side in the pond, he'd held her hand and stroked her cheek. And then he had done so much more to her, had touched her in new places and in such exquisite ways.

"The kisses," she repeated. She closed her eyes to savor the memory. "First you kissed one corner of my mouth, then the other. And then your lips met mine."

She hadn't even finished speaking the words when she felt the first kiss on one corner of her mouth, then one on the other corner. And then, just as she remembered it, he pressed his lips against hers. But this was different from her memory of it. Better. There was no gentle teasing and coaxing into a kiss. He was hard and demanding. She met the pressure and parted her lips. His mouth was so familiar, yet the sensations were intense in a way their kisses hadn't been years earlier. Each nip and lick and taunt sparked along every nerve ending in her body.

Hours earlier, she'd thought she was going to die. But now, here, in Daniel's bed, she was alive. She needed to savor every moment of it.

"Please, play the game later." She wriggled to reach the hem of her chemise and pulled it over her head. Heat flooded her face again, but she pushed off her drawers, now naked in front of him for the first time. She savored the softness of the sheets against her bare skin. "Touch me now, the way you did then."

He stroked her shoulder, his gaze fixed on her face. "I can't. We can't. You've had a shock. I can't take advantage of that."

She grabbed his wrist, pulled his hand beneath the

thin sheet that covered her, and pressed his palm over her heart. "Daniel, I want you. Can't you feel it?"

He closed his eyes and drew a shaky breath, then traced one finger across her breastbone and over the nipple of one breast. He moved his fingers to her belly, pausing at her navel. She watched the outline of his hand under the sheet as it went lower and he ran his finger up the inside of her thigh. "Tell me what you want, kitten."

She could barely form words. "I want...what you're doing...only more. And your lips on my skin."

He placed kisses down her neck, then whispered again. "What else?"

She longed for the release he could give her, but this time she wanted more. "I don't want to stop. I don't want you to stop."

"I won't stop," he whispered as his fingers stroked her ever more intimately. Two of his fingers touched her wetness and slid inside her.

She gasped and tightened around him.

"Hells bells, Emme, you'll be the death of me."

With his lips tracing their way down her neck and breasts, she arched in anticipation of the next pleasure that awaited her. He stroked his fingers inside her. She bit her lip and moaned. "Daniel. Daniel! Oh..."

Her entire body clenched of its own accord. The pressure between her legs and in her lower belly rose to an unbearable crescendo. She feared he'd stop, as he had years ago, when they'd thought they'd have a lifetime together to finish what they'd started. Blissfully, this time he continued. He rubbed and stroked and drove her so far into her need, she didn't remember any other way of being, until the unbearable pressure crested and broke and heat radiated out from a place deep inside her.

"Emme," he whispered. "You're so beautiful, so passionate. Oh God, the sight of you."

She slowly returned to her senses. When she opened her eyes, he was watching her.

"Did I make you happy, kitten?"

"Mmmm. So happy."

She rolled onto her side and traced a fingertip from his cheek down to his neck, then lower to his chest that was revealed by his partially unbuttoned shirt. She deftly undid the rest of the buttons and slid the shirt off his shoulders. He moved to let it drop to the floor. Emme explored the muscles of his chest, remembering how it had felt when he'd pulled her against him in the water. She compared him to her memory. His chest was broader and stronger, and there was more hair sprinkled over the smooth skin, but his nipples still hardened when she stroked them. Before he could know what she planned to do, something she'd regretted not doing the summer they'd fallen in love, she ran her fingers down over his tight abdomen and cradled his erection through his trousers.

His eyes closed on a moan, but he pushed at her hand. "No, Emme."

So, he thought that would be the same as well, that he would explore and pleasure her body, but she would barely touch him? He had argued they had to restrain themselves, that he wasn't about to ruin her, that she should remain a virgin until marriage. It had sounded like a reasonable case that night in the library, but things had changed. She grasped him more tightly, and he cried out in pleasure.

"I'm no longer the innocent girl I was when you knew me last." She slid her hand up to his waist and under his clothing as she spoke. It was the first time she'd ever felt the velvety-smooth skin of his erection under her fingertips. He lay motionless, his arousal belied only by his hardness in her hand and his quick breaths.

"If you believe that, kitten, it's proof you have no idea what more I could do to you. What more I want so desperately to do to you, especially when you touch me that way."

"Nothing is stopping you."

"There's propriety, for one. Your reputation, your future."

"To hell with all those things."

"Emmeline!"

She sat up and pulled the sheet tight against her. It was now or never. She wanted him, needed him so badly, and it seemed the only way to have him was to tell him the truth. Even if she were able to convince him without an admission of her guilt, he'd know soon enough.

"Daniel, I'm not a virgin."

He sat up next to her and ran a hand through his

hair. The way several strands stood on end enticed her, begged her to run her hand over them to smooth them.

"Kitten, what we've done hasn't taken your virginity."

She grimaced. "I know that. I'm not a ninny."

He wasn't going to make this easy for her. She'd have to say it. All of it.

"There was a fiancé. My fiancé, for a short time. Before I went to Spain."

Shock registered on his face. He grasped her hands. "Did he force you? Did he hurt you? Where was your father?" He clenched his jaw. "Where was your brother?"

"There was no force. There were extenuating circumstances." Her heart sank when she saw how he looked at her, and he didn't even know the worst of it. And he wouldn't. The part she'd played in orchestrating her own ruination would remain her secret.

She pulled her hands away from his. "I suppose it changes everything. I'm sullied."

He pressed his lips to her palm. "I'm not a virgin, either, and just so you understand, I don't consider either of us to be sullied. Kitten, look at me." He stroked her chin as she looked up into his eyes. "I wanted to be your first, but there were reasons we couldn't. Those reasons haven't gone away. I'm relieved you weren't coerced or hurt, but he used you badly, I'm afraid."

She pressed a finger to his lips. "That's not what happened."

He pressed a kiss to her finger. "You were grieving. It was hardly fair to you."

She ran her hand over his cheek and down the side of his neck. When she reached his collarbone, he stayed her hand with his.

He looked away from her. "Nor would this be fair. You're still grieving. And there are other considerations."

Emme took his hand in hers. "Daniel, what is it? Are you still grieving? You lost both your parents in such a short time. And then...then you had to leave."

He ran his hand through his hair again and let up a long breath before meeting her gaze. "After what I've gone through with my uncle, I won't burden a child of mine with being a bastard."

"But those were just ugly rumors started by your uncle, and you've prevailed. Your title has been reinstated."

"Not yet. There will be discussions and conditions." He stared down at their joined hands. "And even though my uncle prevailed, it doesn't make the rumor untrue."

Emme gasped. They sat in silence for a moment as she tried to make sense of what he'd just said. When she could finally speak, she didn't have any wise words to say. "I'm sorry. It's quite a shock."

"To me, too. My mother told me when she was dying. She and the marquess had tried to have a child for years. And then one of my father's—the marquess's —old Army mates got a young lady in trouble. They all thought it was the perfect solution. No one counted on me looking so much like my real father, or on my uncle's suspicions about his brother and sister-in-law finally conceiving after more than a decade of marriage."

Emme wanted to say something. She needed to close the chasm that his heart-wrenching story was opening between them, but no words came to her. She squeezed his hand.

"I'd met him, my real father, over the years. He was exciting, fascinating. An adventurer who rarely returned home. Perhaps having his blood in my veins has made it easier for me to stay away from England so long."

Now he squeezed her hand. "And a part of me will always be sad for losing the illusion of my childhood, of being the marquess's and marchioness's blood son. But they loved me, as does my real father. For them, I'll go home and pretend to be the true heir and live the life they all wanted for me. So yes, I'm sad, sometimes melancholy. But no longer grieving."

She shook her head. "I'm sorry for all of it. For what you had to learn. For the way society and my own family treated you. For not being there for you as you grieved for your parents and your past."

How would she feel to learn she wasn't her parents' daughter, to be disconnected from the identity she'd had her entire life, to have it snatched out from under her in an instant? She couldn't imagine how deeply it must have cut. She wrapped her arms tightly around

Daniel, trying desperately to provide solace to him now.

He stroked her hair. "But you, kitten, you *are* still grieving. You're still wearing mourning colors." He held her shoulders and gently pulled her away from him. "And as much as I want this, as much as I believe you want it, too, we can't do this. Not this way. I won't risk your feelings."

She pulled out of his arms. "I'm an adult. My feelings are my own concern."

He closed his eyes for a fleeting second and shook his head. "You must at least concede a pregnancy would be both our concerns."

"There are precautions. Surely, you're aware of them. You said yourself you're not a virgin."

"That would have required planning. And what has happened over the past twelve hours is nothing I'd planned. I'm sorry, Emme."

The shock of his refusal hit her like the sea waves had hours earlier. Once again, he was rejecting her. It came so easily to him.

"I should go back to my cabin." She lurched toward the side of the bed.

He grasped her shoulders. "No. You need rest. Lie back down."

She twisted, but couldn't break free from him. "Please, don't make me stay here with you."

"Emme, it's not—"

"Please." She choked out the word. "It's humiliating."

"Don't." He dropped his hands. "Please, just lie back

down and rest. I'll go, if that's what you want, but the medic said you must rest."

She didn't want him to see her this way, but she didn't want him to go, either. She sat with her back to him, staring at the wall beside the bed, unsure of what to say or do, only knowing that if she'd still had the ability to cry, the tears would be streaming down her face by now. At least she was spared that embarrassment.

"Go," she finally said.

The mattress shifted as he rose from the bed. "Please, lie down."

With her face still turned away from him, she obeyed. She curled onto her side and he laid the blankets over her.

"I'll make sure the medic checks on you regularly."

"Don't..."

Don't go, she wanted to scream. *Don't leave me. Don't reject me.* But she couldn't ask that of him, that much was clear.

And he was right. She had just temporarily lost her senses. It had to be the shock of the events of the day, of the events of this entire interminable journey that had almost sent her down the same destructive path she'd already traveled. She was past those bad choices now and well on her way to redemption.

"Don't what, kitten?"

She swallowed the lump in her throat that made it almost too tight to speak. "Don't make a fuss."

"Just rest," he said, and then the cabin door swished open and clicked shut again behind him.

Alone with nothing but the sound of the waves lapping against the ship, Emme longed to cry, to release her angst and take the edge off her anger. But the tears refused to come, as they had since the day of Eleanor's death.

*D*aniel paced along the edge of his stateroom, then stopped to lift the shade from the porthole for at least the fourth time to check the status of the sunrise. This time, the clouds on the horizon were pink and the lower half of the sky was gray. Daybreak was finally underway. Soon Emme and he would look at each other in the bright light of day. Outwardly, they would look the same, but in truth, everything had changed last night.

He'd told her his deepest secret, the truth he'd only ever shared with Granston and Swimmer, and then only because he'd been drunk and desperate to unburden his soul. When he'd accosted her in the dark passageway just over a week ago, he'd believed her unworthy of ever earning his trust again. But this was Emmeline. Emme. *His* Emme, back in his arms and his life, and just as he'd felt five years ago, he trusted her with his truth and, much to his own shock, his heart.

And she'd trusted him with her secret, as well. Her virginity was no longer an issue, but her innocence—

and she might not realize it, but she was still innocent
—was. He still meant to have her. But not in the way
she'd offered herself to him, the way he'd wanted to
take her. This time, they would do things properly. The
moment she woke from her much-needed slumber,
they would agree upon his new plan.

"No doubt she's of the same mind," he told himself.
She'd always had a way of making him desperate with
wanting her, and desperation had almost led to care-
lessness. Again.

"Daniel? What time is it?"

Just the sound of her voice, still thick with sleep,
made him want to climb into bed with her this minute.
They were just days from England, and then they could
formalize everything. It would still take months. Too
long to be reasonable, but soon enough that he could
wait. And soon enough that if she asked him to make
love to her again, he'd only find the strength to refuse
her through knowing he'd remedy the wrong in due
time.

He adjusted his frock coat to ensure she couldn't
identify the evidence of her effect on him, and turned
to face her with a smile. She'd already sat up and
propped herself against the pillows.

"Good morning." He sat on the edge of the bed and
leaned over to kiss her chastely on the cheek. "How do
you feel this morning?"

"Better."

In truth, she didn't look better. Her eyes, so bleary

from salt water yesterday, were now bloodshot and swollen.

She shifted under his scrutiny and pulled the blanket up to her chin. "I didn't expect to see you today."

"Emme, we need to talk."

She wriggled a few inches farther away from him. "No, there's really no need. We said all that needed to be said last night."

He stood and stepped closer to the window, giving her the courtesy of modesty and distance she seemed to need this morning. "Not yet. We need to discuss what nearly happened last night."

"But nothing happened." Her shoulders dropped, just an inch, but it was progress. "It was rash to suggest. I apologize. I don't want you to think I went into...that I did what I did with my former fiancé in such a rash way. We were eloping, and on our way to Scotland, we had to stop for the night. He suspected my family was on our heels, and it was the only way to...well."

Her words were like a knife in his heart. The thought of her with a scheming man who'd taken advantage of her grief was enough to drive him utterly mad. Given the chance, he would throttle Meriden for allowing such a thing to happen. A small voice in his head mocked him for his own hypocrisy. Hadn't he thought to ruin her himself? But for now, there was nothing he could do about it.

"Extenuating circumstances, as we discussed. But that's in the past. We need to discuss—"

"He wasn't a suitable match in my father's eyes," she continued. "He had no title, but a bit of wealth, so he had entrée into some of the finest events. The first time I saw him from behind, with his thick, dark hair, I thought he was you."

She'd been engaged to a man she'd originally thought was him. With money but no title. No doubt her father had thought the man as worthless as he'd deemed Daniel.

Emme continued. "When he turned to face me, of course I knew he wasn't you, but he was handsome enough, and a talented dancer, and he took a shine to me."

"That was big of him."

"Of course, if you'd still been in England, I wouldn't have given him a second look."

Daniel's heart did a little trill in his chest. They were of the same mind, as he had presumed.

"Anyway, I didn't regard his lack of pedigree as a problem. We just had to convince my father, which is where our, er, *indiscretion* came into play."

Seducing a woman to force a marriage. It was shamefully close to the designs he'd had on her at first. He clenched his fists in anger at Sanderson, but mostly at himself.

He willed his hands to relax. "Was he careful?" he asked quietly.

"Yes, as I told you, he didn't hurt me and – oh. Oh, I see." She stared at the distant wall. "Fortunately, it turned out he hadn't left me with child when he ran off and married an obscenely wealthy heiress."

But the lack of a pregnancy had been sheer luck. The reprobate hadn't even taken care to protect her. Daniel wanted to hunt down the man and pull him limb from limb, but he calmed himself enough to take her hand gently. "I'm sorry about last night. I might have given you the impression I didn't want you. Nothing could be further from the truth. I still want you. Desperately."

Her eyes widened. "Right now?" She glanced at the window where the morning light leaked in around the edges of the curtains. "In the light of day?"

Still clasping her hand, he knelt on one knee beside the bed. "Lady Emmeline Radcliffe, will you do me the honor of marrying me?"

"Marry you!" She snatched her hand away from him and jumped out of the opposite side of the bed, blankets still clutched to her breast. "I can't marry you. I've written letters, made plans. I'm officially a spinster."

Her words made no sense. Perhaps she was still in shock from yesterday's events. "Emme, please sit down. You look pale."

She held up one hand to warn him to keep his distance. "I will not sit down. I will not stay here with a…a…marriage-minded bachelor for one more minute!"

"Last night we nearly…" He shook his head. It was as if she had no idea how a woman was to react to a marriage proposal. He'd have to persuade her, and time was not on his side. Soon her aunt might rise and come looking for her. "What if we'd never been separated five years ago? Do you suppose you might have married me if I'd had the chance to ask?"

Tears shone in her eyes. "What does it matter now? As you've said, it's in the past."

"Do you truly believe that? Because after last night, I'm more inclined to believe fate reunited us to finish what we started years ago."

"Fate." Her face was unreadable.

He cursed under his breath. "Yes, fate. Kismet. Alignment of the stars and all that." He reached out his hand to her. "What will it take, Emme? Just tell me. What do you want?"

"To be a spinster! Really, it's like you haven't even been listening."

Daniel squeezed his eyes shut. The throbbing in his temples made the rum hangover pale in comparison. "This might be the most muddled conversation I've ever had."

When he opened his eyes, Emme had moved out from the side of the bed and picked up her now-dry dress from a chair. "At least we can agree on that," she said as she pulled the thin gray frock over her head.

He'd never bothered to be there in the morning after a night of pleasure, so he'd never watched a woman dress before, but he was quite sure Emme was making a mess of it. He strode to her side and helped her struggle her arms into her sleeves. "You have to marry me."

She glared at him as she stepped back and tugged at the laces of her bodice. "Because you've helped me with my gown?"

He clenched his jaw and stepped close enough to feel the heat of her skin. She was supposed to have agreed by now, the stubborn woman. He knew it was desperately unfair of him, but he was, after all, desperate. "Because we spent the night alone together. What if someone were to learn of it?"

"Nothing happened. I was indisposed and given no choice."

"That will hardly matter if tongues start wagging. Trust me, I know how whisper campaigns can destroy a reputation."

"No one will learn of it. The other passengers are nowhere near your stateroom, you pay every sailor on this ship, and my aunt will never mention it. No one will ever know." She stalked to the door, then turned abruptly toward him. "Unless you plan to tell someone."

It crossed his mind. Heaven help him, if he couldn't entreat her, he could force her. And what would that make him? Just as bad as that lout of a fiancé.

"Emme, I'm sorry. I thought we were of the same mind. I misunderstood."

"I should say so." She straightened the skirt of her dress and pushed her untamed hair out of her face. "Now if you'll excuse me, I'm sure my aunt will want to be apprised of my health on this fine morning. Good day, Mr. Hallsworth."

In all the years they'd known each other, she had never addressed him so formally. Daniel gave her a slight bow. "Good day, Lady Emmeline."

And with that, she swept out of his stateroom and closed the door soundly behind her, taking with her his last hope for love.

CHAPTER 7

*E*mme had been avoiding Daniel for the week since he'd proposed. Now that they'd reached England's shores and she was about to walk away from him forever, she was seized by a desperate urge to throw herself into his arms

"It will improve shortly." Aunt Juliana gazed at the looming shoreline of Brighton.

The gray mist pressed in against Emme's skin and made it hard to catch a proper breath. "Will it? As I recall, this weather's just as to be expected."

"Not the weather. Your mood. Being farther from *the sea* will make you feel better."

Emme nodded. "I'm sure it will."

"And if it doesn't, you could always consider the alternative."

"Becoming a pirate?"

Her aunt shot her a sideways glance. "I was trying

to be tactful, but if I must be blunt, you could just marry the boy."

"Maybe once upon a time." Emme focused on the crowds and carriages gathering on the dock.

Once upon a time, she hadn't lost her virginity to a cad she'd never planned to marry. Once upon a time, she hadn't stood at the brink of ruin. Once upon a time, she hadn't carried a secret that could pose a threat to Daniel reclaiming his title.

"Things have changed," Emme said. "I've found my calling with the spinsters. It's important work. Not to mention, marriage isn't something my family does well, is it?"

While it wasn't the most important reason she'd never marry, it was no small consideration.

"Your parents were very happy once. They've had some setbacks, but they'll come through it."

"Ah, marriage. Something to *come through*."

"No need to be saucy," Aunt Juliana chastised her.

Emme laid her hand on top of her aunt's. "I know you're only trying to help. I'm just in a sour mood over the thought of being trotted about London like a thoroughbred horse instead of riding one across your estate. Do you remember how Edward and I used to ride?"

Riding was the one thing—other than her family and friends—she'd missed while she'd been away. The freedom of the wind streaming through her hair. The hypnotic comfort of horse hoofs pounding over the ground. Of course, she hadn't been allowed to ride like that since she'd been a child. Ladies did not ride fast steeds flat-out across country meadows, as she'd been reminded endlessly by every member of her family. She wondered if those rules applied to spinsters as well. She certainly hoped not.

"It will be a good life," she said, more to herself than to her aunt. "A quiet life, but a good and meaningful one."

And a safe one, where no one would be moved to uncover her illicit past and ruin her future with it.

"And will it be enough?" her aunt asked.

A month ago, she would have easily answered yes. Now, she didn't know how to answer.

She squeezed Aunt Juliana's hand, taking comfort more than giving it. "It shall have to be enough."

※

"You want to *marry* the governess? Have you gone soft in the head?" Granston snatched the glass of rum from Daniel's hand and slammed it on the table in the captain's quarters. "Maybe you've just had too much of my good stash."

"You're the one who advised I take a wife."

"After we've had time to raise the devil in every debauched port town in England. And London. And several small countryside villages. Besides, the wife of the future marquess needs to meet exactly three criteria." Granston counted off on his fingers. "One, she should be a ninny. As a man who's taken on far too many intelligent mistresses, trust me on this. Two, she must be of a high station. Neither a governess nor a lady's traveling companion will do. Third, she must be a virgin who is above reproach. Seeing as you're racing hell for leather, I'm assuming you've had something to do with this girl's downfall and are now having an attack of conscience."

"That's not it." Daniel propped his arms on the table and held his pounding head in his hands. The truth, Emme's truth, was a confidence he'd never share with anyone, even his closest friends.

"Don't tell me you have *feelings* for this girl?"

He hadn't planned to tell Granston before he could say the words to Emme, but she'd managed quite the disappearing act for the remainder of their journey. Now they sat in the port of Brighton and she'd disembark any minute, without a backward glance at him.

"I probably didn't have a prayer from the first day I met her. Well, maybe when she was fourteen. But by the time she was seventeen and I kissed her that first time, it was all over for me."

Granston's narrowed his eyes. "Emme. Emmeline. Meriden's sister." He mulled it over for a minute. "Lady Emmeline Radcliffe. History with the girl, indeed. Well played, Hallsy. That will stick it to the earl, marrying her right out from under him. Explains why you want to do it post-haste as well, before he can put a halt to it."

"That might be how it started, but one way or another, I plan to marry her. I just need a plan."

Granston grinned. "Ah, I see."

Daniel shot what he hoped was a withering look at his friend. "See what?"

"The reason for the rum. Turned you down flat, did she?"

He tightened his grip on his glass. "The lady seemed confused."

"She doesn't strike me as the type to be easily confused. Nor easily persuaded, it would seem. Yet you still look hell-bent on dragging her off to Gretna Green."

A shiver ran down Daniel's spine as he thought of Emme at the hands of the fiancé who *had* taken her there and then used her so badly. "That wouldn't help my reputation, now would it? The plan is to woo her, make a respectable match of it. The Committee for Privileges will be impressed."

"Hallsy, this is a complicated game you're playing, winning over a girl who doesn't want you." He rubbed his hands together. "It will require the touch of a master."

Daniel shook his head and instantly regretted it when the room went temporarily out of focus. "You'll steer well clear of this, Granston."

Granston slapped his friend on the shoulder. "While you're in such a mood to take my advice, which I will admit is infallible, let me give you one more piece of it."

"Your ability to misunderstand is matched only by your arrogance." Daniel rose unsteadily to his feet and

Granston had to lay a hand on his shoulder to steady him.

"For now, I advise you to sleep off that half bottle of rum you swallowed. And sober up, man! You hardly need the *ton* gossiping about your propensity for drink. Regarding your problem, I'll begin working on the solution."

"Where are you going? And what the hell do you plan to do?"

Granston grinned much too wickedly for Daniel's taste. "As captain, I must fulfill my obligation to see our fine ladies safely ashore."

Daniel meant to go after him, but he wasn't steady on his feet. He dropped back into the chair and reached for the second half of the rum. If he couldn't stop Granston, the least he could do was be too obliterated for the rest of the day to hear about his friend's exploits.

❧

"*A*h, so pensive, Miss Trent." The captain offered an arm to Emme and one to Aunt Juliana. "No doubt you're distraught over leaving this fine vessel that has delivered us safely to England's bonny shores."

"Returning home will be an adjustment," she said, smiling politely.

"I, for one, am just thrilled to be back on dry land." Aunt Juliana sighed. "I mean no offense to the SS

Lizette, Captain, but I think I shall do quite nicely without the ocean beneath my feet."

"And you, Miss Trent, are you just as anxious to be rid of my swift schooner and humble hospitality?"

Emme smiled. "No, sir. I shall quite miss the hospitality. You are a fine captain and ever the gentleman."

"I beg of you, don't let word of it get around London," he said as they made their way down the gangplank to the dock.

Somewhere in the crowd were Emme's parents and brother, the last of her relatives outside of her dear great-aunt, waiting to receive her back into the bosom of the family. A family without a sister. Parents without a civil word to say to each other. A brother chastising himself for his younger sister's downfall.

A brother she'd forgiven days ago for his part in separating her from Daniel. He had never acted with anything but her best interest at heart, and the scandal plaguing Daniel's family would have made a match impossible. Her father would never have allowed it. Emme didn't doubt Edward had stepped in to keep her from giving her heart to a man she'd never have been able to marry. How could he have known she'd already lost her heart, since she'd never confided it to him? And Daniel still would have left. The scandal and his grief over his parents' deaths had sealed that fate.

Her stomach twisted as she stepped onto British soil and knew that, this time, she was the one leaving him.

"Miss Trent, you've gone quite pale," the captain whispered.

"Just getting my land legs."

He sent her a sidelong glance. "You're not feeling faint at the thought of being escorted by a man of my reputation, then? Hallsy hasn't been telling tales out of school about me?"

Emme shrugged. "Mr. Hallsworth and I haven't exchanged a word since my rescue." That wasn't precisely true, but it was enough to appease the captain.

"Good, then. It's just as he promised me. He's kept my counsel. He's a respectable man, that Hallsy. A good man. Some woman will be lucky to have him for a husband.."

Emme's pulse beat in her throat and she hoped her modest neckline hid it. "I take little notice of such things. I plan to become a spinster myself. But as you hold him in such high esteem, perhaps you'll help him find a suitable match."

Before he could fashion a response, Emme dropped his arm and raced toward another gentleman she'd spotted among the crowd. There was no more need for pretense. She was Lady Emme Radcliffe, returned home, and she'd just caught a glimpse of the one man in her life who was always there for her.

Her brother saw her in the same moment and stepped toward her with his arms open wide. Caught up in his embrace, Emme let her reservations about the reunion with her loved ones slip away. By the time

Edward let her out of his grasp, Aunt Juliana and her father were beside them, the latter taking both her hands in his in an uncharacteristic show of public affection.

Emme could hardly remember when her father had last held her hands. Possibly just after Eleanor's funeral. Before that, she couldn't even guess. Probably sometime in her childhood. He withdrew and cleared his throat. Balding and bespectacled, his gray mustache slightly longer than when last she'd seen him, he was once again the picture of the aloof and fashionable gentleman.

"Granston? How long has it been?" Edward said. The two old friends shook hands. "I had no idea it was your ship bringing my sister home to us."

The captain showed no surprise to learn his old school mate was Miss Trent's brother. She wondered how long he'd been onto her ruse.

"It

"It's been the better part of a year," the captain told Edward. "Since we watched poor Alcott's sad descent into matrimony."

Emme arched an eyebrow. "Mr. Alcott married my dear friend, Captain."

The captain bowed contritely. "I meant no offense, Lady Emmeline. The new Mrs. Alcott is divine, of course."

Her father shook the captain's hand. "Granston, we appreciate that you've returned both ladies to shore safe and sound." He glanced about the dock, then at his son. "Where is the hired hackney, Meriden? We must get the ladies to the train."

"It will be along any minute," Edward answered. "In the meantime, perhaps Granston can tell us more about his ships."

"You have other ships, then?" her father asked.

The captain stood up straighter. "Five altogether, sir."

Emme held her breath, waiting for the captain to mention his business partner.

"It sounds like you've done quite well for yourself, Granston," her father said. "The navy rescued you after all, then?"

Emme bristled at her father's insensitivity, all but throwing in the man's face the fact that the previous Earl of Granston had lost the family fortune at the card tables. The captain, whom she already quite liked despite herself, rose even more in her esteem when he smiled at her father.

"Taking my commission was the best thing I ever did, sir. After that, I took on a business partner, and we've done quite nicely."

Her father continued staring at the ship, seemingly oblivious to the discomfort of everyone around him. "Once a man has had such success, he typically begins thinking about marriage."

Emme's heart caught in her throat, wondering what on earth her father could suspect about the captain's marriage-minded business partner. Her worry turned to embarrassment when the captain shot her a wink and a grin, and her father's meaning became clear to her. She'd been on British soil for less than five minutes and already her father was trying to marry her off to the first man he could find with a title and a fortune.

It was Aunt Juliana who saved the day, stepping forward to take the arm of her nephew-in-law. "Limely, I fear I need to sit down soon. Shall we find that carriage?"

Her father, reminded of his duties, gave his wife's aunt a slight bow. "How thoughtless of me, Aunt Juliana. Yes, we'll take our leave now."

They said goodbye to the captain and Emme thanked him for the safe journey.

Edward shook his old friend's hand. "Good to have you back in the country again. We'll make plans when you get to London."

"The best of plans, indeed. Be sure to prepare Swimmer," the captain said. He gave Emme another surreptitious wink. "I'll be sure to call on you and your lovely aunt as well, my lady."

"We'll look forward to it," Emme said.

And as long as he didn't bring his business associate with him or encourage her father's misguided attempts at matchmaking, she actually meant it.

The captain strode away from them, looking quite pleased with himself, Emme wasn't sure for what reason.

"We'd better not keep Father waiting," Edward said.

Emme took his arm. "And Mother. Why did you leave her waiting alone? Is she at a nearby café?"

"Emmeline, she's not here."

"Call me Emme. You know how I feel about that. And what do you mean, Mother's not here? Her daughter returns after a year abroad, and she misses the homecoming? I hardly think so."

"It wasn't her intention. When I visited her a month ago, your return was all she could talk about. But we had frightful storms last week that washed out some of the roads."

"Visited her? What does that mean? And if the roads are washed out, how did you and Father get here?"

"We took the train from London," Edward said. "You did read my letters, didn't you? I told you, Mother has moved to the country house. Permanently. And Father is staying in London. *Permanently*."

Emme stopped short and whirled to face her brother. "Edward," she said in a hushed tone, "are you telling me our parents are separated?"

He nodded. "Permanently."

"Stop saying that word! It can't be so. We have to do something about this."

He placed a hand on her shoulder to move her toward the carriage. "It's a blessing, believe me. You remember how awful it was when they were under the same roof."

"Yes, I remember. I'd assumed it would improve once I'd left."

Emme's thoughts were spinning. Knowing her

parents' deteriorating marriage was proceeding to its natural conclusion only bolstered her belief that she was making the right choice for her life, passionate night with and confusing feelings about Daniel aside. But it also threatened to ruin her plan.

What if her mother no longer had any influence over her father, just as her aunt had suggested during their voyage? Emme was counting on that influence to mollify him. She'd need all the support she could get when told her father his only remaining daughter—at the perfectly marriageable age of twenty-two—was leaving the marriage mart to become a spinster.

CHAPTER 8

*E*mme tried to focus on her needlepoint, but her fingers trembled. She laid aside the travesty of wide, looping stitches. She'd always hated needlepoint. She'd only ever taken it up in the first place to please Eleanor and appease her father.

With a deep sigh, she moved from her chair next to the fireplace in the sitting room to the window and stared out at the drizzling London rain. It had been one week since she'd gotten safely off the ship and comfortably far from Daniel, but time and distance hadn't made her think of him less often. And the nights...the sleepless nights had become unbearable.

"Still missing the sea?" her aunt asked from behind her.

Emme turned and smiled at her only confidante, now that her mother's journey had been further delayed by the interminably bad weather. "It shall pass, I'm sure."

"And if it doesn't?" her aunt asked.

As Emme opened her mouth to respond that things would improve because they simply must, the door burst open and Edward practically flew into the room from the hallway. "We have visitors. Just arrived on the afternoon train, returned from a trip to the countryside."

With a flourish of his hands, he presented Tessa and Lucinda. Tears welled in Emme's eyes as she threw her arms wide to hug the friends she hadn't seen since the day she'd left London for her year abroad.

"You both look wonderful!" Emme said as her friends embraced her.

It was true. Tessa, blonde and petite, still looked and moved like a little yellow bird. Luci, buxom and golden-haired, hovered somewhere between sweet English girl and exotic temptress. Together, they were the most welcome sight for sore eyes.

"We're sorry it took so long to get here," Tessa said. "With all this terrible weather, the roads were impossible, and the trains were overbooked."

"I'm just glad you're here now." Emme brushed away a tear, hoping no one noticed it. "Tessa, I'm sorry I couldn't attend your wedding. And Luci, I can't wait to hear all the gossip I know you'll have." She leaned forward and hugged her friends again.

"I wish I'd stepped into the room quickly enough to be in the midst of that embrace."

Emme jerked her head up at the sound of the familiar voice. Captain Granston stood framed in the doorway. In her last week on the ship, she'd grown so accustomed to spotting Daniel in his company, albeit always from a safe distance, that now she was prepared for the shock of seeing him enter the room.

Still, when he actually did, she realized she hadn't prepared enough. It took her several seconds to remember how to breathe.

"I would take credit for delivering your friends, instead of just precipitously finding them on your doorstep, if I thought it would curry favor with the ravishing Lady Emmeline," the captain said.

He smiled as he looked past Emme and her friends. "And Lady Kendall." He stepped forward and took her aunt's hand, gallantly lifting it to his lips. "It is indeed my lucky day. You remember my business partner, Mr. Hallsworth, of course."

"I didn't know you'd returned to England, Mr. Hallsworth," Edward said.

Daniel nodded, but his face remained unreadable. "I have, Lord Meriden. I have pressing business."

"And how are you finding London?" Aunt Juliana asked him before Edward could say something cutting, which he looked for all the world about to do.

"More crowded than ever, and I do miss the Spanish sun on days like today," Daniel said. He glanced at Emme. "But England has its charms."

Emme hoped she wasn't blushing as she fixed him with a steely-eyed stare.

"Ladies, Granston, Mr. Hallsworth, since we're all

here, let's move to the sitting room and have a proper drink," Edward said.

"Perhaps just one, before we spirit Meriden away for a night of...respectable gentlemanly pursuits," the captain said as he held an arm each to Tessa and Luci.

"Yes, strictly respectable, I'm sure," Luci said with a laugh.

Edward led the way out of the room with the captain and Emme's friends following close behind him. Daniel held out his arm to Aunt Juliana.

"You young people run along without me," Aunt Juliana said. She picked up her needlepoint and busied herself over it.

"Shall we?" Daniel held out his arm to Emme.

She swished past him. "I'm perfectly capable of walking unescorted through my own home."

When they reached the hallway, she slowed down enough to keep pace with him. "What are you doing here?" she whispered.

"You already know, Lady Emme, I have business with the House of Lords in a few days' time."

"Not in England." She resisted the urge to point out he was being a ninny. "What are you doing in my home?"

He glanced at Edward, now well ahead of them. "Visiting an old friend."

"Who seems less than happy to see you."

Daniel's smile faded. "I suppose there will be a lot of that these next few weeks. But while I'm working out the conditions for restoring my title, I'll need to ingratiate myself with respectable members of the *ton*."

The hint of melancholy in his voice gave her a twinge of contriteness. She clasped her hands behind her back as she walked more slowly beside him. "I don't envy you that. I'm doing my best to avoid that lot myself."

"Ah, the luxury of an unimpeachable lineage." He smiled again as they reached the entryway of the sitting room, and he stopped to let her step past him.

He had no idea just how precarious her own reputation was, and she wouldn't bore him with the details, no matter how much she longed to confide in him. She put the irrational desire down to foolish nostalgia for what they'd once been to each other and the secrets they'd once shared. Their confidences had been innocent then. Now they were both burdened with a history of terribly consequential transgressions, and the less said about them, the better.

Two footmen had appeared without needing to be summoned, a testament to the disciplined household her father ran, and quickly set out scones and portions of sherry for them.

As they drank a few toasts and made polite chitchat, the gentlemen—including Daniel—were charming company, but Emme longed to be alone with her best friends. More than that, she longed to be alone with Daniel, but that desire was another sin she would bury and never show in the light of day, and she wished him away from her so she could regain her equilibrium.

"How are you finding life back in London, my lady?" Daniel asked her.

She should give a polite and vague answer, but her nerves were too on edge to keep up that great a lie. "It's rather stifling. The poorer parts of town are even more overcrowded and lacking in the basic necessities than when I left a year ago, and the blasted rain won't let up long enough for me to join the other spinsters to visit our charges—the women and their families we help."

He stared at her with one eyebrow cocked.

"I shouldn't have said any of that." She did her best to offer him a fake smile. "I should say it's lovely to be home."

Daniel scowled. "Please don't. Then I'll feel more the heel for my own opinions of the place. You were gone one year. Imagine if you hadn't seen the city for five years."

"I suppose it hasn't aged well in that time," she said.

He shrugged a shoulder. "Perhaps my memory of it was too charitable. And speaking of charitable, I've been very impressed by the good things I've heard about the charitable work done by the Spinsters' Club."

"Are you?" she asked.

It was hardly an organization discussed much at society events. The women they assisted hardly lived up to society's expectations of those deserving of help, but she wouldn't flatter herself to think he'd gone out of his way to inquire about it. What good would it do her—or him, for that matter—to know he was thinking about her even half as much as she was thinking about him?

"And about the work Lady Tessa and her husband, my old friend James from Harrow, do with their scholarship foundation," he said. "It's allowed me some measure of optimism about this place that's supposed to be our home."

Her heart tripped when he said "our home." It was private and intimate, and she wanted to step closer to him and speak in whispers and share confidences.

She took a few steps to her left to move closer to the loose circle made by their friends. Daniel shifted a bit to his right, immediately caught and responded to something the captain said, and just like that, their intimate conversation was finished. It was the right thing to do. She just couldn't fathom why the pain of it had to cut so deeply.

The captain glanced at Emme and flashed a smile. "We've made plans for your brother this evening, Lady Emmeline, but you and your friends are such charming company, perhaps we should stay a bit longer."

"Oh, that would be delightful," Tessa said, rolling her fan opened and closed. "We're going to discuss Darwin's theory of pangenesis, and I would so love your input."

"Pan what?" The captain widened his eyes while Daniel and Edward grinned.

"But we also have to discuss the latest fashions," Luci said, "and who looks terrible in them."

Tessa nudged Luci in the ribs.

"And who looks lovely in them," Luci added.

The captain looked more horrified. "I'd hoped we'd have a friendly game of cards. I've learned a fascinating American game. Poker."

Luci clapped her hands together. "Oh, I've heard of it. I'd love to learn it."

Tessa nudged her ribs again.

"Another time," Luci said.

Emme reached for Tessa's hand. "And we're going to discuss the work Luci and James are doing with your scholarship foundation. I've been reading up on conditions in the workhouses and—"

"They can't be serious," the captain said to Edward.

"They can and they are," her brother answered with a look of pride on his face.

Daniel patted the captain's shoulder. "Perhaps the ladies are best left to their own devices, after all."

"Besides, the rest of London would be so chagrined to be deprived of your charms much longer," Edward added.

The captain polished off his sherry and ceremoniously set the glass back on the serving tray. "I'm afraid my compatriots are correct, ladies." He touched his forehead as though tipping his hat. "And so, sadly, I bid you adieu."

As the servants retrieved the gentlemen's coats, hats, gloves, and umbrellas, the small group said their goodbyes. Edward stepped into the hallway, followed by Captain Granston. Daniel left last, shooting one quick look at Emme as he reached the door. They locked eyes, but didn't smile. Then he was gone, and the noise of the three old Harrow friends eventually faded into the street.

Tessa pulled Emme into a quick hug. "I hope it wasn't too terrible for you."

"Terrible?" Emme smoothed down her skirt and did her best to appear unfazed. "You mean because of Mr. Hallsworth?" She shook her head. "That was so long ago. Who even remembers?"

"We do, as do you," Luci said. "Your brother said there'd be dinner when he fetched us from the train station, but I suppose that won't be for at least another hour. That gives you time to tell us everything."

Emme couldn't even be vexed with Luci, having missed her straightforward manner so much.

"About your time in Spain," Tessa said. "And the work you plan to do with the Spinsters' Club."

"And about Mr. Hallsworth and the voyage home." Luci arched an eyebrow, daring either of her friends to argue with her.

Emme exhaled a sigh and picked up the sherry. "Fine. But we're going to need more of this."

Tessa took the full glass Emme offered her, but she frowned. "Let's not be injudicious, though. We have all evening, after all."

Emme hoped to keep any discussion of Daniel and the trip home as brief as possible. Otherwise, Tessa's warning aside, she might need to drug herself with the rest of the bottle.

*H*aving survived seeing Lady Emme without being able to touch her and enduring dinner with her less-than-welcoming brother the previous evening, Daniel relaxed in Swimmer's private room in the Reform. As a servant entered bearing another bottle of fine Bordeaux, Daniel settled back into the deep leather cushions and observed the well-appointed, dark-paneled space. The servant filled the duke's glass, offered more to Daniel, who refused it, and withdrew.

Daniel smiled, remembering a long-ago night. "This is a far cry from the last establishment where we shared a drink."

Swimmer laughed, no doubt having only the vaguest recollection of the crowded cantina in Bilbao where Daniel and Granston had celebrated with him on his last night of wild abandon. "To this day, I can't recall how I made it onto the ship the next morning, although I do remember the rough seas aiding and abetting my hangover for what seemed like a week. It was the beginning of a very long year."

Daniel hesitated for a moment, then spoke. "I'm sorry I was unable to attend your father's funeral to pay my respects in person."

Swimmer waved away Daniel's regret. "As much as I hated being summoned home for my own wedding to a woman I scarcely knew, I was glad to have that last year with him." He sighed heavily, and Daniel could see the weight of his title and its responsibilities lay heavily on his old friend.

"And of your late wife—"

"That's enough talk of ghosts for tonight." Swimmer tossed back half his glass of wine. "Granston tells me you're on a mission."

Daniel took the last small sip of wine left in his glass, holding the sublime taste on his tongue, while he considered just how much of a pummeling Granston deserved for his lack of discretion regarding Daniel's interest in the recalcitrant Lady Emme. Or he could feign misunderstanding.

"Just making a few charitable donations, trying to do my part," he said. "Seems the least I can do." It truly was the least, and Daniel had some ideas about how to do more, but those might have to wait until the business with his title was settled.

Swimmer raised his eyebrows. "I was referring to you having the marquessate reinstated. Unless charitable contributions are another stipulation the Committee for Privileges has imposed. Granston told me they're making some ridiculous demand that you prove yourself worthy."

The tension in Daniel's shoulders eased. Granston wouldn't need a pummeling for discussing Emme with their other friends, after all. "The committee never used the word 'worthy', and they didn't mention 'charity', only 'respectable behavior'. They've set out a few guidelines, made a few suggestions. I'll play their game for a month or so."

"Tell them to go to bloody hell!" Swimmer said. "There's no appetite to let the title languish. They're just trying to extract a pound of flesh for their own amusement. Or perhaps one of their wives is a judgmental old bird and her kowtowed husband is trying to earn her favor. It's an abuse of their power."

Daniel grinned. "Thank you for your affront on my behalf, but whatever the reason, their goal aligns with mine. No reason to cause a fuss or challenge them over something I plan to do anyway."

Swimmer frowned. "Surely the Hallsworth name doesn't need that much rehabilitation. But if that's your plan, tread carefully where Granston's suggestions for entertainment are concerned. You can't have the first mention of your name in the society pages be for any reason that's less than pious."

"Yes. The last time I was mentioned in the papers..."

"Not to worry. I have some contacts who will run a very flattering piece on the once and future Marquess of Edensbridge the moment I give them the word. Probably early next week. That'll give you a chance to get your wits about you and be seen at the most stylish places, raising just enough interest to whet the insatiable appetite of the *ton*."

Perspiration pricked Daniel's underarms and back. "Stylish places?"

Swimmer waved his hand in the air. "I have a list of them. I also have a list of the matrons it's most important to impress."

Daniel leaned forward and propped his elbows on

his knees, studying his old friend's face. "When did you become so socially savvy?"

"When I no longer had a choice."

"But lists, Swimmer?"

"Those are courtesy of the duchess. She remembers you fondly, Hallsy. I must give you fair warning, my mother might well make your redemption her personal crusade."

"Did I hear mention of the Duchess of Wrexham?" Granston's voice boomed from behind Daniel. "Such a handsome woman. And I do so love a handsome widow. Perhaps I should stop round to pay her a visit."

"Not without me there." Swimmer rose to his feet at the same time as Daniel to shake Granston's hand. "Otherwise, I'll have to call you out."

Granston clapped Swimmer on the back. "Still a barbarian, just like I told you, Meriden."

At the sound of the name, Daniel froze in place. He caught Granston's look, the slightly raised eyebrow, the cocky grin. It seemed his old friend might need a sound trouncing after all. Unless it was a joke, a truly terrible one, the kind only Granston could find amusing. Granston had promised Daniel he'd need only spend one evening in the company of Steady Eddie, dangling the lure of some time with Emme as bait when Daniel had needed more prodding. Now it seemed Granston planned to make their interaction a daily occurrence.

Daniel sat down, hoping if he wished it hard enough, Meriden would disappear. Or better yet, all his friends would disappear and Emme would appear in their stead.

"Hallsy." Granston clapped his shoulder hard. "Don't be an ass. Shake the man's hand."

Daniel stayed seated, but obliged, and the rest of them each took one of the luxurious leather chairs set in a semi-circle in front of the hearth, with a low fire chasing away the bone-chilling dampness of the English spring. The servant stopped 'round again to fill the wine glasses, and this time, Daniel didn't refuse. The four former mates sipped wine and kept the conversation light. Daniel, for his part, was taking the measure of each man, of what they'd become, when Granston mentioned the elephant in the room.

"Has anyone had word from Harry?"

The other three shook their heads.

"Not for months," Swimmer admitted. "I thought perhaps he'd stayed in better touch with you and Hallsy, his fellow adventurers abroad."

"Granston was the only one who ventured that far," Daniel said. "When did you see him, Granston? About a year ago?"

Granston nodded. "Give or take."

"You've been to Argentina?" Meriden shifted to the front of his seat. "I've heard it's quite beautiful."

Daniel gave him a wry smile. "Daddy never did let you out of jolly old England, did he, Steady Eddie?"

Meriden sat up straighter and glared at Daniel.

"Hallsy," Swimmer warned, but Granston flashed an encouraging grin.

That look in itself was enough to stop Daniel. He wasn't about to provide Granston with cheap entertainment. "I didn't mean that the way it sounded," he lied.

Meriden gave one curt nod, accepting the lie.

Daniel meant to leave it at that.

"One tends to be more careful when one has a lineage and a title to consider," Meriden countered.

Swimmer and Granston both leaned forward, but Daniel held up his hand. His friends relaxed, seeming to believe his indication of a truce. He wouldn't disabuse them of the notion.

"How fares Lady Emme today?" Daniel asked, only partly to annoy Meriden.

Granston barely tried to conceal the nudge of his foot against Daniel's boot, but Daniel continued to smile placidly in Meriden's direction.

"My sister is none of your concern." Meriden took a swig of wine and stared into the fire.

Daniel thought about how satisfying it would be to push his former friend into the flames. Only for a second or two. Only long enough to make him scream in agony. It was kinder than the man deserved after what he'd allowed to happen to his sister at the hands of a scoundrel. One more thing Daniel couldn't forgive.

"I do so hope *someone* is looking out for Lady Emme," Daniel said.

Meriden met Daniel's gaze with fury glinting in his eyes. "My family has been through enough, *Mister* Hallsworth. You will do well to steer clear of them."

"I knew it," Granston said. "I knew it was too good to be true, the friendly pretense the two of you kept up last night." He winked at Swimmer. "That's why I poured half a bottle of my best rum into Meriden before I brought him here. Time to clear the air so the two of you can get up to your old antics again."

"Granston, you're an ass," Daniel said. He'd had more than his share of Swimmer's wine, and was far from the paragon of sobriety he'd been last night, which was making it harder to keep his own emotions in check.

"I have to agree with Hallsy," Swimmer said.

Daniel leaned forward and spoke to Meriden. "As for you, Viscount Meriden, you can stop being such a self-righteous prig. The dispute over my title has nearly been settled, and I'll soon be a marquess again."

Swimmer lifted his glass in the air. "And so, a toast is in order!"

"Hear, hear!" Granston lifted his own glass.

Neither Daniel nor Meriden moved, their gazes locked. Daniel could only hope the man could read what he felt about him, about his inability to protect his sister's virtue and her fragile heart. *Better she'd have married an untitled bastard who loved her than run off with a social-climbing lecher.*

It was Meriden who broke the stalemate. He pushed himself to his feet, thanked Swimmer for his hospitality, and shook Granston's hand. He stopped just in front of Daniel. "I bid you good evening, *marquess.*"

Daniel waited until the man had almost reached the

door before he called out to him. "Meriden, do give my regards to your sister. Better yet, I'll come by and give her my best myself."

"You'll do nothing of the sort!" Meriden took one step toward him.

In an instant, Granston was on his feet in front of Daniel and Swimmer was shepherding Meriden out the door.

A minute later, Swimmer returned and the three men took their seats. Daniel crossed his legs and calmly stared into the hearth. For the first time since he'd set foot on English soil, he felt some measure of peace and purpose.

"Is he mad or just a pompous ass?" Swimmer asked Granston, gesturing to Daniel.

"I'm going to say a bit of both," Granston said. "But love will do that to you."

Daniel snapped his attention to Granston. "Stop right there."

Granston shrugged. "I'm not going to keep your secrets if you're so hell-bent on wearing them on your sleeve."

"Lady Emmeline?" Swimmer asked. "After all these years, that's what that little exchange was about?"

Daniel shifted uncomfortably in his seat. If he'd been so transparent after all, Meriden might come to the same conclusion. "I was once interested in the girl."

"You were a hair's breadth from ruining her," Swimmer corrected. "Or so Meriden claimed."

"Not to mention, he's *still* interested in the girl," Granston added.

Swimmer shook his head. "Hallsy, you can't expect Meriden and his father to set her out on a silver platter because you've shown up with your title nearly restored. And whatever that was between the two of you, it damn well didn't help your cause."

Daniel scowled. "She's twenty-two. She can marry whomever she chooses."

Granston peered at him over the top of his wine glass. "Exactly. And she didn't choose you. You would do well to remember that. You need an ally, and Steady Eddie might just be it."

"The day I need anything from Steady Eddie is the day I'll declare myself ready for Broadmoor."

"There was a moment there when I was going to suggest it myself." Swimmer laid a hand on Daniel's shoulder. "But now that I know what truly ails you, you'll suffer no such fate, for I, dear boy, have all the answers. On your feet. We have ground to cover while the night is still young."

Daniel groaned.

Granston leapt to his feet and downed the last of his wine. "That's more like it. What's first? An underground boxing match? A burlesque review?" He rubbed his hands together. "Perhaps the newest house of the great social evil. I know for a fact they're quite motivated to attract a certain clientele. With the likes of a duke in tow, we'll have the run of the place."

"Granston, we're here to build up a reputation, not

destroy one," Swimmer said. "We're going to have evening coffee with the most venerated and respectable woman I know."

Granston's grin turned into a frown. "Not your mother. I was only joking earlier—"

"Yes, my mother." Swimmer pulled Daniel to his feet. "If there's one thing my mother knows, it's how to make a respectable match. Lady Tessa and Alcott can vouch for that."

Daniel stopped his progress toward the door. "Why are you so anxious to involve the duchess in the plans for my redemption?"

"For his own preservation, no doubt," Granston offered.

Swimmer shrugged. "What can I say? I'm just an affable fellow hoping to do my part in clearing the path to true love."

Daniel glanced at Granston. "While avoiding a marriage of his own. Still, I'm in no position to turn down help." He turned as Granston opened his mouth to speak. "Unless it's from you."

Granston made a show of straightening his cravat while Swimmer chuckled, and Daniel led the way as three-fifths of Harrow's Finest Five filed out of the room, looking for all the world like London's most respectable gentlemen.

29 March, in the Year of Our Lord 1870

To Mr. Daniel Hallsworth, son of the late Marquess of Edensbridge:

Pursuant to the request made of you by the Committee of Privileges on 18 March 1870, we are pleased to see your progress toward establishing a respectable household on English soil. We are most encouraged by your association with the Duke of Wrexham, and his mother, the Duchess of Wrexham. We remind you that engagement to the daughter of a peer in good standing in the House of Lords will do much to prove your ability to faithfully execute the duties of the Marquess of Edensbridge, and we look forward to learning of your progress on the matter in the near future.

Respectfully yours,

The Hon. Mr. Charles Alby
Clerk of the Committee for Privileges
House of Lords
London, England

CHAPTER 9

*A*fter several more restless days passed on British soil, Emme was thrilled to finally be doing something worthwhile.

She stepped down from the hired hackney and landed her booted foot in a puddle of something murky, smelly, and well outside her realm of experience. She picked her way across the rutted road, holding her skirts up to her ankles and stepping more carefully as she followed Lady Abigail to the front door of a narrow, gray house stuck among a row of connected buildings, one more dilapidated than the next.

She smiled to cover the shock of seeing this part of the city for the first time, and reminded herself of the virtue of their cause.

"How many children did you say live here?" she whispered over her shoulder to Lady Rachel, who brought up the rear of their small entourage.

"In this house? Three, with another one on the way. Probably dozens on the whole of the street."

Emme glanced up and down the narrow street. It was an alleyway, really. A fierce sadness gripped her as she wondered where in this fetid landscape the children could play, how they could learn, looking out of their tiny, grimy windows onto this sad view, what dreams they could hold in a world this grim?

"Don't look for any of them to be about in the street," Lady Rachel said as Lady Abigail, a few feet in front of them, stopped at the door of the house they'd approached and knocked. "The younger ones will be attending to chores."

"And the older ones?"

"Factory work, mostly. I know one of Mrs. Bailey's sons—they live in the house on the corner—has an apprenticeship with a blacksmith a few blocks away. The oldest boy. He's ten now, I think. Those not so lucky will be out begging."

Working in factories. Standing behind kicking horses. Begging. Emme tried to remember what Edward had been doing when he was ten. She'd been seven then. She'd received a gorgeous miniature model of her family's Arlington Street townhouse for her dolls. She'd had so many of them, and each doll had had her own elegant wardrobe. Edward had even carved a small wooden dog for her when she'd pouted for a week that the youngest child of the Doll family was pining for a pet.

The small door opened in front of them and a maid

in a clean and pressed, if threadbare, brown dress stood in front of them. She inclined her head and curtseyed.

Lady Abigail spoke to the woman. "Mrs. Billings, lovely to see you. How do you fare today?"

But Mrs. Billings was no maid of the house. She was one of the two women residing here with their children, one of the down-on-their-luck women they were here to help. Of course, there would be no servants in a house of so little means. Emme couldn't fathom how she could be so obtuse. She was not only on the opposite side of London from where she resided, she was in an entirely different world. She smiled at Mrs. Billings, whom she knew to be about her own age, but whom by looks could have passed as ten years older than Emme.

The woman invited them into the house, which began with a dark, narrow hallway, then opened to reveal a cramped sitting room to the right with a pitched, narrow staircase to the left.

"Please, m'ladies, have a seat."

Mrs. Billings's accent was not what Emme expected. It was quite refined, better even than a ladies' maid.

Emme took an unsteady breath as she sat on a worn black divan whose seat cushion sank further under her than she expected. According to Lady Abigail, Mrs. Billings had come from good circumstances, married a working man who supported her well. But after he'd died, she'd been reduced to living in a shabby house with another family, with barely a ha'penny to scrape together between them.

The other woman living in the house, one Mrs. Carter, had two children and a third was on the way, while her husband served a term in debtors' prison. It was unlikely they'd see Mrs. Carter that day, as she was close to her confinement and no longer going up and down the stairs. Lady Abigail had proudly reported the woman was able to keep up with the small sewing repair projects that earned her some semblance of an income while she lay abed.

As Mrs. Billings excused herself to check on the tea kettle and turned to leave the room, she bumped into a small, cherub-faced child with long, blonde hair plaited into two neat braids, who couldn't have been more than six years old. Mrs. Billings bent and whispered something to the child, who curtseyed in front of the spinsters, then backed away and disappeared up a dark staircase.

"My daughter, Jeannette," Mrs. Billings told Emme. She turned toward Lady Abigail. "She'll ensure Mrs. Carter is ready to receive company."

"Lovely." As Mrs. Billings left the room, Lady Abigail leaned closer to Emme. "While Lady Rachel and I check on our mother-to-be, you can chat with Mrs. Billings. There are rather cramped quarters upstairs. I hardly think the three of us will fit into her bedchamber."

A minute later, the little girl returned, curtseyed, and motioned for the spinsters to go up the stairs, and Mrs. Billings arrived with a tea service—shabby, with

dings and scratches, but polished to a luminous shine—
and set it on the tiny table in front of Emme.

"Jeanette will serve us." Mrs. Billings took a seat
across from Emme.

The little girl poured tea into Emme's cup and
motioned to the cream and sugar. Emme requested one
lump, which the girl stirred into the tea. She then
repeated the ritual for her mother, who took her tea
black, curtseyed to both women, and disappeared out
the door.

"That was lovely." Emme took a sip of tea.

"We've practicing the skills she'll need in a few
years' time. We don't have the connections to find her a
position in the home of a peer, but perhaps a successful
tradesman. Someone kind who runs a safe and
respectable household."

Emme furrowed her brow, not mentioning that
cleaning and cooking skills were more important to a
maid seeking a position, as footmen were charged
with serving duties in the respectable households
she'd mentioned. But perhaps it was different in the
home of a tradesman's wife. And she kept her counsel
on what an unsafe or disreputable household might
mean for a young maid, sure that Mrs. Billings wasn't
naïve. Without a peer's money and a father's name to
protect her, the world posed an untold number of
threats to the girl, and the most her mother could dare
hope for Jeanette was a safe place to earn a living
wage.

As Emme sipped her tea and tried to think of something more to say, a few small portraits propped on top of a rickety sideboard caught her eye.

"Oh, those are lovely." She stood slowly, taking care not to bump the table that butted up to her knees. "Is this one a portrait of your daughter?"

"It is. She was three then. It was the first time I could get her to sit still for more than one minute at a time so I could get the sketch down."

Emme glanced at Mrs. Billings. "You painted these? All of these?"

"Yes, m'lady. They're of Jeanette and Mrs. Carter's two boys, and a few neighborhood children. I did the small portraits first, and now I'm practicing miniaturizing them."

In front of each of five small portraits, none of them bigger than a foot high, were much smaller, circular-shaped paintings, each an exquisite replication of one of the larger pictures.

"For lockets." Emma had never seen such fine and detailed work up close.

"Yes, ma'am." Mrs. Billings cleared her throat. "M'lady, while we have a few minutes alone, I wonder if I might impose upon you."

Emme looked up from the paintings to see the woman staring intently at her with wide eyes in a pale face. "Mrs. Billings, what is it?"

The woman fidgeted with her hands. "It's about Mrs. Carter." She glanced at the staircase as if assuring herself no one was in earshot. "After the babe is born, Mr. Hartman has a mind to send her back to the factory where she worked. You are familiar with Mr. Hartman?"

Emme nodded. She had recently learned of the arrangement. The spinsters donated their initiation fees into a fund that was used to supply housing, food, and care to needy women and children, but women who were able-bodied were expected to earn at least some of their own keep. Instead of overseeing these employment requirements themselves, the spinsters employed a small group of solicitors, led by Mr. Hartman, to act as liaisons between the women needing jobs and employers looking to save money by hiring out some of their work to women for a fraction of the cost of employing men. Hence, Mrs. Carter worked at hemming and repairing clothing for a number of tailors, and Mrs. Billings worked with a house painter, blending custom paint colors for the walls of the wealthy.

"She'd make more money in the factory." Mrs. Billings wrapped her hands around her middle and Emme feared the woman would be sick. "But she can't return to that horrid place. The long hours away from her children, and on her feet, no less. And the beatings. She nearly lost the babe early on because of them."

Emme felt ill herself. She lowered herself back onto the divan. "They beat her? And while she was pregnant?"

The woman nodded. "It's not the worst thing that happens in those places. Not even close to it. I've been able to avoid the fate of working in such a place through sheer luck of having a knack for color and paints. Sewing is a much more common and low-wage skill, so Mr. Hartman doesn't encourage it as a means to income unless there's no other choice."

Mrs. Billings dropped her voice to a whisper. "I implore you to have a word with Lady Abigail, convince her that Mrs. Carter should continue her sewing, despite the lower wages."

"Yes, there must be something we can do." Emme closed her eyes for a minute, desperate to settle the morning tea and toast that now churned in her stomach. She opened her eyes and glanced at the table stacked with Mrs. Billings's paintings. "Do you sell these, then?"

Mrs. Billings stared at her, barely blinking, no doubt thinking Emme quite addle-brained for jumping from such a serious topic with no warning. Or perhaps she thought Emme hard-hearted. Still, she answered. "No, ma'am. No one in this neighborhood could afford to spend money on such frippery. I give them as gifts. Many of the women on our street have been so helpful to us. It's a way to thank them."

"You could sell them, though. That's what I'm getting at." Emme turned to face Mrs. Billings, whose face flamed pink at the edges. "To ladies of the *ton*. The miniatures as well as the larger portraits. My mother had portraits of my sister, brother, and me commissioned about five years ago. It was very lucrative for the artist, and I daresay he had significantly less talent than your work displays."

"You're very kind, m'lady. But I have neither the contacts nor the appropriate background for such work. Besides, how many peers would hire a *woman* to paint portraits of their children?"

Emme shrugged one shoulder and squinted at the delicately rendered, tiny picture of Jeanette. "Any who hoped for such fine work." She turned a bright smile on the woman. "You must paint a miniature of the portrait of my sister, my brother, and me so I can give it to my mother in a locket on her birthday."

Mrs. Billings protested, but Emma stopped her.

"I'll pay you the going rate for such work. And don't expect it to be the last. Such a piece will create excitement among the other ladies of the *ton*, and they'll be clamoring for their own miniatures painted by you in no time."

"I couldn't possibly." Mrs. Billings twisted her hands in her lap. "Mr. Hartman assigns us our work."

"I wouldn't ask you to turn away work." Emme touched her hand, hoping to calm what looked like fear. Whether it was fear of crossing Hartman, angering the spinsters, or interacting with ladies of the *ton*, she didn't know. "You can do the portraiture work on your own schedule, around the demands of Mr. Hartman's clients."

Mrs. Billing hadn't yet agreed, but normal color had returned to her face and she'd ventured a glance at her handiwork on the sideboard. "I do love painting children's faces. They're so full of innocence and mischief at the same time."

Emme stood and clasped her hands in front of her. "May I take that as a yes?"

Mrs. Billings rose slowly to her feet. "Yes, m'lady, I'll do the locket portrait for you."

She held out her hand and Emme shook it, then held onto it. "And if others are interested in engaging your services…?"

Mrs. Billings bowed her head. "I would be honored."

Emme grinned. "Perfect."

Perfect, indeed, because when it came to setting a trend among the *ton*, Emme knew just the woman to do it.

*T*hat afternoon, Emme stood in Picadilly on the doorstep of Her Grace Helen Wellesley, the Duchess of Wrexham, and Emme's best hope at making her mark on the Spinsters' Club. She twisted the handle of her large parasol, reminding herself that she really must muster the energy for a shopping trip, if only to get a more suitably-sized accessory.

To her left stood Tessa and Mr. Alcott, linked arm and arm, heads bent together. She'd ridden to the duchess's house in a rented carriage with them, and had come to regret the decision. As far as she could observe, the couple spoke mostly in couplets and quoted poetry to each other. Still, Tessa looked radiant and the height of fashion in a bustled royal blue skirt and lady's waistcoat, matched perfectly to the blue ribbon of her hat and the stitching on the edges of her white gloves.

To her right stood Luci, who had arrived separately, escorted by her father, Viscount Fairbank. Emme drew back her shoulders to stand straighter. She had never felt at ease in the man's presence. Tall, slender, and guarded, he was ever the perfect gentleman, now aging gracefully and graying at his temples. But there was something intense about his dark brown eyes, and rumors about his clandestine service to the Crown had swirled for years. But to Luci, he was just her overprotective father, which no doubt explained her demure, pale blue gown with the neckline all the way up to her collarbone.

Luci must also have been assessing their assembly, as she reached out to touch Emme's wrap, which was the same lavender color as her simply cut gown. "It's nice to see you in something other than gray."

In truth, Emme would have happily participated in the afternoon's outing wearing her simple gray frock from the morning's trip with the spinsters, but she'd tread in something unidentifiable and decidedly foul during her morning trip with the spinsters and had carried it home on the hem of the dress.

The front door cracked open and the duchess's butler bowed in welcome. Fairbank checked his timepiece. He and Mr. Alcott both motioned to the ladies to precede them. The coolness of the large entryway, no doubt helped by the pale gray marble of the floor and stairs, felt refreshing after the minute they'd spent waiting under the unseasonably sunny sky, which had finally revealed itself after more than a week straight of rain.

Servants took hats, gloves, parasols, and Lord Fairbank's walking stick, then the butler led them to the duchess's sitting room. The woman herself welcomed them into the room with wide open arms, looking timeless with her blonde hair swept up and off her barely-lined face, and dressed in a deep purple gown, the design of which was the height of and fashion, the color the symbol of royalty. It was rumored to be the duchess's favorite color, whether for the way it announced her power in society or the way it set off her alabaster skin, no one could be sure.

The duchess hugged first Tessa, then Emme, and then Luci. Emme had enjoyed the pleasure of meeting the duchess frequently over the years, as she was close in age to Emme's mother. Mr. Alcott took the duchess's proffered hand and bent over it gallantly. Luci's father kept his distance.

"Fairbank, I had no idea you would grace us with your presence. What an honor."

"The honor is all mine." Fairbank bowed slightly, but it hardly seemed reverent.

"I do fear I must let Cook know we have one more guest for tea, though." The duchess seemed to accomplish this by raising an eyebrow at one of the myriad of servants hovering at the edges of the large, sumptuously appointed room.

"There's no need," Fairbank said. "I'm merely here

to ensure my daughter will be appropriately chaperoned during her visit."

The room went deathly silent. Luci, looking mortified, squeezed her father's arm. The duchess smiled slowly and mirthlessly. "I'm sure you're not insinuating—"

"Your Grace!" Their heads swiveled in the direction of Mr. Alcott, who held a limp Tessa in his arms. "Might I trouble you to show me where my wife might lie down? She seems to have been overwhelmed by the sudden change of weather."

"Of course." The duchess conducted servants with brief words and hand gestures, and at the same time, invited her remaining guests to be seated.

"Do you think she's all right?" Emme whispered to Luci.

Luci pulled her by the hand. "Come and sit. She's fine. We've learned we sometimes need to distract the duchess and my father when they put each other in these foul moods."

"Does that happen often?"

Luci shrugged. "Only when they see each other, which they do as rarely as possible. Don't look so concerned. He'll leave shortly, then you can bend the duchess's ear."

In fact, Emme didn't need to wait that long. As soon as she returned from assisting Mr. Alcott and a butler with situating Tessa in an adjoining room, the duchess reached for Emme's hand.

"My dear, I need your opinion. I'm redecorating my

son's study for him. I'd like to add a bit of Spanish flair, an essence of Madrid, if you will, and I'm sure you could lend some insight."

Emme stood, not sure about any such thing. She barely concerned herself with decorations and appointments, even less so since she'd decided she'd never run a household of her own. But a trip to the duke's study would provide the moment alone with the duchess she needed.

"Fairbank, would you be so kind as to entertain your daughter for just a moment?" the duchess said as two servants arrived with trays of tea service and scones.

The look Fairbank shot the duchess hardly matched his polite response. Emme hoped he would leave soon or poor Tessa might spend the entire afternoon feigning swoons.

A short walk brought them to a large mahogany-paneled, leather-furnished room. From the thick brown rug on the wide-planked floor to the scent of brandy and cigars in the air, this was indeed a masculine retreat. Emme furrowed her brow, wondering just how pleased the duke would be to have his mother apply her feminine touch to the decor of his study.

"I don't know what I can suggest, ma'am," she said as the duchess closed the door behind them.

"For decorating?" The duchess widened her eyes. "Nothing, of course. My son would have my head if I dared touch a single tome in what he calls 'the last refuge in his own home'. I just wanted a quick word with you, alone. You see, my dear, I'm in need of your help."

"My help? But not with decorating. This is fortuitous."

"Is it? How so, my dear?"

Emme clasped her hands in front of her and tried not to appear overeager. "I, too, have need of a favor."

"I see." The duchess narrowed her eyes and nodded ever so slightly. "Let's have a seat, shall we?"

Emme would have preferred standing. Sitting somehow made their discussion seem so formal and binding, when all Emme wanted was a quick, easy agreement from the duchess to help her rally portrait painting opportunities for the young widow she'd met just hours earlier. But the duchess wanted formality, and so Emme obliged.

Despite wanting to launch right into her request, Emme remembered her manners and her upbringing once they were seated. She bowed her head in the direction of her hostess. "How might I help you, duchess?"

The older woman silently assessed Emme, making her shift uncomfortably in her seat. Finally, seemingly satisfied, she smiled at Emme. "I should like to hear your request first, Lady Emmeline."

Excitement bubbled inside Emme and she made no pretense of trying to draw out the duchess's proposition instead. "We've spoken of my desire to join the Spinsters' Club."

"A devoted group of women working for a wonderful cause."

Emme smiled. "Yes, I think so, too. In pursuit of that, I spent the morning at the home of two women, both with young children, whom the spinsters are helping. I'd like to do something special for them, but I need your influence, ma'am."

"I appreciate your candor."

Emme bit the inside of her lip and wondered if that was the duchess's subtle way of saying Emme lacked diplomatic skills.

"But I'm afraid I cannot imagine what you could possibly need from an old woman such as I. I'm hardly the epicenter of influence."

Emme fought to control a laugh, unsure of whether the duchess was being falsely modest or playing a part for some reason. In truth, the Duchess of Wrexham was the epicenter of all of the most important business of the women of the *ton*.

"But if you think there's something I can do..."

"Oh, yes." Emme folder her hands in her lap and squeezed them together to focus her energy and tamp down her excitement. "One of the women I met this morning, a Mrs. Billings, is a remarkable artist. I fear her talents are being wasted in a workaday world." Emme weighed telling the duchess the long story of the solicitors and their shortsighted views of how to help the women in need, but opted for the charm of brevity instead. "I've hired her to make a miniature copy of a portrait of my siblings and me so I can give it to my mother in a locket."

The duchess leaned back and rested her arms on the chair, striking a pose Emme imagined the Queen herself might strike when holding court. "I've heard such work can be exquisite."

"Yes, ma'am, as is the case with the work of Mrs. Billings."

"And you, my dear Lady Emmeline, should like me to spread the word of this incomparable talent whom the ladies of the *ton* might find interesting."

Emme nodded. "Yes, ma'am."

"Then you are correct. These events are fortuitous. You see, I'm in a bit of a quandary, and if I'm unable to resolve it, I hardly think I'll have the time or opportunity to discuss your Mrs. Billings with the influential ladies I know." She leaned forward in her seat, her bright blue eyes shrewd and sharp. "If, however, you were to relieve some of the burden of my own current project, I'm sure I could find the time to help you with yours."

Emme smoothed the material of her dress over her lap, wondering why the hairs on the back of her neck stood up in warning, when all she was doing was having a perfectly lovely discussion with the duchess. "Whatever I can do to help. Short of decorating advice, I'm afraid."

The duchess shook her head. "It is a project of an entirely different sort. A social project, if you will. I have a young acquaintance in need of making a good match."

"A match, as in a marriage?"

"Exactly."

Emme twisted her hands in front of her. "I hardly think I can be of service when it comes to marriage, never having made such a match myself." Despite entertaining proposals three times, with ever-worsening results.

"You needn't be an expert. Just a young woman with the ability to say kind words regarding our subject to your peers. I wouldn't ask if the situation weren't desperate. Our goal is a wedding by midsummer. That will give the newlyweds time to make their appearance as a married couple at all the best events of the late Season."

Emme arched an eyebrow. "Midsummer. Oh, I do hope it doesn't become a Shakespearian comedy of errors."

The duchess gave a wan smile, indicating this was no lighthearted matter. "Will you help my poor, dear friend with this important task?"

Emme furrowed her brow in a look of utmost seriousness as she wondered what sort of social misfit the duchess had agreed to help. Society could be so cruel, and the maiden must be in dire straits to admit her own shortcomings so baldly. Spinster or no, Emme wouldn't be able to bear the sight of herself in the mirror if she were to turn away from a woman who so desperately needed her aid.

"Of course. I would be honored to help your friend."

The duchess clapped her hands together and rose to her feet. Emme followed her lead. "Then it's settled. We shall help each other. You shall meet my friend this very afternoon and begin discussing your plans."

"Plans?"

"Nothing elaborate. Just advice regarding what to say, where to be seen, whom in your age group to meet, all from a young woman's perspective. I'll handle all the society hostesses and invitations to the best events. For you, too, of course."

Emme hurried to keep pace with the duchess, who was now hastening to the drawing room. "Invitations? But I don't plan to participate in the Season." Heaven have mercy, what might happen if her father saw the chance to parade his daughter about at every event in London?

"Just the first half of the Season, dear." The duchess stopped outside the drawing room and patted Emme's hand. "A wedding by midsummer, remember?" The woman grinned when she heard conversations rising from behind the closed drawing room door. "It sounds like my other guests have arrived, and you can meet the man at the center of our project."

Emme nodded, then began to shake her head as the duchess pushed open the doors and entered the room like the indomitable hostess holding court that she was.

"Man?" Emme asked. "Did you say man? Don't you mean woman?"

But the duchess was out of earshot and busily

greeting guests. Mr. Alcott and Tessa had returned from the ante-room, and Luci stood chatting with them, her father still hovering, despite the arrival of two other powerful society hostesses. No doubt the appearance of one very disreputable Captain Granston —engaged, by the looks of it, in charming the stockings off the society mavens—had raised the overprotective father's hackles.

Emme's heart sank. Where Captain Percival trod, others of Harrow's Finest Five were likely to follow. The duke was rumored to have resumed hiding from his mother at his country estate, Lord Harrison was still abroad, and Emme's brother was spending the day with their father. What were the odds the captain might be on his own that day?

Out of the corner of her eye, Emme caught the movement of the duchess, being escorted on the arm of the last guest. Far too late, her hackles went up. She'd already pledged her support to the duchess, and to the young *man* who was to be married off by midsummer. For as long as she was able, Emme kept her eyes forward, refusing to acknowledge or believe the identity of that man. But then the two of them were upon her, and she had no choice but to turn and smile.

"My dear Lady Emmeline, I must introduce you."

"Of course." Emme pictured herself a sharp-toothed fox, suddenly surrounded and rendered tame by a pack of hunting hounds. And one of those hounds had the most intriguing, deep blue eyes. She'd be able to sleep much more soundly at night if she never had to think of gazing into the depths of those eyes again.

The duchess released her companion's arm. "This is the young man we discussed earlier, the one with the dilemma you and I can help solve. Mr. Daniel Hallsworth, the future Marquess of Edensbridge, once you help him find a suitable wife."

CHAPTER 10

"*L*ady Emmeline, it's so lovely to make your acquaintance again." As Daniel held out his gloved hand to her, she went pale, as pale as she'd been the day he'd pulled her from the water, and he half-worried, half-hoped he'd have to catch her in his arms again.

Emme rallied quickly and grasped his fingers for the merest second before releasing them. "Mr. Hallsworth."

Her skin, pale but with color slowly returning, only served to set off the deep emerald green of her eyes and the auburn highlights of her hair. She wore lavender today, a lovely color against the soft skin of her throat, and a welcome change from gray, albeit still a reminder of her mourning.

"Do the two of you know each other?" The duchess folded her hands together over her heart.

Daniel hoped his conspirator wasn't overplaying her hand as Emme nodded at the duchess.

"You'll recall my brother is acquainted with both the duke and Mr. Hallsworth."

"Yes, but I didn't realize you'd met your brother's school friends," the duchess said. "I recall my son saying he'd only met you once."

"The duke didn't join us at the Radcliffe's country home during the summer months we spent there." Daniel watched Emme's face carefully and was rewarded by the slightest blush in her cheeks at the mention of those summers.

"Well, you can catch up on old times, then, this afternoon." The duchess squeezed Emme's hand. "You'll be happy to learn you share a passion with your brother's old friend."

Heat flooded Emme's cheeks, instantly turning Daniel's thoughts to their passionate indiscretions.

"You're both deeply involved in charitable causes," the duchess said. "Mr. Hallsworth has become the patron of several worthwhile causes in the short time he's been back in London."

Emme studied the man in front of her. There were still traces of the privileged boy he'd been, the boy who'd so boldly and confidently plied her with his seductions. But now there was a hint of world-weariness, of the same sadness that afflicted her when she thought about how much need existed in the world and how little she could do to affect it.

"Several causes?" Emme said. "There's always so

much to be done, isn't there, Mr. Hallsworth? And not enough hours and money to do it. I should like very much to hear about what you're doing."

"I've been inspired by those with kinder hearts than mine," he said. "It's hardly worth mentioning."

More like he didn't care to discuss it, not here among all this frippery. Her words resonated. In a short time, he'd come to understand her devotion to her own cause and the women she could help. But could it ever be enough? Besides, not everyone in high society, nor on the Committee for Privileges would approve of his support of some of the city's most desperate cases. It rarely occurred to those who disapproved that poverty might drive poor behaviors and not the other way 'round. But Daniel had to keep his counsel on all of that while he rebuilt an unassailable reputation.

The duchess turned in the direction of her other guests and announced that tea was served on the terrace. Daniel flashed a devilish grin at Emme and held out his arm to her, glad to leave weighty matters for another day and eager to enjoy the next few hours he would get to spend in her company.

In front of them, James took his wife's arm and the two of them smiled as they gazed at each other. They were a living, breathing testament to the joy of matrimony, and Daniel hoped Emme was paying attention to them. Unfortunately, she seemed to be drawn to and amused by the sight of Fairbank with his daughter on one arm, put in the uncomfortable position of having an unescorted duchess in proximity to his other arm. Fairbank inclined his head in the duchess's direction, who took his arm with even less enthusiasm than he'd shown in offering it.

The three of them led the procession down the hallway, followed by the society mavens, one on each of Granston's arms, then Lady Tessa and James. He and Emme followed the Alcotts. Somehow, despite being several steps in front of them, the mavens managed to take turns glancing at Emme and Daniel. He sighed under the weight of the watchful eye of London society on him.

He kept their watchfulness in mind and spoke softly to Emme as they entered the hallway. "As you've so generously agreed to help me, I should probably tell you what I desire in a wife."

"Desire?" She choked out the word. "I was under the impression this was a desperate situation. Should you expect to have some sort of wish list fulfilled?"

"Hm. Desperate might be too strong a word. I think my future title and a few other attributes will recommend me well to society's maidens, so, yes, I have a few wishes I expect to have fulfilled."

Every carefully chosen word seemed to have its effect on Emme, as looks of surprise, anger, and something else—dare he hope desire?—chased across her face.

"I hesitate to ask," she said.

"Well, to begin, she should be blonde."

Emme nearly stumbled and he gripped her arm tighter. "Blonde? Why on earth should she be blonde?"

"It seems very British, doesn't it? And blondes can be so lovely." Daniel rested his gaze on Lady Lucinda in front of them. He even made a discreet-bordering-on-inappropriate appraisal of her form. He hardly needed to have his arm twisted to do it. Lady Lucinda was quite comely, and her high-collared dress, covered what could only be described as an ample bosom. Far from being modest, no doubt what its wearer intended, the gown was enticing.

"I'll thank you to stop leering at my friend."

"Sorry. Got lost in my thoughts for a moment." Daniel fought to control a grin when Emme gasped indignantly.

"There are plenty of well-bred Englishwomen with dark hair. And I have it on the best authority that the last woman to whom you proposed was not blonde."

"Well, times change, proposals get rejected, men must move on." He wondered if Emme realized just how tightly she was gripping his arm. He grinned to cover the grimace elicited by her fingertips digging into his flesh.

"Well, move onto someone who is not Fairbank's daughter. If I'm to help with this project of yours, I'd prefer it end in a marriage rather than a duel."

"Perhaps the duel would end in my favor, and a marriage would ensue."

Emme snorted quietly and gracefully, as only a well-bred Englishwoman could. "Rumor has it, Fairbank has been dispatching worthy opponents since before either of us were born."

Daniel instinctively pulled her arm tighter against him, not enjoying what could be construed as admiration for another man. "Perhaps it *is* best to set our sights elsewhere."

They arrived on the terrace, where a servant pulled out a seat for the duchess at the head of a beautifully laid table that could have served a formal dinner as easily as high tea. Daniel held out Emme's chair, then took the seat beside her, as they'd been assigned by the placards beside their teacups. Fairbank was seated at the opposite end of the table, as far from the duchess as he could be. He was flanked on one side by his daughter and on the other by Lady Tessa and James. The mavens were seated opposite Emme and Daniel, one on each side of Granston, who, as Daniel had hoped, was distracting them from speculation about what might be going on between Lady Emme and Mr. Hallsworth. While he wasn't above plotting subterfuge to win a stubborn woman's hand in matrimony, Daniel was deadly serious about restoring the reputation of the Hallsworth name.

One of the servants poured tea for Emme, then offered sugar and cream. She requested sugar cubes, then amended her request to none, which Daniel found curious. He took his own cup strong and black, which was the only way he could stand it after falling out of the British habit of tea while abroad. When they'd been served finger sandwiches and scones, for which he'd never lose his taste, Emme glanced in his direction. She set her jaw and narrowed her eyes, and he braced for the joy of the lady's set-down.

"Other than the requirement regarding her hair color, what criteria have you set for your helpmeet and lifelong companion?"

There was an edge to her words that made him hopeful. This was the duchess's scheme, after all, and he had little sense of whether it would work on such a headstrong woman as Emme, but already there were positive signs. "She should be..." *intelligent, stubborn, passionate,* "...amenable."

"Amenable? As in docile?" She fixed him with a mirthless smile. "Like the Queen's collie?"

He sipped his tea, then shrugged one shoulder. "Collies are also known for their agility and stamina."

That drew a full blush from the base of Emme's throat to edge of her hairline.

"For keeping up with the children." He clicked his tongue. "Please do keep your thoughts pure. I'm trying to rebuild a reputation."

She widened her eyes and coughed on her sip of tea, drawing the attention of the others at the table. "Pardon me," she gasped. "I'm fine, really."

The duchess motioned away the two servants who had rushed to Emme's side to attend to her, but that didn't break the stare of the mavens who now watched them more closely. Ah, well, Daniel could perform with an audience. It would be a pleasure to learn whether Emme could as well, as he planned to put her through her paces over the coming weeks. In public and in private.

～※～

*T*he next evening, Emme wrapped her fingers around the stem of her aperitif glass. She stared into the fire the servants had laid in the sitting room to ward off the chill of yet another rain front that had moved in over the city. A quiet dinner with her aunt and two best friends and the first glass of sherry hadn't yet calmed her, but perhaps the second glass would do the trick.

"And do you know what he had the nerve to say to me?" she asked her friends, her aunt having long since retired and left them to their own devices.

Tessa, sitting ramrod straight and looking dutifully demure, her first glass of sherry sitting untouched beside her, tilted her head. "Was it something about blondes, dear?"

Emme blinked slowly and sighed. "I'm sorry. I must be a terrible bore tonight."

"Of course not!" Tessa gave her a sweet smile.

"Perhaps a bit." Luci finished her sherry and helped herself to a second glass. Tessa cleared her throat, and Luci shrugged. "Well, she is. And what kind of friends would we be if we weren't honest about it?"

"The terrible kind." Emme grinned.

She'd missed Luci's straightforward manner. When she wanted, Luci could bluff her way through the most spirited game of whist, but she was never less than brutally honest with her best friends.

Tessa lifted her glass of sherry and took a sip. "In the interest of being good friends, let's discuss why you feel the need to discuss it."

"Endlessly," Luci added, then raised her eyebrows at the cutting look Tessa gave her.

"Luci's right, Tessa," Emme said. "I know I've gone on and on about it. My mother would be mortified by the kind of hostess I'm being, not asking after your husband, or Luci's Season, or your families."

Tessa shook her head. "Don't try to change the subject now. You can't stop talking about Mr. Hallsworth, and I think I know why. You haven't been totally honest about what transpired between the two of you on your voyage from Spain."

Emme blushed. She hadn't been honest with them, not completely, and she never would be. Even her closest friends couldn't know the truth about her. No matter how much they loved her, she couldn't expect them to stand by a fallen woman, a disgrace to her family. A shameless harlot who'd tried to seduce a second man, only to be rebuffed by *his* sense of propriety.

"Come, now, Emme, we've figured it out." Luci leaned forward and laid her hand over Emme's.

For a moment, the horror that they knew what had happened in Daniel's stateroom made her stiffen with fear. But the fear was soon replaced by relief at the prospect of having someone with whom she could share her deep, dark secret about their shameful tryst. Perhaps it was even time to tell them what had happened on that night more than a year ago, the night that had spurred Edward to convince their parents to let her travel abroad with Aunt Juliana. The night she'd surrendered her virginity to the cad who'd flattered her with flowery promises and lies about everlasting love and devotion, while she'd pretended to want those things so she could use him for her own ends.

Tessa leaned forward and laid her hand on top of both Emme's and Luci's. "It's obvious the two of you still have feelings for each other. James has noticed it. Granted, he's keenly attuned to love, like all the great Romantic poets."

Luci glanced at Tessa. "But this is about Emme and Mr. Hallsworth." She turned her attention back to Emme. "You're not the first lady who has let a man steal kisses from her. And out on the ocean, under the stars—I can't imagine the temptation!"

Tessa sighed. "What Luci is trying to say is that you mustn't judge yourself so harshly. If you have feelings for Mr. Hallsworth and he has feelings for you, why not let him court you?"

Because as much as he said her sordid past didn't matter to him, of course it did. Or it would, someday. She was soiled and damaged. The kind of woman he could take for a lover? Maybe. The kind of woman he could marry, with his quest to restore honor and respectability to the family name? Never.

"I don't think he's interested, not anymore. He

seems quite set on finding a wife. A blonde wife. And I'll help him find someone appropriate as a favor to the duchess." And for him, so he could have what he needed most—a respectable match.

Tessa leaned closer and gave her a quick hug. "You're too kind-hearted for your own good, which is how I know you'll do the right thing. If you won't have him, you owe it to him to let him go."

"The right thing?" Luci huffed. "Tessa's right that you're kindhearted and noble. *And* you deserve to be happy, which is why you shouldn't let him go at all!"

Emme nodded, agreeing to everything and nothing all at once. Their opinion of her was a lie. Noble, indeed. But what could she do except go along with the ruse? A flirtation, a kiss, even a near-seduction were all forgivable. But what Emme had done would have her labeled an outcast. She had no choice but to give up any hope of a happy marriage and respectable wifehood. But she couldn't bear the thought of losing her dearest friends as well.

Before she could formulate some response to their conflicting advice, noise from the front of the house drew their attention.

"Father's home earlier than expected."

Emme scooped up the sherry bottle Tessa gathered the glasses, and they tucked them into the hiding place behind a needlepoint bag in a low cabinet drawer. As they took up their still full tea cups, they heard a woman's voice asking the servants about "my dear daughter."

Tessa took Emme's hand. "Your mother!"

"Finally." Luci shook her head. "How did she manage to take a route that delayed her this long?"

Tessa nudged Luci in the ribs.

"I don't even care," Emme said as she rushed to the door. "I have to see her. Come with me."

"No," Tessa called after her. "We'll see ourselves out. Have your reunion in private, and give the countess our regards."

Emme stopped and smiled at her friends. "Thank you. We'll have you 'round for tea as soon as my mother is settled in."

"And tell her about Mr. Hallsworth." Luci said.

Tessa nudged her again.

Luci groaned. "What? Perhaps her mother can talk some sense into her."

A few days after embarking on the duchess's plan for him to win Emme, Daniel once again sat ensconced in a large, leather chair by the fireplace in the private room at Swimmer's club. He stared into his half-empty glass of fine Scotch whisky and listened to Granston and their host banter.

"I can't understand why you're avoiding her. I find the duchess's company delightful." Granston lifted his glass. "A toast to the Duchess of Wrexham."

Swimmer lifted his glass half-heartedly. "I enjoy my mother's company in small doses. And in addition to being good company, she's a shrewdly intelligent woman who sees right through your boyish charms."

"Ha! She resists me only because I've reined in my considerable appeal around her," Granston retorted. "How would it look, seducing my old friend's mother? But if you're truly concerned, and well you should be, you should join us at the ball this Thursday."

"Not on your life! That's exactly the kind of event my mother dreams of attending with me. She's probably already scoured the guest list to identify all the suitable prospects for the role of the next duchess." Swimmer gave a mock shiver. "All the more reason for her to keep believing I'm at the country estate."

"Well, you do have a duty to the title to provide an heir," Granston said.

"All in good time, Granston." Swimmer lifted his glass again. "But for the next year or two or five, I'd prefer practicing begetting an heir to actually having one."

Granston guffawed. "Hear, hear!" He slapped Daniel on the back. "Come on, then, lift your glass."

Daniel did so, albeit with little enthusiasm, resenting the interruption to his thoughts of Emme and the afternoon they'd spent together. The way she'd gripped his arm so tightly and had widened her eyes and blushed when he'd teased her about his preference for blondes. He must remember to use that to his advantage in the future.

Granston slapped him harder on the back and startled him out of his pleasant reverie. "You're quite the bore tonight, Hallsy. Come on, be a good guest and toast our host's sordid plans."

"Leave him be, Granston." Swimmer patted Daniel's shoulder. "The man is in a bad way. He has all the signs the most dreaded of diseases."

Granston widened his eyes in a pathetic imitation of an innocent. "The French disease?"

"All right, the second most dreaded."

"Ah." Granston nodded. "Of course. Love sickness."

Daniel tossed back his whisky and scowled. "The pair of you really should tread the boards. This *amusant* commentary of yours might play well as a bit of theater."

Swimmer filled Daniel's empty glass, then topped off his own. "That would go over worse with the duchess than my plans for a few years of debauchery."

Daniel grinned at his incorrigible friends and lifted his glass high in the air. "To the duke's impending debauchery." He glanced at Granston. "And to your never-ending pursuit of it."

"Hear, hear!" Granston said again, and tossed back the rest of his drink.

Someone knocked at the door, and Swimmer bid them entrance. One of the club's managers bowed in the doorway, then announced Viscount Meriden.

Daniel's lighthearted mood evaporated.

The manager left, closing the door behind Steady Eddie. Daniel clutched his glass and stared into the fire, hoping if he wished hard enough, the bloody man would prove to be a figment of his imagination.

Swimmer and Granston greeted him warmly and poured Meriden a drink, but Daniel remained seated and silent. After a few minutes of camaraderie, Meriden spoke to him.

"I have need of a word."

"Of course," Swimmer said.

"With Hallsworth. Alone"

Swimmer nodded. "I see. Well, take the room, then."

Granston's seemingly perpetual smiled faded. "Are you sure that's a good idea?"

Swimmer exhaled loudly. "I'm sure we can trust these two to be civil. Hallsy?"

Daniel continued his best imitation of a rock until Swimmer slapped him on the back every bit as hard as Granston had earlier.

"Yes, I'll be civil." He stared at Eddie. "Although I can only speak for myself."

"I haven't come here to call him out," Meriden said without taking his eyes off Daniel.

"All right," Swimmer said. "We'll be outside."

"Right outside," Granston added. "And if anything untoward happens, I'm prepared to break down this door."

"Oh, are you?" Swimmer asked. "Now that I would like to see."

"Don't believe I can, do you?"

Their voices were cut off as the heavy door closed behind them. Daniel motioned for Meriden to sit, then poured whisky into one of the clean glasses on the serving table in front of them and held it out to his nemesis.

Meriden hesitated.

"I hardly had time to poison it," Daniel said. "And it's Swimmer's hospitality, not mine, so you won't be beholden to me."

Meriden took the glass. "Neither of those were my concerns. I was contemplating whether I trust myself to remain civil with a good glass of whisky in me."

For his part, Daniel was curious about what had brought the man here. Being hostile probably wouldn't be conducive to finding out. He lifted his glass in salute. "To a truce."

Meriden nodded. "Fine, a truce." They both took a swig. "As long as can come to an understanding."

"Which is…"

"You are not to see my sister again."

"Word does travel fast in this town, doesn't it?"

Meriden scowled. "Especially when Lady Lucinda Fairbank is a dinner guest. As soon as my sister left the room for a few minutes yesterday, her friend couldn't resist regaling my aunt with the details of your afternoon tête-a-tête with her."

Daniel wondered if that were true, or if Meriden had stooped so low as to set spies upon Emme. "Lady Lucinda didn't strike me as the type to gossip."

Meriden gave a mirthless laugh. "Not within her father's purview. But when he's out of earshot, she's quite the talker. And she couldn't stop talking about you and my sister."

"You needn't make it sound so base. We were both invited to take afternoon tea with the duchess and a few other guests and found ourselves seated next to each other."

"A happy coincidence, no doubt." Meriden took the last swig of his drink and eyed the bottle, then shook his head and set down his glass.

Daniel considered being tactful, a feint, perhaps, but decided a lunge would be the more satisfactory course. "Lady Emmeline and I were merely discussing a project. She has agreed to help me find a wife."

Meriden jumped up from his seat. "You will not marry my sister, and I will not allow you to ruin her reputation."

Daniel set down his glass very slowly and stood as well. "Where was all of this brotherly protection a year ago, when a blackguard preyed on your sister and you allowed it to happen?"

Meriden's face went red. "Whatever you think you know, trust me, Hallsworth, you have no idea. Never speak of that again. Not to me, not to Lady Emme, not to anyone, or I will come for you."

No one had ever looked at Daniel with murderous intent before. If Meriden had come armed with a pistol or a blade, Daniel might be meeting his maker this very minute.

Meriden stalked to the door and turned to face him again. "Never, Hallsworth. Do you understand me?"

Daniel nodded and watched Meriden leave, then let out a long, slow breath. Perhaps he'd judged Meriden too harshly. Perhaps the man had done his best to protect his sister, but had fallen short. And perhaps some of the hatred he felt for Meriden was really for himself.

"No blood that I can see." Granston stepped into the room and circled slowly around him.

"Meriden looked intact as well," Swimmer added. "Although, I wouldn't want to be the poor sod who says one wrong word to him tonight, given the look on his face."

Granston shook his head. "You really do bring out the worst in him, don't you?" He glanced at Swimmer. "Pity, isn't it?"

"Hm." Swimmer nodded and poured another shot of whisky for himself and Granston, and they clinked glasses.

Daniel looked back and forth between them. "What meaning am I to take from that?"

Granston sighed. "You want the girl. The girl adores her older brother."

Daniel waited, but Granston offered no more explanation. He glanced at Swimmer.

"What Granston is trying to say is that you're a fool. If you want to win the hand of Lady Emmeline, you'll need all the help you can get." Swimmer sloshed whisky into Daniel's glass and handed it to him, then clinked his against it. "There's one man in all of England who might be able to help you, but you insist on making him your enemy."

CHAPTER 11

*E*mme entered the breakfast room at an impossibly early hour. The spinsters believed in "early to bed, early to rise," and if Emme hoped to be one of them, she had to adopt the habit, even if she did startle more than one of the servants who hurried to set a place for her at the breakfast table. It all would have been easier to manage if she and Aunt Juliana hadn't stayed up late two nights in a row with Mother, but even a day-and-a-half after being reunited, there still seemed to be so much more to share about the year they'd been apart.

She could tell by the unused place settings that she'd arrived even earlier than her father and brother this morning. And from the missing one that her mother didn't plan on joining them. The only one Emme could never have beaten to breakfast had been Eleanor.

As the footman poured a cup of tea and served her a plate salmon and eggs fresh from the kitchen, she could almost picture her sister there, in the seat just across from hers, peeking at the morning papers before Father arrived to tell her ladies don't read at the breakfast table. Emme smiled, remembering the few mornings she'd had breakfast alone with her sister. Eleanor was always full of good cheer, but never more so than first thing in the morning. Except when Emme vexed her, as she had that fateful summer she'd made the dastardly mistake of falling in love.

Emme had risen at the crack of dawn, full of energy she couldn't contain, despite the late hours she'd kept to rendezvous with Daniel in the library. She'd found her sister in the breakfast room with a nearly finished plate of food in front of her and a book balanced on the edge of the table. Emme had forced herself to slow down as she'd entered the room, not wanting to rouse her sister's suspicion that something was amiss.

"Good morning, sister," Emme said.

Eleanor surveyed Emme silently, sweeping her eyes from Emme's head to her toes with a penetrating gaze. As Emme piled eggs, bacon, and fruit onto her plate, Eleanor didn't speak. When Emme sat down opposite Eleanor, her sister leaned back in her seat.

"What have you done now, Emme?"

Emme struggled to swallow the forkful of eggs she'd shoveled into her mouth. Daniel's late-night attentions had left her famished, but now she worried her older sister would deduce the reason for her early-morning appetite. Emme longed to confess to Eleanor, to share her delicious secret, but she only wanted to share her hopes for a bright future with Daniel, not the details of what had passed between them. Those should remain between lovers.

"Why do you assume I've done something?"

"Because I'm not an idiot, nor am I blind." Eleanor leaned forward and dropped her voice to a whisper. "It's Edensbridge, isn't it? What happened? And where were you yesterday afternoon when you asked your maid to lie and say you'd taken to your room with a headache?"

Emme's face flushed hot. "How do you know? Does Mother know? Does *Father*?"

"She knows you were gone, he guesses, and they both assume you simply went off into the woods by yourself, despite being told a thousand times not to do it. And while you were taking dinner in your room to avoid scrutiny, I was listening to them *speaking* about you in Father's study."

Speaking, said about the earl and countess and in that tone, was code for arguing. Loudly. Usually about yet another of their younger daughter's transgressions.

"I don't know what happened between you and Edensbridge, and I don't care to. But if you can't bring your behavior to heel for your own sake, think of how others might be affected. A friend of Edward's, let's say. A young man who, were he to land on the wrong side of a man of Father's stature, might be irreparably damaged."

Emme closed her eyes and took a deep breath. If Father ever learned what had transpired between Daniel and her, the way she'd met him while wearing only her shift and whisper-thin wrap, both of which had, at some point, become half undone, damage to his reputation wouldn't even be the worst of it. While not fully debauched, she had enjoyed carnal pleasures with a man not her husband, not her fiancé, not even her suitor. Once again, she was unredeemable.

"At least have the decency to look less guilty," Eleanor whispered. "And next time you think of doing something so selfish, think of Mother."

Eleanor didn't have to elaborate. Father blamed Mother for Emme's behavior. He said she'd become too permissive after the twins had died of the fever. Emme didn't know if that was true. All she could remember from that time was the deep, quiet loneliness of the house with the twins' laughter gone, Edward off at school, Eleanor with her tutor or hunched over her needlework, Mother taken to her bed for days at a time.

The sounds of the woods—birds singing, the brook babbling, furry creatures digging for food or shelter— had comforted her. She'd talked to the forest creatures when there'd been no people around her who would to listen to a ten-year-old girl. It wasn't until the following year, when Mother had arranged to have Tessa and Luci join her for studies with her tutor, that the loneliness had abated. Soon after that, Eleanor's own pleasant nature had returned, and life had seemed hopeful again, but never more hopeful than the summer she and Daniel had fallen in love.

If only Emme had learned the lesson Eleanor had tried to teach her that day over their early-morning breakfast. But after Daniel had disappeared from her life and Eleanor had died a few years later, Emme had returned to her reckless ways. If not for Edward rescuing her from Gretna Green as she'd counted on him to do, she could have found herself doing penance in a disastrous marriage. Now she had the opportunity to do her penance in her own way, working with the Spinsters' Club. She'd make Mother proud of her, and perhaps even mollify Father. But first, she had to get Mother's blessing, secure the duchess's support, and find her first love a respectable wife who was worthy of marrying him.

She stared down at the eggs and salmon on her plate and wished she'd stayed in bed.

"Emmeline, how lovely to see you so bright and early." Her mother swept in behind her and dropped a kiss on the top of her head.

Emme's spirits lifted immediately. "And you, Mother. It's wonderful to have you home. But I didn't expect you at breakfast."

"I couldn't wait to see you again. And I just had a lovely chat with Aunt Juliana. She'll be down shortly. Today, I hope the two of you will tell me everything about your time in Valencia. Then tomorrow, we must go shopping. You're so thin. Do your dresses even fit you anymore?"

Emme rolled her eyes. "I'm exactly the same size I was when I left for Spain. And I don't need many things."

As Mother sat down, a servant stepped forward to pour her coffee, then disappeared back into the kitchen.

"What about the ball on Thursday?" Mother asked. "Surely, you don't plan to wear something from your Season three years ago."

Emme planned to do exactly that. After all, she was only attending to fulfill her obligation to the duchess. It wasn't as though she need impress anyone. The only man she'd ever cared to impress would be looking for a wife, not at her.

Her mother stirred sugar into her cup, then sighed. "Emmeline, you know your father expects you to entertain suitors this Season."

Emme reached for her mother's hand and gently squeezed her fingers. "We wrote about this. There are other things I'm doing right now, women in need whom I'm helping."

"It's a lovely thought," her mother said, despite not knowing the half of it, "but it's not in your father's plans."

"Then you must help me with him. Talk to him. Convince him. I'll make both of you proud of me, I swear it. I just can't do it as someone's wife."

Her mother leaned back in her chair while Emme

waited for her promise. Before Mother could give it, Edward and Father's voices echoed in the hallway.

Emme's mother jumped to her feet and gave Emme a kiss on the cheek. "My darling girl. We'll discuss this later with Aunt Juliana. But right now, I must get more rest. Ask Edward to stop by my room before he leaves the house."

"Of course, Mother. Sleep well."

The countess slipped out one door while her husband and son entered through another. Emme greeted Edward and Father, then sank back into her own morbid thoughts. She'd done this to her parents, to their marriage. And now there was nothing she could do to save them. She could only hope to save herself and some poor, unsuspecting man from the same fate. If a woman like her mother—upstanding, respectable, chaste until wed—couldn't find happiness in marriage, what hope could there be for a woman like Emme, who was so undeserving?

❧

Perhaps Emme didn't deserve to witness Daniel's behavior, but he was so enjoying her look of disapproval. which didn't quite mask her jealousy. For his part, he had trouble keeping his eyes off her, though he hid it from her as best he could.

She'd arrived at the ball in a stunning dark green gown, the color of a forest at dusk. He'd seen her in that color before, but this dress was cut lower and included intricate gold stitching along the sleeves and bodice that drew the eye, or at least certainly drew his. Her hair was swept up into a ridiculously intricate mass of curls piled onto her head, revealing the fine bones and flawless skin of her face to glorious effect. It had taken everything he'd had to hold himself back from rushing to her side and kissing her hand, as a few other bachelors had been moved to do.

After a suitable time away from her, he approached, where she sat with some of the married ladies along one side of the dance floor. She still clutched the glass of punch he'd brought her during his last brief respite from dancing with blondes. The duchess had done a fine job of convincing their hostess to keep him partnered for every dance. Perhaps too good a job, his weary feet reminded him. But it was worth it to see the way Emme openly glared at him, just barely slipping a mask of serenity over her scowl when he was within a few feet of her.

He bowed in her direction. "Are you enjoying your evening, Lady Emmeline?"

She nodded. "Of course."

Beside her, Lady Tessa watched them carefully. Daniel took the empty seat on Emme's other side and dropped his voice. "I must thank you for heeding my wish. I believe I've danced with every eligible blonde lady under the age of thirty who is in attendance tonight."

"Trust me, Mr. Hallsworth, I had nothing to do with it."

"Didn't you? Well then, what are the odds? You were the only brunette I danced with all evening."

"Hm. That was so many hours ago, one hardly remembers."

Ah, but that statement alone was proof of just how well she remembered. "I do hope you'll forgive me for treading on your toes that one time. I'm afraid I am a bit out of practice."

Emme refused to meet his gaze, staring instead at the dancers still on the floor. "It was three times, and I must say, you made a remarkable recovery. With every partner since me, it's appeared as though you're floating on clouds when you dance."

Daniel leaned closer to her. "So, you've watched every one of my dances?"

Lady Tessa gave a little snort and quickly flicked her fan over her face.

"I've not *watched.*" Emme shook out the full skirt of her dress with undue force. "I've merely *noticed.* I *noticed* your dance with Lady Lucinda looked especially effortless."

"Yes, well, how can one go wrong with such a divinely talented partner?"

The mark hit home, as evidenced by the flush of color to Emme's cheeks. Lady Tessa reached for Emme's hand. When Emme clamped down hard on her friend's fingers, the lady winced behind her fan.

"That's not to disparage your talent, my lady." Daniel bowed his head slightly, as though begging her indulgence. "It might just be that we were both so woefully out of practice."

Lady Tessa lowered her fan and extricated her hand from Emme's. "I'm sure that's it. Perhaps you should have another go of it, now that Mr. Hallsworth has had an opportunity to hone his skills."

"Oh, I couldn't possibly." Emme shifted uncomfortably in her seat.

"Nor could I." Daniel rose to his feet. "It seems I have the good fortune of having Lady Lucinda as my partner for the next set." He leaned toward both ladies and whispered. "My understanding is her father entrusted her two older brothers to chaperone her this evening, but neither of them is half as attentive as her overly protective father."

Emme gave the smallest gasp and covered it with a delicate cough. Daniel bowed to them again, then excused himself. Only when he'd reached the opposite side of the room and held out his hand to the lovely Lady Lucinda for the next dance did he allow himself a well-deserved chuckle.

*E*mme stopped just inside the entrance to her home and surveyed the havoc the muck-covered streets had visited upon her boots and hemline. Somehow, even her gloves and her oversized parasol had splashes of mud on them. But for all the dirt she carried, she walked with a lightness in her step she hadn't felt in ages.

"Has my father asked about me?" she asked in a hushed tone to the footman who took her parasol, hat, and gloves from her.

"No, my lady. Guests arrived not fifteen minutes ago, in the company of your mother and brother. It was at that time that Lord Meriden reminded your father you were not due home from tea with your friends for another half-hour."

Bless Edward. He didn't hide his concern about her work with the Spinsters' Club, but he'd agreed to create a cover for her, as long as she took either him or —when he was unavailable—James and Tessa with her when visiting Mrs. Billings and Mrs. Carter. His stretching of the truth would give her enough time to clean off the evidence of an afternoon spent at a more industrious enterprise than enjoying tea, even if it had meant missing a chance to her best friends.

"Please send my maid to my room, Harold."

The footman bowed and hurried off into the bowels of the house while Emma flew up the stairs.

Fifteen minutes later, wearing a fresh skirt and satin slippers, she strolled into the atrium to find three men looking out through the bank of windows at the back of the house, taking in the garden. Edward and her father she'd expected. Daniel, on the other hand, never ceased to surprise her. Not so much his presence, perhaps, but her own happiness at discovering it.

They hadn't spoken since the ball two days earlier, but when she hadn't been annoyed recalling his boorishly flirtatious behavior there, she'd wondered when their paths would cross again. It would only be to plot their next move for procuring his redemption, of course.

Daniel separated from the other two men and met her halfway into the room. "Lady Emme, always a pleasure. I'd hoped to see you today to inform you that I've been moving forward with our plan." Daniel bowed in her direction.

For all her hope of seeing him, she was suddenly unable to think of anything suitable to say in his presence, as he stood tall and solid and real in front of her, with his dark hair and wild blue eyes. And the truth of it hit her. She had *missed* him over the past few days. How had she managed without even knowing where he'd been for five years before that? She shook her head. She had no right to miss him.

"Are you all right, Emme?" he asked quietly.

"I'm fine." But she wasn't at all sure it was true. Perhaps she was just looking forward to the excitement of undertaking their scheme. She pressed a cool hand to the side of her neck. "You were saying something about our plan."

He nodded. "The day after the ball, invitations began arriving from parents interested in having the future Marquess of Edensbridge court their daughters."

"And you've accepted these invitations?" She focused on smiling to prove she was pleased with his progress.

"A few." He observed her closely. "Are you sure you're all right? You didn't wear yourself out on your adventure, did you?" He touched her elbow.

It sent a shockwave through her flesh, emanating from the points where his bare fingertips had pressed against her exposed skin. She glanced at his hand, and he quickly withdrew it.

"Did Edward tell you about my afternoon?" she asked.

"He'd hardly be inclined to share your secrets with me. The Duchess of Wrexham, on the other hand..."

"The duchess is here? Is that what's so interesting in the back garden?"

"Yes and no." Daniel took a sip of port and glanced at Edward and the earl. "She's here and is no doubt interesting, but your father is much more intent upon her son."

"Her son. The duke is here, visiting my family?"

Daniel nodded. "So great is your father's pleasure, he allowed me, with my questionable past, through the front door, based on the duke's recognizance."

Emme sniffed. "Don't be so dramatic. My father is a fair man."

Daniel didn't offer an opinion on the matter. Instead, he changed the subject. "I gather you saw your charges this afternoon. How are the widow and her housemate and their children?"

"First, Mr. Hallsworth, I believe there's something you need to tell me. Something about a factory you're buying, and the labor changes you plan to make."

She grinned when he raised his eyebrows in surprise.

"That's not common knowledge," he said. "How did you learn of it?"

"I have my sources," she said.

She nearly had to blink back tears, remembering how excited the women were by the prospect of improved conditions at one of the major factories, changes that could ripple out to other workplaces as well. She wanted to kiss him for his generosity. And for his kindness. And for the way a lock of his dark hair now fell across his forehead.

"Do you know just how many lives could see a positive impact from your decision, Mr. Hallsworth?" she asked instead.

"I suppose. I mean, I hope so." He held out his arm to her. "Enough about that. Shall we take a turn in the garden? You can tell me how the widow's miniature portrait of you is coming, and at the same time, we can delay the fate of meeting your suitor by fifteen minutes or so."

She rolled forward on her toes as she remembered the joy on Mrs. Billings' face just hours earlier, when Emme had brought more paintings for the woman to recreate into miniature portraits, as well as the down payment on the fees for the work. "Not just a portrait for me, but for three other ladies as well. Mrs. Billings has almost completed—" She turned abruptly toward Daniel. "Did you say *suitor*?"

Emme's hands shook and she willed herself to stay

calm. What was the duchess about, bringing her son here like an offering to her father's fevered dreams of Emme's future married state? The betrayal cut deep, followed by horror as her mind leapt forward to a wedding night with a powerful duke who had just learned his virginal bride was, in fact, no virgin.

Daniel dropped his proffered arm. "Emme, it's fine. No one other than your father expects that the duke will court anyone this Season. Granston has designs on his time, and the duke seems only too happy to indulge him."

She let out a long breath. "Thank you, Dan—Mr. Hallsworth. That could end badly."

He bent his head close to her and spoke in a low tone. "I won't let anything end badly for you, not again."

She wanted to hug him for saying it. They now shared secrets. If they couldn't be lovers, perhaps they could be friends.

Until he finds a blonde who strikes his fancy.

He was well on his way to courting someone who could help him bring honor to his family name. The plan was working. The thought left her cold again, and she excused herself, flashing a smile that she hoped covered the pain in her heart, a pain she had no right to claim.

She stepped away from Daniel without saying another word and walked toward her brother and father. They would discuss more details of his plan later, when she had the strength to deal with it. Perhaps she'd worn herself out on her visit to Mrs. Billings and Mrs. Carter after all. In the meantime, it seemed she would have new plans—these laid out by her father—to foil. And it occurred to her that she already knew how to do it and—at the same time—to turn the whole unfortunate circumstance to her advantage.

4 April, in the Year of Our Lord 1870

To Mr. Daniel Hallsworth, son of the late Marquess of Edensbridge:

Pursuant to the request made of you by the Committee of Privileges in correspondence dated 29 March 1870, we are pleased to see your progress toward courting the daughter of a peer in good standing in the House of Lords. However, it has come to our attention that several young ladies are under the impression that you intend to court them. Please be advised that the Committee would find it unacceptable of you to mislead such fine women with a promise of marriage you do not intend to keep. The Committee therefore recommends you settle upon a respectable match before our next scheduled correspondence on 25 April, and court one lady with the intention of proposing marriage in short order.

Respectfully yours,

The Hon. Mr. Charles Alby
Clerk of the Committee for Privileges
House of Lords
London, England

CHAPTER 12

*E*mme walked slowly toward the breakfast room, surprised at how bright the hallway was at such an early hour. She couldn't determine whether it was the early hour or the remnants of her disturbing dreams that made her head ache so this morning. Whether the dreams had affected her head or not, the essence of them lingered enough to leave her agitated. She'd dreamt of Daniel, which wasn't so unusual. But this time, he hadn't even known Emme was there watching him as he'd stood in the center of a ballroom surrounded by blondes. Blonde country maidens. Blonde debutantes, asking him to court them. Blonde brides in their wedding finery. Blonde babes being handed into his arms.

But Emme would be damned if she'd let that ninny of a man and his lust for blondes ruin her waking hours as much as they had her sleeping ones. She tucked a stray tendril of her own disappointingly auburn hair behind her ear and steadied her step until she was practically marching into the breakfast room. There, she found her father sitting alone at the table, his breakfast dishes long since cleared by attentive servants, poring over the morning paper. With Daniel's quest for a blonde-haired, ninny wife well underway, the duchess would be amenable to helping Emme with her own quest, and Emme had to be prepared. She threw back her shoulders and pasted on a smile.

"Good morning, sir." She gathered toast, cheese, and jam from a sideboard while a servant poured a cup of tea for her.

The footman left Emme and Father alone in the room, but Father didn't notice, as he had yet to lift his eyes from the pages in front of him. Emme took her seat to his right and audibly sipped her tea. He glanced at her with a half-smile, then lifted his head and removed his readers.

"You look well this morning, Emmeline. London air agrees with you, after all. It's good to see color in your cheeks."

She widened her eyes, unable to hide her surprise, quite sure the choking London air had no positive effect on her health. But her father was in a jovial mood, and she was happy to use it to her advantage.

She chewed and swallowed her first bite of toast, then smiled at him. She longed to mention Mother and the happiness of being back in the bosom of her family, but she feared the mention of it would sour Father's mood. "It's lovely seeing Tessa and Luci nearly every day."

"They're a good influence, getting you out and about town. And the duchess—I had my doubts about her at first, but now I understand her motives." Her father winked as though they shared a secret.

"Motives, sir?"

"Her search for a new daughter-in-law."

The one bite of toast she'd eaten seemed to have stuck in her throat. She gulped down half her cup of tea to clear it. "Oh, I hardly think that's her interest."

She slowly set down her teacup, pondering how to steer the conversation away from the Duke of Wrexham. "Lady Tessa and Mr. Alcott have been giving me poetry recommendations, so I've been expanding my repertoire of verses."

"That's splendid." He patted her hand, the way he used to pat Eleanor's when she'd done something to please him. "And I noticed the needlework on the kerchief you carried yesterday. Your improvement is nothing short of miraculous."

In fact, it was quite short of miraculous, as the handiwork he praised was attributable to Mrs. Carter. But basking in the glow of his approval, she couldn't see the harm in letting him believe his only remaining daughter had finally done something to inspire his pride.

Her father beamed at her. "It's been such a welcome change, Emmeline, seeing you smile when you leave the house to attend an event."

"Do I?" Perhaps it was true, although it doubtless had more to do with the anticipation of telling Daniel about her adventures than with any proclivity for interacting with the *ton*.

"Yes, and I think I know who's behind it."

Emme's heart skittered, fearing he'd read her thoughts.

"Don't think I haven't heard the duke has started turning up at events you attend."

"The duke? But we're not—"

"No need to play coy. I couldn't have found a better match for you myself."

Emme, for her part, couldn't think of a worse match than any of Daniel's friends. Not to mention the shame that would be visited upon her entire family if a duke were to discover he'd married damaged goods. But she'd been expecting this conversation since the duke had visited their home, and had planned how she'd redirect it.

"There's something else I'd hope to discuss, Father, besides the *ton*." She took another sip of tea while her father watched and waited. She couldn't remember ever holding his rapt attention this way. "I'd like to do good works. Help those less fortunate. Many of the most respected ladies are so engaged these days."

Her father nodded. "I think that's a fine idea, Emmeline. The duke might appreciate a wife who patronizes a charitable cause or two."

She shook her head. "I don't want to patronize charities. And the duke has no interest in courting me."

He patted her hand again, then checked his pocket watch and jumped to his feet. "I must get to the House. Tell your mother...Never mind." He kissed Emme on the top of her head. "This was lovely. I hope you'll join me for breakfast again soon."

"Yes, sir. But can't we discuss—"

"I was going to make this a surprise," he interrupted her, "but I might as well tell you now."

Emme's heart raced in anticipation. Would he pledge his support of her good works? Announce he was proud of her for wanting to help others? Tell her he loved her?

"Your mother and I are going to escort you to the duke's soiree next week. She'll help you choose a new gown for the event. Something cheerful."

"But I can't—"

Her father left the room before she could finish.

Emme hunched over her toast, her appetite flagging. Their talk hadn't gone at all as planned. Instead of securing her freedom, she might have just convinced her father he was about to become a father-in-law to a duke.

*D*aniel leaned against the mantelpiece in the duke's salon and gripped a glass of his friend's finest cognac, all the while cursing his own cowardice for not throwing himself into the Bay of Biscay when he'd had the chance. Granston had been wise enough to turn down the duchess's dinner invitation, claiming a pressing previous engagement. In his position, Daniel couldn't afford to turn down any respectable invitation, and few invitations in town were more coveted than an intimate soiree at the reclusive duke's home, with the duke himself finally in attendance.

But it had been a long week of keeping up pretenses, with far too few opportunities to bend his head close to Emme's and share the secrets of their plans, his for marriage, hers for rescuing every damsel in distress within the city limits. Those few times though—at an outdoor theater performance, a chance meeting in the park, another afternoon tea—had made the drudgery of society life bearable, he dared think even exciting.

Now he stood apart from the twenty or so guests—intimate being a relative term in the duchess's world—who laughed and chatted and drank the best liquor in London. As far as he could tell, none of the younger ladies in attendance were unmarried except Lady Lucinda, whose ever-watchful father shot enough furtive glances in Daniel's direction to assure him he was neither expected nor welcome to court her. All in all, Daniel should have been enjoying the pleasant evening, but he couldn't shake a bone-deep melancholy. Emme was late. What if she didn't attend, after all?

"Not to worry." Swimmer joined Daniel and motioned for a servant to refill both their glasses.

"Your luck and your mood are both about to improve immensely."

Swimmer glanced at the entryway and Daniel followed his line of sight. The cognac he'd just sipped suddenly warmed his throat. There she was, finally, on her brother's arm and followed by her parents, stepping into the salon. As the butler announced the earl and his family, the focus of the room shifted and came to rest on her glowing face with those bright green eyes.

"Oh no. It's as bad as Granston said it is. I do so hate it when he's right." Swimmer took Daniel's glass out of his hand and set it on the mantel. "That's so you can keep your wits about you. What's left of them, anyway."

"Hm?" Daniel caught most of Swimmer's words, or at least some of them, as he watched Emme's progress through the room. "Did you mention Granston?"

Swimmer nodded. "He said your sickness is worsening, and if we don't get the girl to agree to marry you soon, we might be smuggling spirits into Broadmoor for you."

"Have you noticed Granston has a flair for the dramatic?"

"Undoubtedly. But that hardly makes him wrong." Swimmer groaned. "It appears even the earl and countess have mended their rift for the goal of presenting their lovely daughter to the duke on a silver platter."

Fear shot through Daniel and he grabbed Swimmer's sleeve. "You haven't changed your mind about courting her?"

Swimmer's eyes flashed with annoyance, but his voice was calm. "Don't be daft. Even if you weren't madly in love with her, I've no interested in courting or marrying, regardless of my mother's thinly-veiled intentions. Not now, not a year from now. If I thought I could get away with it, not ever. But I can hardly be rude to my mother's guests, can I?"

"No, I suppose not." He held up his hands in a gesture of conciliation he didn't feel.

"I'll put in a good word for you." Swimmer frowned and shook his head. "But I'm sorry to say, I'm not sure it will help."

Swimmer was wrong, of course. Emme was coming 'round to his way of thinking. Swimmer and Granston simply couldn't see it, as it was something Emme and he shared, just the two of them. As if she could feel him watching her, she glanced at him, and in that moment, he was sure she read every lovelorn line written on his heart.

*E*mme knew she shouldn't stare, but Daniel had never looked at her the way he was right now. In fact, no man she had ever met had regarded her with such a mix of passion, possessiveness, and something else. Was it fear? If her own emotions rose in response to his, then it had to be, for those were the three overwhelming sensations that made it nigh on impossible to tear her gaze away from him.

"Emme, the duke approaches," her brother whispered.

She managed to shift her attention away from Daniel's intense scrutiny, but then she smiled too broadly and laughed too loudly. If she kept up this behavior, by the end of the evening she'd have everyone worried she was afflicted with some form of madness. She wished she had some poetic words to describe it, as James or Tessa would, but she was no student of poetry, and any words that could adequately capture what had passed between Daniel and her in the space of several heartbeats would cause a scandal.

If you won't have him, you owe it to him to let him go. Tessa's words came back to Emme, and the room was all at once too warm and too cold.

She exchanged pleasantries with the duke, who was the epitome of politeness to her, but who seemed much more interested in exchanging friendly barbs with Edward about a long-overdue fencing match. The duke then moved a few feet away to speak with their parents, who wore identical looks of fawning mixed with satisfaction. Guilt clogged Emme's throat, but pretending she was interested in the duke's attention did more than provide a means to an end. It offered a respite from her parents' war of silence. She'd torn them asunder, and now she had the opportunity to reunite them. Even if it was a short-lived ruse, being on the same side of something—*anything*—for a few days or a week might be the balm that soothed her parents' wounds long enough to heal.

Emme suddenly needed the comfort of a friend's hand on hers. "Luci is here somewhere. I spotted Lord Fairbank when we arrived. I have yet to see the Alcotts."

"The Alcotts are gaining notoriety as London's most fashionably late couple." Edward smirked. "Shameful."

"Aren't they just." Emme laughed and leaned against her brother's arm, heartened that she already had the comfort of a dear friend by her side.

"But before we find Lady Lucinda, perhaps we should swallow the medicine."

Emme's next step faltered. "You mean…"

"Hallsworth. It seems he's everywhere we go these days. Though I must say you're a good sport about it, indulging him in conversation."

"Mr. Hallsworth and I have no quarrel."

If only they had, it might be easier to help him plan his future without her. Daniel's project was progressing nicely, and soon hers would be, too. No need to avoid him, despite her initial reaction upon seeing him across the room. Now was the time to get used to it. After all, this was how it would be one day when he was a married man and she was a confirmed spinster.

"Let's say hello." Emme squared her shoulders as they crossed the room.

"Lady Emme," Daniel said.

"Mr. Hallsworth." She managed to smile, not madly or falsely, but genuinely.

"Meriden." Daniel stuck out his hand.

"Hallsworth." Edward shook his hand quickly and withdrew it.

The air in the room, still hot and cold all at once, was suddenly stifling, too. Emme laid her hand on her upper chest, willing herself to breathe more easily.

"Your gown is lovely, Lady Emme," Daniel said. "Then again, green is always becoming on you."

She blushed under his intense gaze and easy compliment, and glanced down at the dress that was from a few Season's earlier to hide her uncontrollable reaction to him. The possessiveness and fear, now mixed with a deep yearning, overcame her. She clung to her brother's arm for support.

"Are there spirits to be had?" Edward asked.

Daniel nodded. "I recommend the duke's cognac."

"Sounds perfect for after dinner, with a good cheroot," Edward said.

"Or perhaps now." Emme laid her hand on Edward's forearm. "I could do with a glass of it myself."

Edward patted her hand. "I understand there's a nice punch available for the ladies. I'll get a cup for you. At the same time, maybe I'll impose upon the duke to share some of his stash." He looked intently at his sister. "Care to join me?"

She sighed. "Well, if there's no cognac in it for me, I might as well stay here and warm myself by the fire."

A look passed between the two men, then both gave

ONE KISS FROM RUIN | 189

a nearly imperceptible nod. "I'll be back momentarily." Edward squeezed her hand, then stepped away from her, glancing back over his shoulder almost immediately.

She waved her hand in the air, then smiled at Daniel. "You'll have to forgive him. He's a bit overprotective. Nothing like Lady Lucinda's father, at least."

"Yes, Fairbank's been shooting ominous looks at me all evening. Now that you've been led like a lamb to stand beside the wolf, maybe he'll be a bit less formidable."

She touched his sleeve, then withdrew her gloved hand immediately. "Forgive me. I was merely going to point out that the best way to remove yourself from Lord Fairbank's sights is to become affianced to someone who is not his daughter." *Please, please, please to do not court my dear friend.*

Daniel smiled, though Emme thought it a bit half-hearted. "Trying to marry me off so quickly, Lady Emme?"

She clasped and unclasped her hands in front of her. "I'm trying to help the duchess with her pet project."

Daniel chuckled. "Well, I've been called worse than both a pet and a project over the years, my lady. And how goes your own pet project?"

"Quite well."

Emme rolled forward on the balls of her feet, so pleased he'd asked. *Again.* He never missed an opportunity to ferret out exactly what it was she was doing to help the two families she'd taken under her wing. As ever, she was excited to report her progress in securing work for Mrs. Billings.

"The miniature paintings are coming along nicely. We have several ladies anxious to have their young children's faces immortalized in lockets." She leaned forward and dropped her voice. "I feel almost wicked, preying on the sentimentality of young mothers, but the truth is, if not Mrs. Billings to do their portraits, then someone else, and after all, she needs to support her own child."

Daniel's smile had faded. "Wicked is hardly a word one would associate with you, Emme."

She laid her hand on her chest again. "It's so warm in here, it's difficult to catch a breath."

"Are you feeling all right?" Daniel set down his glass and held out his hand to her. "Just a moment ago, you mentioned needing to warm yourself by the fire."

"Did I?" She waved his hand away. "No, I'm fine." Still, she stepped a few feet away from the fire.

"I was just trying to guilt Edward into sneaking me a quaff." She endeavored to appear more collected. "Have I told you about Mrs. Carter? She and her children live with Mrs. Billings and her daughter. It seems she has quite a hand for fine stitch-work. As you can imagine, there's no end to embroidery needed by the ladies of the *ton*."

Daniel raised his eyebrows. "Founding cottage industries, are you? I wasn't aware the Spinsters' Club operated that way."

"They don't, not yet. I'm hoping to bring them 'round to some new ideas."

He smiled. "You're always a breath of fresh air." His smile faded. "But your father looks less than pleased at the moment. If I had to wager, I'd say you're spending too much time with the wrong marriageable man."

Emme didn't risk a glance in her father's direction. "He still has plans for the duke and me, I'm afraid. Luckily, I have my own plan."

"Oh? I've never met a woman with so many plans. Tell me."

His gentle entreaty sent a delicious spark down her spine. She ignored it and took a deep breath to steady her voice. "We both know the duke won't entertain the thought of new wife this year. He's still in mourning."

"Is he?" Daniel glanced at his friend. "Hm. Perhaps he is."

"Really, do men even pay attention?" She shook her head. "Anyway, all I have to do is seem amenable to my father's plan, then strike a bargain with him. I'll entertain the duke's offer to court me, and will even accept his offer of marriage."

Daniel's face darkened, then he widened his eyes. "Offers which will never come."

"Precisely." She bounced on her toes again, so pleased with her plan, she couldn't contain herself. "The caveat will be that if the duke doesn't propose by summer, or cuts off a courtship at any time before that, my father will allow me to remain unmarried and turn over my dowry to me."

"And why would the Earl of Limely take that offer?"

"Because he knows a good bargain when he hears it." Emme smiled as she watched her father and brother, both now held in place by the duchess's attention. "He knows the duke could find me most unpleasant if I were disinclined to court."

"So, to secure your good behavior and open the door to the possibility of hooking a duke on the line, you believe your father will agree to this plan of yours."

"I do. Mother agrees with me. Edward seems skeptical." She frowned. Her brother actually seemed rather pessimistic, but had agreed to support her. "Don't you think it's a clever plan?"

"Oh, yes. Lord protect me from ever having a daughter as clever as you." Daniel took a swig of his drink, but his glass was already empty. "Damn it."

"I thought you'd be pleased for me." At least she'd hoped as much. She desperately wanted him to be impressed by her cunning.

"Forgive me, Lady Emme. It's just that I find myself parched and in need of another drink. Here comes your brother now, dismissed from his audience with the duchess, and bringing you the promised cup of punch." He inclined his head. "Meriden."

"Hallsworth."

Daniel bowed ever so slightly in her direction. "Have a wonderful evening, my lady."

Emme smiled. "You, too, sir."

Edward took Emme's arm and gently steered her toward Luci, who now stood with the newly arrived

Tessa and Mr. Alcott. Emme was buoyed by their presence, but suddenly she was also exhausted. She stole one glance over her shoulder, in Daniel's direction. But he'd already made his way to the duke, and the two were deep in conversation while the duke poured a glass of spirits for each of them, his conversation with Emme was no doubt already forgotten.

This was how it would be in the coming years. Their eyes might meet across a crowded room, they might have that moment of recognition that neither shared with anyone else, one or both of them might even wish for things to be different. But all would be as it must. They would exchange pleasantries, go their separate ways, and endure their lonely lives.

"*D*on't look at her, not even a glance," Daniel told Swimmer. "She can't know we're discussing her." He focused his attention on the glass of whisky his friend was pouring for him.

As soon as he'd seen Daniel approaching, Swimmer had signaled for a servant to bring something stronger than an aperitif.

"If you need someone skilled in intrigue, perhaps it's time to enlist the help of Fairbank," Swimmer said.

Daniel stole a furtive look at the mysterious man, who had been facing the opposite direction but immediately pivoted to make eye contact. Daniel looked away. "How does he do that? It doesn't matter. This is a job only you can do."

Swimmer sipped his whisky and looked across the room at his mother. "You know this is going to put me in her bad graces for months."

"That'll be nothing new for you. Besides, can you really compare a few months of discomfort to my life-time without Emme?"

Swimmer pointed at Daniel. "That. See, that is what Granston's been warning me about for weeks—that your schemes with my mother would give you false hope." Swimmer took a deep breath and blew it out slowly. "Hallsy, it might be time—"

"No." Daniel tossed back his drink in one swallow and set down his glass. "Not yet, not while there's still a way to stop Emme's ridiculous plan. If she gets her father's permission and her hands on her dowry, it will be over. You can't let that happen. *You* can help me stop her."

"The things I do for the Five." Swimmer angled himself away from the crowd in the room and dipped two fingers into his whisky. He dabbed liquor on his jaw, neck, and the edge of his shirt under his cravat.

"Were you really threatening me with Broadmoor earlier?"

Swimmer took a swig of his drink and set it down. "If I'm going to humiliate myself in front of some of the *ton*'s biggest gossips and draw my mother's ire, I'm going to fall back on the oldest excuse in our book."

Daniel grinned. "Swimmer, old friend, I do believe you're stewed."

"Give me a pat on the back as I walk away, just a small one."

Daniel obliged, and Swimmer stumbled ever so slightly with his next step. He looked back at Daniel and laughed too loudly, drawing discreet glances from those closest to them. As Daniel watched his friend, he was careful not to smile at his performance.

"Anything I should know?" The duchess drew alongside Daniel.

Daniel shrugged. "It appears your son might have had a bit much to drink before dinner, ma'am."

"How odd." The duchess arched one eyebrow. "I've seen him imbibe twice as much and not slur a word."

"That is odd."

"Are you referring to your son's unfortunate behavior, duchess?" Fairbank had crossed the room quickly and quietly.

Daniel was even less comfortable receiving the man's attention up close than when there'd been a room between them. The duchess, however, was unfazed.

"No need to be dramatic," she told him. "He's enjoying himself, something he doesn't do often enough these days."

"I'll remind you, madam," Fairbank said, fixing her with a withering stare, "there are young ladies present."

The duchess sighed. "Your daughter hardly seems interested in the duke's animated conversation with the Radcliffe men." She glanced at Daniel. "A conversation that might be quite interesting, isn't that right, Mr. Hallsworth?"

Daniel kept his eyes straight ahead, fixed on Swimmer, not venturing a look at either of his current companions. "I couldn't say, madam."

Out of the corner of his eye, he saw Fairbank give the woman a respectful bow. "If I may, duchess, I'd like to escort my daughter and her friends to another room."

The duchess glanced at Emme, who looked pale and perhaps even unsteady on her feet. "The butler will show you to my sitting room down the hall." She made eye contact with the servant across the room.

"Of course." Fairbank gave a curt nod and slipped away from them, moving along the edge of the room and arriving at Lady Lucinda's side in the space of a few heartbeats. After a brief word, he escorted her and Emme out of the room, followed by the Alcotts.

"Whatever do you suppose my son might have said to the earl that has made him go so quiet and still?" the duchess asked.

Just enough, Daniel hoped. Meriden, for his part, looked far from surprised. When the duke finished his long speech, he made a sweeping bow. The duchess touched Daniel's arm.

"It appears we're ready to move to the dining room, Mr. Hallsworth. Would you do me the honor of escorting me?"

"Of course, madam."

Escorting the duchess meant, of course, waiting for the servants to inform the guests of the next event and corral them into position, then to take her arm as they proceeded through the stately halls of the duke's London home. These duties didn't afford him the opportunity to catch a glimpse of Emme with Fairbank and her friends.

As the guests filed into the dining room, gentlemen helped ladies into their seats, then waited for the rest of the party. Daniel played his gentlemanly part, but he fidgeted with impatience when Emme and her friends didn't arrive with the other guests. When almost everyone had made it to their seats, Fairbank entered the room with Lady Lucinda on his arm. He seated his daughter, whispered something to one of the servants, and took his own seat far from the duchess. The servant reported to the duchess, who gave him whispered instructions. The servant then whispered something first to Emme's mother, then to her father, while more servants hurried to the table and removed three place settings so efficiently, it was as though the duchess had never intended to entertain three more guests.

Daniel tried to catch the duchess's eye, but she was ever the gracious hostess and had duties that didn't include placating his curiosity. He ventured a glance at Swimmer, who widened his eyes as though to say he knew nothing more than Daniel. Only after the first course had been served did Lady Lucinda, who was across from Daniel and two seats down, catch his eye.

She waved her hand at her face and rolled her eyes back, mimicking a faint. Daniel nearly jumped out of his seat, but Lady Lucinda shook her head firmly. If Emme had taken ill and neither of the Alcotts had joined them for dinner, it stood to reason they'd taken her home.

Daniel spent the entirety of dinner barely speaking, feeling he was taking ill himself. But his malady was borne of anger. Emme had been pale and flushed in turns, and had claimed she was too cold and then too warm. She'd been cavorting about town in her quest to save downtrodden women and their children, putting herself in jeopardy. Again. And the men of her family had done precious little to protect her. *Again.*

Over an hour later, Daniel finally saw his opportunity to leave. As the ladies and gentlemen separated for after-dinner drinks and tea, Daniel made his sincerest apologies to the duchess, who gave him her most concerned motherly look, and to Swimmer, who warned him to proceed carefully. He didn't speak to anyone else in attendance, not owing any of them an explanation.

As he waited at the front door for his hat and coat and for his coach to be brought to the front of the house, one of the guests accosted him.

One look from Meriden had the duke's servants receding from the front hall. When they were alone, Meriden turned to Daniel. "Tell me you don't plan to go to my family's home."

"Who knows what disease she's caught, gallivanting about on the wrong side of town?"

Meriden crossed his arms over his chest. "Don't be ridiculous."

"Your sister has fallen ill, and you don't even give a toss. You don't deserve her. None of you do."

"Oh, and you do!" Meriden gave a mirthless laugh. "Stop being such an ass, Hallsworth, and leave her alone, as she's asked you to do so many times."

Daniel shook his head. "No, she hasn't. You have, acting on your father's behalf or your own, I don't know or care, and then—"

"She's fine."

Daniel's heart pounded. He crossed his arms over his chest to keep himself from grabbing hold of Meriden's jacket. "You and your father, both of you just—"

"Hallsworth, she's fine! Emmeline's fine. She made a show of falling ill, quite like Swimmer's show of inebriation."

"It was a ruse?" He dropped his shoulders and unclenched his fists. It wasn't difficult to fathom. After all, Emme had spent more than a week during the journey from Spain holed up in a small stateroom, feigning seasickness.

"When Swimmer, in all his drunken glory, informed our father he wouldn't be seeking a new wife any time in the foreseeable future, he shattered a plan my sister had been concocting. You wouldn't know anything about that, would you?"

Daniel held his tongue.

"Of course you wouldn't, because if you did, I'd have to suspect you orchestrated this whole charade just to thwart her. Now she fears she's running out of options, and her heart is breaking. Surely you wouldn't be so monstrous as to break her heart *again*."

Meriden took a small step toward Daniel. Daniel held his ground. Part of him actually hoped Meriden would punch him. It would sting much less than his words, and if Meriden's words were anywhere close to truth, if he'd caused her pain again, it was less than the thrashing he deserved.

"I have to see her."

Meriden shook his head. "Leave it alone, Hallsworth."

"I can't. Just a word, a chance to apologize. Please."

Meriden glared at him.

"If not for me, then for her. She deserves an apology."

Meriden groaned and rubbed his hand across his jaw. "Fine, an apology, *if* she agrees to see you."

Daniel held out his hand. Meriden hesitated, then finally shook it, declaring a temporary, if fragile, détente. The two former friends set off to find Emme together.

CHAPTER 13

*E*mme held tightly to Tessa's hand as they sat side by side on a hard bench in King's Cross Station. They were in a private waiting room with glass in the upper half of the walls, giving them a view of the few people waiting for late-night trains while protecting them from interacting with those of the lower classes. It wasn't lost on Emme that she hoped to help people like those she now watched through glass —respectable, hardworking people like Mrs. Billings and Mrs. Carter—yet her position didn't allow her to be among them in most circumstances.

"Shall I check whether the train is still on time?" Mr. Alcott asked. He stood by the wall at the back of the room, giving the women privacy, despite the fact that they'd sat in silence for the past quarter hour.

"Yes, please do." Tessa glanced over her shoulder at her husband and smiled. As soon as he'd left the room and closed the door behind him, she sighed and leaned her shoulder against Emme. "All right, out with it. What is so pressing that you can't even let us bring you back here tomorrow at a respectable hour to take a morning train to your aunt's country house?"

"Respectable." Emme snorted at the word. "That's what it all comes down to, doesn't it? Respectability. Every moment of our lives is dictated by it. What's the point of leaving tomorrow morning, knowing I'll arrive in Cambridge after dark, and oh how damaging that will be to my reputation!"

"I'd say you have a point, but I fear you might bite me."

Emme sighed. "A rabid dog, now, am I?"

"Nonsense. You know what I mean." Tessa snapped her fan open and closed in quick succession, a sure sign she was annoyed. "You're like a sister to me, and I had hoped I'm like one to you, as well. But you refuse to tell me the truth."

"About?"

"About everything. About anything." Tessa turned to Emme and took both her hands. "Emme, darling, I know you're in love with him."

Emme pulled her hands away and rubbed her palms on her skirt. "In love? With whom?"

"Don't play coy with me." Tessa took her hands again and held them firmly. "You love the man who asked you to marry him. Don't deny it. James learned of it straight from the captain. But you refused him. Why?"

She couldn't tell her friend the truth. Or she

shouldn't. She might lose Tessa, and probably Luci, too. And then she'd be alone. She'd have Aunt Juliana and her mother, and even the spinsters if she could get her dowry money, but none of them would ever be best friends. Like sisters. Like Eleanor.

"Stop that right now." Tessa squeezed Emme's hands hard. "Stop shutting me out of your conversations with yourself. Have some faith in me."

Emme lifted her eyes to Tessa's and saw tears.

"Trust that I might know much more than you think I do, and I love you just the same," Tessa said.

Emme held her breath for a few heartbeats, then exhaled slowly. Her dear friend had stood by Emme through her siblings' deaths and her ill-advised decisions and the brief run to Gretna Green. Her loyalty had earned her the right to the truth.

Emme nodded. "I'll tell you. After all Daniel has been through—the scandal about his parentage while his mother lay dying, his uncle's treachery of spreading gossip, the dispute over his right to inherit—he needs an upstanding, respectable wife. A woman above reproach." Emme stared down at her hands clasped in Tessa's. "I am not a respectable woman. I'm a fallen one."

She lifted her eyes to meet Tessa's gaze, ready to receive the harsh judgment she'd see there. Instead, she saw only tears and a slight nod of Tessa's head. And all the while, Tessa never let go of Emme's hands.

"Mr. Sanderson," Tessa said. "The ill-fated trip to

Gretna Green, when Edward arrived just in the nick of time."

Emme took a deep breath to steady herself. "In truth, he arrived a few hours too late. So, I can never be the wife Daniel…a future marquess needs. I have to let him go so he can find a worthy woman who can give him back what his uncle and the society gossips took from him."

Once again, she couldn't share the whole truth, that the elopement had been her idea, not Sanderson's, and that marriage hadn't been part of her plan. She couldn't bear for her friends to know the true depths of her depravity.

"Oh, my poor darling." Tessa pulled Emme into her arms and held her like a mother comforting a small child. "My poor, poor darling."

Emme let herself relax into the hug and willed the tears to come—tears of pain and shame and repentance. But once again, she could find no relief because she had no tears to cry.

"Thank you," she whispered. "Thank you for not hating me."

"Of course not! I'll always love you." Tessa pulled out of the hug and took Emme's hands. "I'll take your secret to the grave with me, but if this is truly what is standing between you and Mr. Hallsworth… It's been more than a year, Emme, and no one else knows."

"Except Mr. Sanderson."

"Who married well and moved away from London. You can't let him haunt you this way."

Emme looked down at her gloved hands, which were shaking. "There are others. The innkeeper, for instance. There were a few stray whispers among the *ton* at the time. If someone really wanted to find out the truth of that night…"

"The innkeeper would have nothing to gain by having his establishment associated with the story of a young lady's misfortune. And why would anyone seek him out, anyway? You don't have an enemy in this world."

Emme shrugged, not wanting to rehash what she'd spent months sifting in her own mind, but needing to make her friend understand. "Because I've posed no threat to ambitious young ladies or marriage-minded parents."

"If anyone ever asks questions, I'll tell them you were with me. Together, our story will be stronger than theirs."

"You'll tell them I was with you at your father's house? And will he and your brothers tell the same story?" Emme watched understanding dawn on her friend's face. "I've turned this over and looked at it from every angle. I cannot see a way out of it. While I remain on the edges of society and do good works, no one will notice me enough to cause trouble. But if I were to become the marchioness…" She shook her head. "You know how it would go. Every detail of my life would be scrutinized by jealous women, or their irate mothers, perhaps even a business rival of the marquess. An opportunist might see a chance to exploit that. His reputation would never be safe with me. He might not even *become* the marquess if word got out."

"Have you considered telling him what happened?"

"I have told him."

Tessa's eyes flew open wide. "What?! What did he say? He obviously doesn't think any less of you, based on what James and I have observed."

"No, I suppose he doesn't. He wouldn't have proposed if he held it against me."

"He knew before he proposed? But don't you see? He still wanted to marry you."

"Because he thinks it can remain our secret," Emme said. "That's what he said when he proposed. But what if it doesn't remain that way? He promised his mother he'd restore not only his title, but the family's reputation. It means everything to him. I can't take that away from him."

Tessa hugged her again. "I can't pretend to understand what you're feeling, Emme, but I'll stand by you, as will Luci."

Emme clung to her friend. "Thank you."

"Darling, I can see through the glass that James is returning."

Emme pulled away from Tessa sat up straight, once again taking on the air of a self-possessed, respectable young lady.

"And he's not alone," Tessa said.

"Is it Edward? My father?" Emme knew from Tessa's wistful smile that it was neither of them. She sighed and leaned against the hard back of the bench. "Daniel."

*D*aniel and James stopped outside the small room where Emme sat with Lady Tessa.

"Hallsy, it's not my place to say anything." James glanced through the glass at his wife, who was hugging Emme.

Daniel's heart sank to think how defeated she must be right now, and at his own hands. He rubbed his temples and groaned. "Say it, James. Whatever terrible things you think of me right now, they're probably all true."

James chuckled. "In that case, I wish I'd come prepared. I was just going to suggest you not try to talk her out of this. Tessa has tried, and if my wife can't convince Lady Emmeline of something, I'm not sure who can. Her brother, perhaps, but I doubt even he can dissuade her from escaping to her aunt's country house."

Daniel watched the women through the glass, wishing he could see Emme's face, but she was turned toward Tessa with her back to him. "It's a safe place for her, full of childhood memories of her siblings, without the painful reminders of her sister's death."

"Terrible thing, that. Tessa says it changed Emme." James shrugged a shoulder. "I always remember Meriden's little sister being a headstrong tomboy, but Tessa says there's something else now, a melancholy that hasn't lifted."

"Your wife is perceptive, and a good friend." Daniel patted James's shoulder. "As are you. Thank you for leaving the note for Meriden."

Emme's note to her brother had simply outlined her plan to take refuge at their aunt's empty country house. James's addendum had assured him, and by extension Daniel, that the Alcotts would keep watch over Emme, get her safely on the train, and send a message ahead to her aunt's servants to prepare for the lady and to escort her from the train station. Whether Emme knew just how much information James had included, Daniel couldn't say, but he was grateful for the breadcrumb trail that had led him here.

"Thank you, and thank your wife for me, too, for looking out for Lady Emme."

"I'd have it no other way. She's like a sister to my wife. And speaking of Mrs. Alcott, you can thank her yourself."

Lady Tessa emerged from the waiting room, leaving Emme alone amongst the six rows of benches reserved for the better classes of British society. He could see her profile now as she turned to face straight ahead, looking out through the glass at the sparsely populated train platform. He longed to run to her side and kneel in front of her and beg her not to look so sad and lost, but he had no right. After all, he'd caused that pain etched into her lovely face.

"Lady Tessa." Daniel extended his hand and she touched it briefly with her gloved fingers.

"Mr. Hallsworth, how good of you to come." She smiled at him, revealing one charming dimple.

Her comment took him aback. "Is it? Good that I've come, I mean."

His friend's wife appraised him swiftly, then nodded. "James has said wonderful things about you, Mr. Hallsworth, and I very much look forward to making your acquaintance further, now that you're back in London." She glanced at her husband. "James is a fine judge of character, so I knew you were a good sort, even before."

Daniel smiled as he waited for her to say more. When she didn't, he raised his eyebrows. "I beg your pardon, my lady, before what?"

She smiled again and fluttered her fan, and Daniel could easily see how his friend had been so charmed by her. "Time can heal most anything," she whispered, then turned to her husband and took his arm.

The newlyweds walked closely together and in perfect step, and disappeared around a corner, leaving Daniel alone to face Emme.

He turned back to find her looking at him, wide-eyed and sad. With his heart breaking, he pushed through the door and sat beside her. Long, dark ringlets of hair fell around her face. She'd changed into her simple gray travel dress, cloak, and bonnet. Gray. The color that had come to define his sad, lovely kitten's life.

Emme stared down at her gloved hands. "If you've come to persuade me to stay, it won't work."

Yes! Yes, you must stay in London, be near enough for me to flirt with you at high tea and make you jealous from across a crowded ballroom.

He rubbed at an imaginary spot on the knee of his evening suit pants. "I've just come to keep you company and to see you safely installed into a private car on the train. It was me or your brother, and he didn't seem likely to be good company after reading your note."

"Then I should thank you for saving me from his foul mood."

"No, you shouldn't. You shouldn't thank me for anything." Daniel leaned against the back of the bench and stared up at the ceiling, wondering how to formulate the truth for her without engendering her disdain. He hadn't been able to come up with it on the mad carriage ride to the station, and no flash of brilliance came to him now. "It's all my fault. I asked Swimmer to make his intentions—or lack thereof—clear to your father."

"I see." She brushed a strand of hair away from her face. "I suppose I knew it was you, although I thought it might have been the duke's attempt to save himself."

"I truly am sorry. I ruined your plan. You confided in me, and I violated your trust."

"Edward told me from the start it wouldn't work, that Father would never take the bait. He was probably right." Her hand fluttered over his, ever so briefly. "But thank you for saying that. No man has ever apologized for overstepping his bounds with me before."

An image of Emme entangled with some other man, a stranger bearing some resemblance to himself, crossed his mind. He closed his eyes and willed it away while wondering if that same image haunted her, and if that was what she meant.

"Oh, here comes the train now." She rose to her feet.

"We don't have to hurry. It will take some time to unload passengers and luggage before they even think of boarding for your trip."

She smoothed down her skirt. "Yes, I suppose, but perhaps we should make our way to the platform."

Daniel stood and picked up the small valise that sat on the bench beside her. "I've never seen a lady travel so lightly."

"There's a trunk with the porter, but I won't need much. It's a simple life at Aunt Juliana's country house."

He held out his arm to her and she took it. "And I suppose Mrs. Billings and Mrs. Carter are all set in their new lives, so your absence won't affect their plight."

She hesitated. "No, there's still much to do. But Tessa has promised to check on them when she can."

"Hm. It's a pity, though. Lady Tessa is so busy. She and James work dawn to dusk on their scholarship projects."

"Yes, they do. But Luci has promised to help, as well."

"Ah, then Lady Lucinda has devised a sneaky way to avoid her father's watchful eye?"

They'd only made it past their bench when Emme stepped away from Daniel and leaned her hand on the back of it. "Oh, yes, that is a problem, isn't it?"

She furrowed her brow and chewed her lip, giving the appearance of having a deep dialogue with herself. Daniel prayed for the voice that agreed with him to win. With a deep breath, she straightened her back, looking far too resolved for his liking.

"I shall send a telegraph to Lady Abigail tomorrow, asking that while I'm away, she continue the work with Mrs. Billings and Mrs. Carter." She took Daniel's arm again.

They took a few more steps.

"And your mother won't miss you too terribly, after seeing you for less than two weeks?"

Tessa stopped walking and frowned. "My mother will miss me, and I'll miss her. I assume she and Aunt Juliana will come to join me soon."

"From a conversation at the duke's dinner party, I was under the impression she'd gone through quite an ordeal to get here by coach and was not looking forward to traveling any time soon."

Emme leaned her hip against the side of another bench. "Yes, and she stubbornly refuses to take the train. She's almost as bad as Aunt Juliana when it comes to trusting new things." She shook her head and threw back her shoulders. "It will be a bit dull and perhaps lonely, but I have plans to make and treatises to write, so I'll fill the days until they come to see me, or I return to town to join the Spinsters' Club."

She took his arm and they moved forward another few feet before she stopped. "But what of Edward?"

"What of your brother, my lady?"

"I'm leaving him in a terrible position, aren't I?"

Daniel took a slow breath before speaking so as not to appear over-anxious. "He'll be the one who will have to explain your flight to the countryside to your parents."

She sat down heavily on the bench closest to the door. "And then try to keep the peace between them. They'll each blame the other, as they always do when I cause a stir."

Daniel widened his eyes, then worked to present a composed visage. Could it be that, on top of everything else, she blamed herself for her parents' rift? He would have to discuss it with Meriden. Clearly, there were things happening in that family that were deeply troubling their daughter, yet none of them seemed to care one whit about it.

He sank onto the bench in front of her. "And so?"

"And so, I must stay." She sighed and drooped like a flower that had lost the sun's light.

Seeing her distress, he kept his own happiness in check. "My coach is just outside. I'll have my man see to your trunk."

"Oh, dear. Look at the time." He followed her gaze to a clock on the train platform. "I can't return home at this late hour, especially with you!"

Daniel couldn't deny the sense in that. "Perhaps in a hired coach. My man and I will follow right behind you."

She shook her head. "That won't be much better."

"The Alcotts, then." Daniel breathed a sigh of relief to have it resolved so quickly and easily.

She shook her head again. "You said yourself, they work from dawn 'til dusk. Even society events are little more to them than opportunities to meet with bene-factors. Tessa was exhausted when they left here. If I show up on their doorstep, she'll get out of bed and make a fuss. No, I'll have to stay in a hotel."

An image of scoundrels like her ex-fiancé sniffing around outside her hotel room made Daniel jump to his feet.

"Nonsense." He forced his voice back to calm. "You know how gossip travels in this town. Word will get out and your father will hear about it."

"Yes, you're right. Of course, you're right. It's settled then." She rose slowly to her feet. "I'm getting on that train after all."

Daniel knew what he must say but shouldn't. The solution was simple but dangerous, even if all went according to plan. But the only alternative was Emme leaving town for weeks, or possibly months.

"You'll stay with me." He held up his hand before she could protest. "I have a large house and a small staff of loyal, tight-lipped servants. You'll have your own room where you can bar the door." That made her smile, and just the sight of it made his heart lighter.

"We'll rise before dawn and I'll take you to the Alcotts, after they've had their full night's sleep, and they can see you home."

She picked at the back of one of her gloves, mulling over the idea, opening her mouth and then closing it a few times, until she shrugged. "It appears it's the best plan we have, which illustrates how dreadfully limited our options are."

He picked up her valise and held out his arm once more. "My lady, our chariot awaits us." *Let us pray hellfire does not await us as well.*

But then Emme laid her hand on his arm, and all was right with the world.

CHAPTER 14

"This is terribly wrong, I just know it," Emme said aloud to herself as she paced the length of the lovely bedroom, decorated in pink and gold, that Daniel's servants had set up for her.

Daniel.

She couldn't sleep, couldn't even lie down long enough to try, knowing he was so near and the house was so private and no one would ever know of anything that happened here under cover of night.

The household staff, small as it was, had scurried about to provide her with every comfort, including a light meal, a maid to undo her hair, and a silk night-gown and robe that appeared to be brand new, although that didn't make sense. Then they'd disappeared and the entire house had gone silent more than half an hour ago.

She thought of her own house at this hour. So often, it was still full of life, with one if not all three of the ladies taking tea, Emme reading while her mother and aunt chatted over needlepoint, servants bustling about as her father and brother arrived home from a session at the House of Lords or a dinner at their club.

Daniel had his own duties to tend to, but when meetings ended or balls drew to a close or dinner and drinks with his friends were over, he came here. To this quiet house. Alone.

It didn't need to be that way, even if it took him months to find a bride. A man in his position, with wealth and a soon-to-be-restored title, those intense blue eyes and thick, dark mane of hair...he could take a lover. Any woman seeking to be a mistress, and even some who had no business doing any such thing, would have him.

Emme stopped pacing and stared down at the pale pink silk robe covering a cream-colored chemise with tiny pink roses embroidered on it. Sweet. Demure. Not the seductive garb of a mistress.

At least, not before tonight.

She untied the robe and let it hang loose around her while she ran her hands over the curves of her body, imagining Daniel's hands exploring her. She ran one hand through her unbound hair, but it was his hand she felt caressing scalp, her neck, her shoulder. With a groan, she dropped the robe to the floor, shook out her hair, and threw back her shoulders.

Slowly, carefully, silently, she left her room and moved down the hallway, the floor and rugs alternately cold and smooth, then warm and plush under her feet.

218 | NANCY YEAGER

She stopped outside his door, the entryway to his private sanctum, the place where he would one day bring a wife. But not now. Not yet. For tonight, he could still be hers.

She laid her palm flat on the door and listened, catching what might have been movement on the other side of it. She knocked lightly, and the door opened almost immediately, as though he'd sensed her coming and had been waiting there for her to arrive. His dark hair was tousled, his blue eyes bright, his naked chest and belly taut and lightly haired, his feet bare. He wore silk pajama pants that clung to his narrow hips. Surely the devil himself had never looked so tempting.

"Emme." Her name fell from his lips like a prayer. He blinked slowly, languorously, eyes full of lust, not sleep. "What do you—"

She pressed her palm against his chest and backed him into the room.

"Need." His final word was a statement, not a question.

She pushed the door closed behind her and leaned against it, watching him as his weighted gaze perused every inch of her body, arousing her as if with his touch.

They stared at each other, their breathing heavy, perfectly synchronized, laden with expectation. He didn't move a muscle. Just waited. Heat radiated off his body and made the blood sing in her veins. She leaned forward, straining on her tiptoes to get close to his ear.

"Daniel, I find myself in desperate need of your kiss."

She couldn't have uttered a more seductive phrase. Daniel tried to hold his ground, but she advanced on him and he stepped back in rhythm with her forward progress, in a dance that was ironically familiar, stopping only when she'd backed him against the mahogany footboard of his bed.

From the second he'd heard the soft squeak of a floorboard, he'd known she was coming to him. He hadn't considered for a second barring her entrance or sending her away. He hadn't had time to put on anything appropriate, and now the silk trousers he wore couldn't hide what her touch did to him. And *her* attire. The thin, white shift, despite its color and embellishment with tiny pink roses, was anything but innocent as it clung to her curves and revealed the outline of her taut nipples. It was even more sensuous than he'd imagined when he'd bought it for her at their last port in France on their voyage home, in hopes that she'd eventually wear it on their wedding night.

He closed his eyes and focused on calming breaths that weren't up to the task. "Emme, you shouldn't—"

She pressed her finger to his lips and he opened his eyes. "Don't say that word: *shouldn't.*" She walked around him to the edge of his bed and ran her fingers over the thick crimson duvet turned back to reveal white cotton sheets.

He risked a step, one small step, toward her. He longed to touch her upturned face, to stroke her soft shoulder, to make her breath hitch in her throat. He stopped himself. "Emme, we can't."

She traced her fingertips over the sheets. "A lady shouldn't. A lady can't. I'll add 'a lady doesn't', to save you having to say it. Do you know how many times a lady hears those words by the time she reaches the age of twenty-two? If I had to wager, I'd say at least one of those three words has appeared in most of the sentences spoken to me in my lifetime."

He stood frozen, cut to the quick by the sadness in her voice and his powerlessness to ease her pain.

She sat on the edge of his bed and locked her gaze on his. "A lady shouldn't want a man the way I want you, but I do. A lady can't have a man the way I want you, but I intend to. A lady doesn't beg for a man's affections, but I will. If that's what it takes, Daniel, I will beg you."

He stood in front of her and cupped her face to turn it up to him. "I love you, Emmeline Radcliffe. I'll never make you beg me for anything."

She slipped off the bed and stood in the circle of his arms. "A request then. Make love to me, Daniel. Tonight. And other nights. Again and again, until you've had your fill of me. I love you, too. *Let* me love you."

She loved him.

The thing he'd once hoped, had sometimes suspected, had always needed, had at last come true.

Five years ago, as he'd stood on the deck of a ship and watched the shores of his homeland recede, he'd told himself he could have a new and better life, he could breathe deeply of the salty sea air, and he could be free. But it had never improved. He hadn't drawn a deep breath until she'd said those three words to him.

A month ago, when he'd met her again, when he'd glimpsed the depth of her loss and pain, he'd wanted to return her to the carefree girl he'd left behind. Now he saw the folly in such thinking. The woman in front of him was so much more, not in spite of the life she'd lived without him, but because of it. He no longer wanted to change her. He just wanted her. He loved her.

At last, he was home and truly free. She loved him! And now she meant to give herself to him, and he meant to have her. To have and to hold, and to love until death.

"Emme, kitten, I love you." He said it again and again, between kisses. First gentle kisses, then firmer ones, then passionate explorations of lips and tongues. He said it because he had to make her hear it, and because he needed to hear her say it back to him.

And she did say it, over and over again as he stripped the filmy garment from her body, as he laid her back on the soft, cool sheets of his bed, as he traced his tongue over inch after silky, lavender-scented inch of her bare skin.

When he lingered over her tantalizing breasts, she murmured. When he traced his way down her flat belly, she whispered. When he ran his tongue up her inner thigh, she sucked in her breath and her words turned to soft gasps. Her exaltations grew louder as he slid his tongue over her musky wetness and slid two fingers inside her, stroking her, coaxing her.

He'd promised her he'd never make her beg, and yet she did now, wordlessly. She grabbed the sheets, then his shoulders. She ran her fingers through his hair while she writhed and arched beneath the ministrations of his fingers and tongue, until her hips arched higher, her fingers gripped tighter, her whole body clenched, and her gasps turned into a long, low moan. Daniel didn't stop tasting and touching her until a final shudder rippled through her body and she relaxed with a contented sigh.

He traced his way back up her body with soft kisses and nibbled the base of her neck. She was sated, but he was still afire. He would let her rest for a few minutes, then would tease and tempt her into shared pleasure. He cupped her cheek and kissed her lips. When she opened her eyes, she looked anything but tired. She leaned forward and nipped his lower lip with her teeth, then ran her tongue over the spot as she ran her hand down his chest and untied his silk pajamas.

"Emme."

It was his turn to sigh and moan under her touch, but he couldn't allow it to be one-sided for long. He ran his hands down the length of her body, all curves and silky skin and long loose hair tickling his now-naked body. He slipped his hand between her thighs and she opened to his stroking fingers immediately. She rubbed him and tightened her grip on him in a way that would make it all end too soon.

He pulled slightly away from her. "Slower, kitten, if you want me capable of consummating our love."

She nodded. "Now." Her voice was low and thick with desire, and as much as he wanted them to explore and tease each other more, he knew he couldn't last much longer.

He nodded. "Now." He kissed her and pressed her back into the pillows.

"You'll take care," she whispered.

"Of course." It took a few more seconds for her meaning to penetrate his lust-addled brain. "Yes, of course," he repeated.

Begrudgingly, he slid off the bed and opened the drawer of his bedside table. He pulled out a small package, unwrapped it, and fastened the ghastly-looking thing onto himself. The French letter was far from attractive, but it would keep her safe from pregnancy until she was ready to bear him a child. Perhaps in months, perhaps not for years, but there was plenty of time for an heir. For tonight, for as long as she needed, he would give her pure pleasure and extract no cost.

He climbed back onto the bed and spread her legs so he could settle between them. "I'll be gentle." She wasn't a virgin, but she was hardly experienced. He positioned himself at her opening.

224 | NANCY YEAGER

"Please don't."

He froze, horrified that he'd made her feel forced.

"Be gentle, I mean." She arched her hips toward him, taking the tip of him inside her, to reassure him. "I've waited so long for this. I don't want you to be gentle."

His breath was ragged, but he focused on staying calm as he inched inside her. She thrust her hips again, taking him fully into her on a gasp. She was tight but so wet, welcoming, not resisting. He grasped her hips to still her wriggling. *Christ*, he was so close to release, and he would not embarrass himself like a schoolboy, not with Emme.

"Give me a moment, kitten."

"It just feels so…mmmm." She closed her eyes and raised her arms over her head on the pillow, and he groaned at the erotic sight of her arching, naked body, him buried in her up to the hilt.

With greater control than he'd ever had to summon, he eased almost completely out of her and then back in. She took in the length of him with another gasp, followed by a delightfully familiar moan. With the next stroke, he kept his word to abandon gentleness. She met his hard thrust and moaned deeper and longer. She thrust her hips and tried to set a steady tempo, but this request he refused. He rocked against her at his own will, building her anticipation, catching her by surprise. Only when he was sure he'd brought her as close to the brink of orgasm as he was himself did he settle into a deep, steady rhythm.

She writhed and grabbed the bedsheets. Murmured and whimpered his name. Clenched around him so tightly. And he was so close, too close, sliding to the edge too fast.

She dug her fingers into his back. Her hips arched and her body tightened. And finally, blissfully, Daniel could let go. He thrust into her one, two, three more times, then gave into reckless abandon, letting her release guide his, and together they surrendered to *la petite mort*.

⌘

*E*mme lay in Daniel's bed—*Daniel's bed*—with cool sheets smoothed under her bare back and draped over her belly, her legs still tangled with his. Dawn was just over an hour away. Too soon, she would have to leave him. But sometime soon, she would be able to come back to him, now that they'd agreed upon their arrangement.

"When can I see you again?" she asked.

"Hmm." Daniel grinned sleepily, which was only to be expected, as they'd not slept all night. "As soon as you wish. I could come calling this afternoon, if the lady will be out of bed before evening."

"Calling?" She hadn't thought of that, of the possibility of seeing him socially, toying with him, teasing him. "The lady just might get out of bed for that." She turned onto her side to face him. "But I meant *this*. When will I be able to see you again like this?"

He turned onto his side as well, mischief glinting in his eyes. "Already missing me? Or perhaps I haven't quite satisfied you? Is that a challenge I hear?"

She stretched her limbs, her body tired and aching but strangely full of energy. "You have satisfied me very well, sir, but I hereby do challenge you to do it again and again. As soon and as often as we can arrange."

"How can I refuse such a demand? But I'll need just a bit of time right now, kitten, to recover. Limitations of the male of the species."

She grinned, knowing she'd pushed him to his limits. She turned his words over in her mind, his affectionate term for her suddenly bothersome after the night they'd just spent together. "Daniel, why do you call me kitten?"

"Why do you think?"

She thought back to the summers years ago when he'd visited as one of Edward's bosom companions. He'd started calling her that the very first summer, any time they were out of earshot of anyone else. "Because I followed Edward and his friends like a pet, and I mewled for attention, and I was such a docile creature."

"A pet?" Daniel laughed. "Docile creature?" He laughed harder, shaking the bed.

She wanted to laugh with him, but could hardly find the humor in being seen as so pathetic.

"Oh, Emme." He struggled to catch his breath. "I called you kitten because you had teeth and claws and you weren't afraid to use them. The insults you threw at all of us. And because when I approached you too fast, you ran away too quickly for me to catch you, and hid so well I couldn't find you."

He reached forward and brushed a strand of hair from her face. "But when I coaxed you ever so sweetly, you finally came to me. Eventually, you even crawled onto my lap and purred."

She sucked in a breath as heat flooded her cheeks. Even after all these years and all the passion they'd shared, the thought of her seventeen-year-old self giving in so easily to his seductions, his tempting kisses and less-than-chaste ministrations, embarrassed her.

"Don't," he whispered, running his fingers along her jaw. "Don't ever remember our time together with shame. I can't bear to see it. If you want me to stop calling you that—"

"No." She laid her hand over his where he touched her face. "Now that I know the meaning behind it, I like it. Although I've never met a kitten quite like you describe."

"Ah, well, that's because you've never met the half-feral cats roaming the grounds of my parents' country estate. My country estate now." His face clouded for just a moment, but he quickly covered it with a smile.

She'd never seen the estate and now longed to do so quite badly. She wanted to picture him there as he'd have been during the summer months, after he'd finished his visit with her family. She wanted to imagine him as a small child running over fields, chasing clawed, hissing, half-feral kittens. "I think I

228 | NANCY YEAGER

should like to meet such cats, being their namesake, after all."

He twined his fingers with hers and pulled her hand to his lips. "And you shall."

"Really? You'd take me there?" She didn't know if it was usual for a man to take his mistress to his ancestral home, but it seemed unlikely.

"Of course. I'll take you everywhere with me. To the country estate. To the small but lovely house in Scotland left to me through my mother's side of the family. To a beautiful port city on the Mediterranean coast of France."

He meant to travel with her. In Scotland and France, perhaps they wouldn't even need to hide their relationship, safely away from the prying eyes of the *ton*. "That would be wonderful. Why France, though?"

"There's someone there I'd like you to meet."

She knew then, and her heart melted. "Your parents' dear friend."

He nodded. "My real father."

She was overwhelmed that she meant so much to him that he'd introduce her to such an important yet secret person in his life. Then again, perhaps it made sense. They would both be secrets he had to keep.

"When can we go?" She wished he would say today, this very afternoon. She longed to run far away with him and proclaim her love for him openly and without reservation, and to have him do the same for her.

"Anytime, really. I'd thought to do it after the

wedding, but I suppose if we arrange chaperones, we could go within a couple of weeks."

Something about his words jarred her. Her sleep-deprived mind struggled to identify it. He'd said wedding. *After the wedding.* Did he intend to marry soon, after all? And did he intend to keep her as his mistress as a married man? To have her travel with him, leaving behind his new bride?

She pulled away from him and sat up in the bed, hugging the sheets to her breast. "I didn't think that was our arrangement. I thought you would postpone marriage, at least for a year, maybe longer."

"Postpone marriage? I'd marry you tomorrow if I could. And you can't tell me you want to spend that much time apart, stealing moments or rare hours here and there, when we could be living as man and wife?"

We. He'd said we. Her. He meant to marry *her.* "Daniel, you can't. We can't."

She stumbled from the bed and searched in the low lamplight for her nightgown.

"We can't marry? Then what was this night about?"

Her eyes met his.

"My God, Emme." He rolled out of the other side of the bed and reached for his robe that was slung across the back of a chair. "You intend to be my mistress. How could you think such a thing, given what we mean to each other?"

"How could I think anything else?" She struggled into the nightgown that had slipped over her head so easily hours earlier. "You know I can't marry you. I have work to do. Important work."

"Marriage won't impede that. At least, ours won't. And think of what you'd be doing for me, the respectability of the Marchioness who is out saving the city." He smiled, but she could see the strain in it.

"It's not just the work. I have to atone for..." She thought of Eleanor. Sweet, long-gone Eleanor, whom she had disappointed so often. Some selfish, childish behavior of Emme's had led to their argument that had made Eleanor storm out of the house and to the lake that day. "I have to atone for so much. You can't even imagine."

She had to tell him the rest of it, tell him how she'd lied to Sanderson, promised him marriage and her dowry, knowing all along she only wanted to be ruined for marrying other men. "There's something else, something you well know but seem to have conveniently forgotten."

"Your former fiancé. I haven't forgotten, Emme. But as I've told you before, and as I'll continue to tell you until my last breath, I bloody well don't care!" He stalked toward her and stood just inches from her, close enough for her to feel his heat. "Our first time together last night was not your first time, nor mine. Just as our second time together was not the second time for either of us, nor the third."

She blushed, more from excitement at the memory of what they'd done than from any embarrassment a true lady should feel. Because she was no true lady. "It's not just between us, though. Others know."

"Yes, Meriden. He'll take it to his grave, you know that. Perhaps you mean Sanderson, now happily married to an heiress. What would he possibly have to gain by ruining your reputation?"

"There were others." Her voice faltered just saying it. "The innkeeper. Other guests. Others knew my secret. I made sure of that."

It had made so much sense at the time, but she hadn't been thinking clearly. Soon after, Edward had shown her the folly of it. And now, more than a year later, it seemed the stupidest thing she'd ever done.

"I never meant to marry him," she said. The pressure in her chest eased immediately, now that she'd resolved to tell the truth. "I wanted to be ruined and to be discovered before we could take vows. I wanted word of it to get back to my father, thinking that once he realized no respectable man would want me, he'd stop trying to force me to marry."

"Oh, Emme, that was a dangerous game."

She nodded. "Edward made that quite clear, assuring me Father would assign me a fate worse than marriage if he ever learned the truth. Then he spent most of his year's allowance paying off everyone who might have suspected what I'd done, and came up with the brilliant plan of sending me to Spain with Aunt Juliana to get me out of Sanderson's purview. In the meantime, I'd met a few of the ladies from the Spinsters' Club, ladies who help women who had more in common with me than I could ever admit, and I knew I'd found my calling. I was heartbroken to leave before I could earn my place with the spinsters, but Edward insisted, for my own good. And I suppose he was right after all."

"And all this time, I've wanted to pummel your brother for not doing enough to protect you." He groaned. "I suppose this means I owe him not only an apology, but my thanks as well." Daniel sat on the bed beside her and took her hand. "If you're telling me all this to frighten me away, it's not working. I still want to marry you and support your work with the women who need your help."

His kindness was almost too much to bear, showing her all over again just what she'd lost that night she'd persuaded Sanderson to agree to her reckless plan.

"But you can't marry me. Not when clearing your family name is finally in your reach." She gripped his hand, knowing all too soon she would have to let go of it, and of him. "Edward and I have lived in fear of the day one of those witnesses turns up with just enough detail to be believable, or with other witnesses in tow, to ruin my reputation and the Radcliffe name and in doing so, destroy what's left of our family. Leaving England for a year and leading a quiet life kept my secret safe. But I wouldn't be safe—*we* wouldn't be safe —if I married a soon-to-be marquess, especially one trying to restore his family's name while hiding his own secrets."

His eyes widened ever so slightly. He blinked fast

and tried to cover it, but she'd seen it, the realization of the threat she posed to him and the shadow of doubt that had crossed his face. Maybe until that split second, some part of her had held out hope that things could be different, but now she knew—despite how very much he wanted it not to be so—that he, too, thought her indiscretion could destroy his plan to restore his own family name. And that would destroy him.

"Our lives have to take different paths." She withdrew her hand from him. She no longer had a right to touch him so intimately. She shivered as the reality of the long, lonely years ahead settled over her.

He touched the strap of the nightgown, then withdrew his touch. "I bought this for you at the last port in France, the day I nearly lost you."

She ran her fingers down her sides, over the silky material, then wrapped her arms around herself, knowing he could never wrap his arms around her again.

His eyes shone with tears. "What cruel irony that the night I finally see you in it is the night I lose you in an entirely different way. I don't even know how to go on without the hope of having you in my life."

But he would learn. As would she. They had no choice.

"I'm sorry, Daniel. If I could change everything, make other choices…" She looked out the window, at the slight change of color in the black sky. "Dawn is nearly upon us. I should wash and dress."

He nodded. "I'll deposit you safe and sound with the

Alcotts. It will be as though last night never happened."
His voice broke on the last words. "But swear to me
Emme, swear to me you'll never look back on our night
together with shame."

She met his gaze just for a second, as long as she
could bear, then turned away from him. "It happened,"
she whispered. "With every fiber of your being, know
that every day of my life I will remember it happened,
and I will be eternally grateful it did."

She walked away slowly, putting one unwilling foot
in front of the other, over and over, until she reached
the door. Every muscle in her body tensed, ready to
bolt from the room. But she refused to do it. She was
not a half-feral kitten, running and hiding from Daniel
and the blissful night they'd spent together. She was a
grown woman, walking away from her lover, releasing
him to find someone who deserved to share his life.

CHAPTER 15

*E*mme stirred when an uninvited guest entered her room. She yanked her blankets over her head when the same reprobate pulled open the curtains to send sunlight spilling across her bed. It was the first time she'd been subjected to the morning sun in the week since she'd said goodbye to Daniel at dawn, and it was her sincere wish never to face the morning light again.

Now she lay in a pool of warm sunlight, silently cursing the person who'd subjected her to it. Her father would have sent servants, who would have hesitantly knocked. Her mother or aunt would have spoken to her softly from the doorway. Only one person in the household would dare be so obnoxious.

"Edward, leave me be." She laid her arm over her eyes to block out all vestiges of morning.

"Shall I send this letter back to the Spinsters' Club then, and tell them you've no interest in reading it?"

She sat bolt upright, wincing as her eyes adapted to the bright light, and focused on her brother, now leaning on the doorjamb between her bedchamber and sitting room. He held a cream-colored envelope between his thumb and forefinger. She reached out her hand, but he shook his head.

"When you're presentable, I'll be in your sitting room with your letter." He closed the door behind him.

With a groan, Emme rolled out of her bed, slid her feet into slippers, and pulled on her wrapper. On her way to the bedroom door, she stopped to look in the mirror, horrified by the tangle of her reddish hair and the dark circles under her eyes. It was doubtful she could even come close to the presentable state Edward had requested, but she splashed her face with cool water from the basin and patted it dry with a linen towel, then ran a brush through the worst of the knots in her hair. A minute later, she entered the sitting room to find Edward, legs stretched out in front of him, looking much too large for her pink-and-white-striped divan.

She held out her hand to him. "I'll have my letter now."

He stared at her with wide eyes. "What passes for presentable has taken a turn for the worse this past week." He handed her the envelope anyway.

She sat in the white upholstered chair across from him and broke the seal on the letter.

"It's good to see you can overcome your cowardice, at least for one morning," he said.

She glanced at him. "Cowardice? What on earth does that mean?"

"It means I expected better from you." His face was set in his stern, older-brother look that she and Eleanor had dreaded throughout childhood. "One despicable cad plays fast and loose with your heart, and you take to your bed. Meanwhile, the rest of the world goes on, Emmeline." He pointed to the window he'd just exposed in the next room. "The city is abuzz with life, with humanity. How many others do you suppose are out there this very day, as heartbroken as you are, but without the luxury of lying about in bed all day?"

His words stung like nettles because they were true. Mrs. Billings had lost her husband just months earlier, and yet rose before sunrise each morning to care for her daughter and help with Mrs. Carter's sons and go about her day's work to eke out a living. Mrs. Carter, now confined to her bed, still spent her time there productively, sewing fourteen hours a day, leaving no time for self-pity over a husband in prison and children in need of more than she could provide.

"You're right, Edward." She sank against the back of her chair. "I've been selfish and childish. I will do better, I promise you." Just as she'd promised Mrs. Billings she would help them, another pledge she intended to keep.

She pulled the letter from the Spinsters' Club out of its envelope. Her hands shook with anticipation. This could be the invitation she'd anticipated for so long, the offer to join the club, at which point she'd have more resources at her disposal to help talented women in need set up money-making enterprises. And she'd be able to keep her word to Mrs. Billings. But as she read the lines written in Lady Abigail's neat, tight hand, her breath caught in her throat. Not only were the spinsters unhappy about the alternative work arrangements she'd make for Mrs. Billings and Mrs. Carter, they were "terribly disappointed" in her as well.

"Oh, dear. Lady Abigail says it's unseemly for unmarried women to be running a business out of their home. Which is utterly ridiculous!"

He frowned. "I suppose it might be. Or it might be a bit unsafe, if they're meeting with strangers."

"Oh, pish. I've been taking the commissioned projects to them directly myself." Emme pinched the bridge of her nose. "Except I haven't seen anyone this past week, which means there are ladies waiting for their miniature portraits and personalized kerchiefs, and Mrs. Billings and Mrs. Carter waiting for more work."

Emme wrapped her arms around herself while disparate thoughts joined and gelled in her mind.

"I don't like the look of that one bit." He pushed himself off the divan. "And I believe that's my cue to leave."

"Not another step, Brother." She gave him her most cherubic smile on him. "I'm going to need your help. "

"Unless it involves hot tea and scones—"

"Oh, what a lovely idea! I'm famished, having

missed breakfast. Have Cook send up enough for two, so you and I can discuss this."

"Discuss what?"

"I have a plan."

He groaned.

"It will require a small storefront in a respectable area with affordable rent, a broadminded landlord, and a wonderful man to be my proxy to negotiate the lease."

"I know I'm going to regret this," he said. "But fine, I'll see to tea and scones while you dress for the day. But I claim all the clotted cream as recompense for going along with this...whatever this is you're likely to get me into." He stopped with his hand on the door-knob. "And I want something in return."

In all the years he'd taken care of her, Emme couldn't remember Edward asking for anything in return for his help. "Of course. It's only fair. More than fair, I should say."

"Make Mother happy," He said. "Go shopping with her. You can get a new parasol, as you've been complaining about the one you brought back from Spain for ages. Although I'm sure you have any number of others you could use."

"They're all three years old."

It wasn't the age that kept her from using them, though. It was that they'd been from her last Season before Eleanor's death. Nearly all of her dresses, besides those she'd worn for mourning, had been from the same time. And every shopping trip she'd taken that year had been with Eleanor. Every dress and hat and glove and parasol she owned from that time had been touched by her older sister.

"Mother's been in discussions with the modiste for weeks," Edward was saying. "They've designed gowns for you in blues and greens and pinks—"

"She knows I can't wear pink!"

"And something...buttercup or something. Yellow, I think."

Yellow. It had been so long since she'd worn yellow. And suddenly, it was the color she wanted to wear most in the world. The yellow of the sun hanging above London. The yellow of buttercups swaying in a field. She pictured herself in a yellow bustled skirt with a matching jacket over a crisp white blouse, sitting beside Edward as they hashed out the terms of renting the storefront for her charges.

"I'll do it."

He grinned, a genuine smile that reached his eyes. "I'll let Mother know after I see to the tea."

"But Edward, someday you truly must let me do something for you."

He shook his head. "Just be well and safe, Emme-line. And let me protect you from cads who will break your heart."

"It's not his fault, Edward. Daniel didn't break my heart. I daresay I broke his." And her own in the process, but that was a discussion for another day, a less beautiful day, or perhaps never. "I do hope you haven't done something foolish, like accost him on the street or challenge him to fisticuffs."

Edward smirked. "Foolish, eh? Well, to be honest, I probably would have if I'd been able to find him."

"Find him? Is he gone? Has he left London?" Her throat constricted for no reason she could determine. Daniel was a grown man. If he chose to leave London with nary a word or forwarding address, who was she to question his actions, or to be gripped by fear to think of him gone?

"No, he's still in town. Just not about. And not receiving. Me, I can understand, but even Granston hasn't been able to see him. I assume the malady that's made you take to your bed for the better part of this past week has afflicted him as well."

Her heart was lighter from knowing Daniel was still near. "That is likely a safe assumption."

He nodded. "We'll speak of it no more. And I'll stop sending threatening missives to his house."

"Edward, you didn't!"

She could see by the look on his face that he had. Steady Eddie, as his friends at school used to call him. He'd never much cared for it, which was no doubt why it had stuck, but he *was* steady, a calming presence in her life. And he was her erstwhile protector, doing his best to shield her even from herself.

A minute after he left to seek out their breakfast, Emme's maid arrived to help her dress for what was shaping up to be a busy day. The first busy day of the life she'd chosen for herself, a life without any man except her dear Edward. Other than his penchant for constantly wanting to pummel Daniel, he really was the perfect brother.

*A*nother day, another threatening missive from Emme's unhinged brother. In the ten days since he'd last seen her, the messages had become part of Daniel's daily routine. At least for the past few days, Meriden had only been warning Daniel away from Emme as opposed to calling him out for causing his sister distress. Daniel tucked the latest envelope into his breast pocket, unsure why he'd brought it with him to the café.

Unfortunately, the place was full of mothers and chaperones and married ladies escorting marriageable maidens about town. He knew better than to take his morning tea so close to the best dress shops in the city. It was no mystery to him why he'd done it, though. Granston had mentioned in passing just yesterday that Meriden was helping his sister with "some ridiculous project or other" that involved looking at storefront establishments in the area. What was he hoping for? A glimpse of her hair? A flash of her smile? An acknowl-edgment that some memory of him still survived in her heart?

There was nothing to be done for it. She was better off without him. His shock at her admission, which he hadn't been quick-witted enough to hide, had broken something in her. He'd watch her shatter into pieces in front of him, and hadn't been able to do a damn thing to stop it or to repair the destruction he'd caused. She had her close friends, her brother, the rest of her family. They would have to be enough, would have to do for her what he couldn't.

As for him, he no longer had his family, but he did have the promise he'd made to his mother on her deathbed to keep him focused and alive. As alive as he could be without Emme. Which, come to think of it, was pretty damn near dead.

He stared down at the next letter on his pile of correspondence, the latest unopened missive from Mr. Alby at the House of Lords. He sliced open the embossed envelope and pulled out the thick paper, taking some time to focus his mind enough to understand the words written there. When the meaning revealed itself to him, he read it another time, just to be sure he wasn't mistaken.

25 April, in the Year of Our Lord 1870

To Mr. Daniel Hallsworth, son of the late Marquess of Edensbridge:

Pursuant to the request made of you by the Committee of Privileges in correspondence dated 4 April 1870, we had expected to see progress made toward courting one daughter of a peer in good standing with the House of Lords, with the intention of marrying in a short but respectable period of time. We were, therefore, chagrined to learn that you have ceased all association with the young ladies of the ton to pursue frivolous pastimes such as visiting alehouses and imbibing spirits with young peers who have yet to provide a Writ of Summons to join the House of Lords, and who are, in some cases, in poor standing with London society.

We hereby encourage you, in the strongest of terms, to eschew your disreputable pursuits and take up the cause of a respectable marriage in the hopes of restoring your reputation with this Committee, which, we will remind you, holds the fate of the Marquesette in its hands.

Respectfully yours,

The Hon. Mr. Charles Alby
Clerk of the Committee for Privileges
House of Lords
London, England

"*B*loody arrogant, pompous, miserable son of a hellhound…" He muttered the words quietly, almost silently, so as not to cause a panic amongst the impressionable young ladies in the café, nor draw the consternation of their matronly chaperones.

Besides, he'd agreed to play this ridiculous game with the committee, and now his family name was indeed on the mend. And his prospects, if he chose to take advantage of them, were indeed favorable.

He took a hurried sip of tea, tucked all his correspondence back into his coat pocket, and pulled on his gloves. He rose from his seat with more purpose than he'd felt since the last time he'd seen Emme. No surprise his purpose now came from his need to see her again. If anyone would know her whereabouts, it would be Meriden. And if anyone could help Daniel find Meriden, it was Granston.

She wouldn't want to see him, of course. But this time he had a good reason to insist upon it, one that wouldn't bring shame or ruin upon her or her family name. This time he needed her help to remove the shadow of scandal from *his*.

CHAPTER 16

*E*mme stood by the front window of the storefront, taking in the narrow yet long front room with shelves along the side walls that could hold wares, the well-worn but sturdy floorboards that could be covered with saleable rugs, and the white painted counter where they could install a till. In four days spent visiting every reputable address Edward's solicitor could identify, this was the only storefront that came anything close to what Emme needed to set up her ladies' cooperative.

She pulled off her gloves and tucked them into her reticule, then hung the handle of her oversized parasol over her forearm, then ran her forefinger over a shelf. "The landlord has had it scrubbed, just as he promised. It's the perfect spot, don't you agree?"

Tessa smiled as she took in the space. "It's lovely, and it's in a wonderful location, between a milliner and a modiste."

"It's a bit small." Luci grinned. "But you're right, it's perfect."

Emme's friends caught her in a quick hug between them, then Tessa pulled her back toward the window.

"I simply must see this suit again in the sunlight. I believe it actually shimmers. And the bustle is just the right size for daytime. The countess has divine taste."

"And you look stunning in that color." Luci ran one hand along Emme's jacket sleeve. "Lemon cream, is it? Which reminds me, I'm starving!"

Tessa rolled her eyes. "Are you ever not starving?"

Emme grabbed both her friends' hands, so glad they were with her, that they both now knew the truth about her and loved her anyway, that they fully supported her in the life's work she'd chosen. "Thank you. I wasn't sure about it. It's been so long since I've worn spring colors. And thank you for being here with me. It means the world, it truly does."

"Where else would we be, silly?" Luci waved her hand to dismiss the thought.

The front door swung open and Lady Abigail, followed closely by Lady Rachel, entered the shop.

"Ladies." Emme laid a hand over her heart, hoping their acceptance of her invitation meant they'd reconsidered their stance on the cooperative. "I didn't think you'd come."

"Good day, Lady Emmeline. Ladies." Lady Abigail glanced at her companion. "Lady Rachel pointed out that I might have been hasty in dismissing your proposal for alternative means of income."

"Quite hasty." Lady Rachel smiled at Emme.

"Thank you for reconsidering and for coming to the shop," Emme said.

Lady Abigail held out an envelope with the Spinsters' Club's seal on it, much like the letter Emme had received days earlier. "After much discussion, we've come up with a counter-proposal to help you in your little venture."

Lady Rachel clapped her hands together. "Once you've met the requirements for joining the Spinsters' Club, we'll pay half the upkeep for the shop!"

Her friends grabbed her hands, but Emme took a moment to understand what the ladies were telling her. She'd wanted to make a difference for so long and had come up with what she'd thought was the perfect plan, only to have them reject it. Now with Edward helping her and the Spinsters' Club providing support, her dream was coming true. She'd had to let go of so many other dreams over the past five years, but finally, there was one she could keep.

"Thank you," she said. "That will help the women tremendously. They'll be able to keep so much more of the proceeds they earn."

"They have you to thank." Lady Abigail shook her hand. "We look forward to working with you. Good day, Lady Emmeline. Ladies."

"Good day," Emme managed to say.

Lady Rachel shook Emme's hand firmly. "Good luck!" she said, then followed her leader back out of the shop.

"Well, that was..." Luci stopped. Even she was at a loss for words.

"I can't wait—" Emme finally started, then stopped. She'd been about to say she couldn't wait to tell Daniel. But she wouldn't tell him. She couldn't. They no longer shared each other's confidences. They would never share each other's lives.

As if to save her yet again, Edward stepped out from the office beyond the counter.

"We've worked out all the details," he said.

A small, bald man with an oversized mustache, rolled-up shirt sleeves, and a wide grin full of brown teeth followed Edward. "It'll be a pleasure doing business with you, m'lord."

Not to mention what a pleasure it would be for him to brag to his friends and all who would listen that he was renting property to the future Earl of Limely. Emme bit back a sharp-tongued response to the man who'd refused to allow her to be in the room while the men talked business. Even as the daughter of an earl and countess and sister of a future earl, the landlord, who had not a drop of aristocratic blood, could dismiss her and any other woman with impunity.

"The landlord understands the shopkeepers and their clientele will be women," Edward assured her as though he'd read her thoughts, or had at least noticed the look of contempt she'd shot in the landlord's direction.

"Which means, of course, m'lady," the landlord bowed again in Emme's direction, "we'll only allow the shop to be open for limited hours, and I'll install a man to keep watch over the building when any of the women are on premises."

Which would mean more cost. Emme chafed at the announcement, but in truth, it was wise. Once word spread that the shop was overseen by women, they'd be an easy target for harassment and maybe even crime, even on such a safe street.

"If that's settled," Luci said, "can we have lunch now, I beg of you?"

"Yes, with my apologies for keeping you waiting, Lady Lucinda." Edward pulled open the front door and the ladies filed out in front of him. Outside the shop, Emme quickly recounted to Edward the visit from Lady Abigail and Lady as the coachman helped first Tessa, then Luci, into the carriage.

"That's wonderful," Edward said. "You finally deserve some happy news."

As Edward took her hand and she alighted on the first step, a man stopped just feet from her. He was beautiful, self-possessed, comfortable in his own skin, as well as his place in the world, as he should be. And he was staring straight at her. The depths of his blue eyes made her breath catch in her throat.

"Lady Emme," Daniel said. He looked past her and touched the brim of his hat. "Ladies, good afternoon." He turned to Edward. "Meriden, I need a word."

Edward scowled. "I'll have a word with you another time. I'm escorting the ladies home for lunch."

Daniel shook his head. "Not with you. I need a word with your sister. It's a matter of some urgency."

Emme stepped back onto the sidewalk and between the men before Edward could say something that would start a fight or otherwise cause a scene.

"Mr. Hallsworth, good afternoon. You're looking well." As soon as the words were out of her mouth, she bit her tongue. She hadn't meant to say that.

"As are you, my lady," he said. "I hope your work is going well, and the ladies you've taken under your wing—how do they fare?"

It warmed her heart to hear him ask. It always warmed her heart to have him near her. But she would remain cool and professional. That was who she was now.

"The ladies are well," she answered. She couldn't help smiling. "And we've just had some brilliant news. I've set a new plan in motion..." She caught herself. They no longer shared such confidences. Still, she couldn't help asking about his work. "I understand improvements are well underway at the factory Grayhall Shipping has acquired."

"Going more slowly than I'd hoped, but I think we'll have much to show for it soon. We might..." He shook his head, perhaps coming to the same realization she had, that they no longer had a right to share so much with each other. "I beg your pardon, Lady Emme. I don't mean to take up so much of your time, but as I said, I need your help."

"I'm afraid I have no idea how I can be of help to you," she said.

Daniel watched her with those fathomless eyes as he handed her an envelope. It was the second official-looking missive she'd received in the last ten minutes. It didn't escape her notice that he took care not to brush his finger against hers as she took the letter from him. It was from the House of Lords.

"Read it, please," he said. "You, too, Meriden, so you'll know I have no nefarious intentions toward your sister."

Emme pulled out the letter and skimmed it, then handed it to her brother. "Mr. Hallsworth, while I appreciate the urgency of this matter, I'm as much at a loss as I was a minute ago. How can I be of any help to you?"

Her heart pounded with dread, fear, and something else she didn't want to name, but she recognized just the same. Desire.

"As you've gathered from Mr. Alby's letter, I'm in need of finding a wife post haste." He shifted uncomfortably from one foot to the other. "And as insincere as I might have been in my efforts to court other ladies in the past, it appears I now need to make an honest effort of it."

She swallowed the lump in her throat. It felt as if the entire world had shrunk down to just the two of them. "As I recall, there were several interested young ladies. Surely any one of them would be happy to receive your attentions. Perhaps even a blonde or two."

One corner of his mouth quirked up. "She needn't be blonde. Just kind." He frowned. "And she'll need to be from an impeccable family, and..."

"And above reproach," Emme finished for him when he couldn't seem to bring himself to say it. It was the one thing she couldn't give him: a sterling, unassailable reputation. The familiar sensation of a knife stuck in her gut came back to her.

"It seems I've made a mess of things this past week or so," he continued, "turning down invitations, disappointing some of the more important hostesses. The duchess will do what she can to smooth the ruffled feathers, but she's busy with many things."

"Hallsworth, you can't ask this of my sister." Edward took Emme's arm.

"No, it's all right." She laid her hand over her brother's. She owed Daniel this much for the heartbreak she'd caused him, for the unforgivable sin she'd committed that now stood in the way of their happiness together. "There's an opera performance at Covent Garden on Thursday evening. My mother has insisted we attend. Everyone who's anyone will be there. I can think of at least three young ladies and their mothers who would be thrilled to see you there. We'd be happy to make reintroductions."

It would be hell on earth to see him in his evening finery and not be able to run her hands up under his lapels and tilt her head up for his kiss. Yet she wanted to see him again as he'd looked on the night he'd joined her in her cabin on the SS *Lizette* for their private

254 | NANCY YEAGER

dinner. She longed to see him in the same black tailcoat he'd worn the night he'd taken her home from the train station. That wonderful, fateful, too-brief night.

She cast her eyes on the sidewalk under her feet and took a deep, fortifying breath.

Edward began to repeat his objections, but when she squeezed his arm, he sighed. "Fine, Hallsworth. You'll sit in our family box, of course."

"That sounds charming," Daniel said. "Which opera?"

Emme hesitated, her stomach twisting into knots. "Smetana's *The Bartered Bride*," she finally answered.

The three of them fell silent and exchanged uncomfortable glances.

It was Daniel who broke the saturnine mood. He touched the brim of his hat again. "Thank you. I'm obliged to you both."

He was polite. Kind and polite, and so distant that he was now beyond her reach.

Edward helped Emme into the carriage and exchanged one last look with Daniel, then climbed up behind her. As the carriage lurched forward, her brother laid his hand on top of hers on the seat, and Luci and Tessa chatted amiably about the perfection of the storefront and the lovely spring weather and the luncheon they'd soon share.

Emme smiled and nodded when it seemed appropriate, but she couldn't follow the details of what they were saying. The knife in her gut had been pulled out, leaving a gaping, bleeding wound in its wake. But even with the lifeblood draining out of her, she would smile, as her parents always told her to do. She would put aside her heartbreak, just as Edward had intimated she should. She would help as many women as she could in a way that would make Eleanor proud.

And she would give up every hopelessly romantic dream she'd ever had about being with the man she loved.

*D*aniel watched the carriage until it turned down the next street, taking with it every dream of happiness he'd ever had. His life would now be filled with obligation—to a wife, to the title she'd help him secure, to the children they'd have together—in lieu of happiness. He would put out of his mind how lovely Emme had looked today, wearing a pale-yellow skirt and matching jacket, a crisp white blouse tied into a bow at her neck, and a cream-colored hat with the ribbon matched to her dress.

When had he last seen her in yellow, or in any color other than those of mourning or dark forests? He couldn't recall. But it wasn't just bright colors that gave her a different appearance. She looked pale and sad, and her eyes belied a longing that resonated in the core of his being.

As happy as he'd been just to stand near her on the street for a few minutes in time, he'd also felt monstrous for making his request of her. If there'd been any other way to meet the demands of the Committee for Privileges, if the duchess hadn't been so overwhelmed with her social duties and obligations, if there'd been another upstanding family to take up his cause...but he'd had nowhere else to turn.

Through it all, though, Emme had carried herself with an air of self-possession, of purpose. She was resigned to their decision and their fates, which would now and forever diverge.

With his heart in his throat, he finally took one step forward, then another, then a few more, until he found himself stopped again, this time in front of the building from which Emme had emerged. He was surprised it was empty. What could she and her companions have been doing in the deserted shop? It didn't matter. Or at least it shouldn't. How she spent her time was none of his concern.

Seeing movement through the large glass window, he pulled open the front door and stepped into the small, neat space set up for commerce. He stopped beside the empty shelves to his right, sure he caught a hint of Emme's lavender scent.

"May I be of service to you, m'lord?"

Daniel turned to see a small, weasel-like man with a ridiculously unfashionable mustache, wearing a decently cut but ordinary suit without the jacket. Now his curiosity was piqued, indeed. "Are you the owner of this establishment?"

"Yes, m'lord, of this entire building. Storefront and offices below, rooms for rent above."

"I see." Daniel took off his hat and gloves as he took in the details of the small, barren shop. "Then yes, I should say you may be of service to me. The gentleman and the ladies who just left—why were they here? Tell me everything you know about them."

But he didn't really care what the man could tell him about *them*. He only wanted to know about *her*. In that moment, he caught a glimpse of his future and how long and lonely it would be, despite the companionship of a wife. Because no matter who else was in his life, it would always be about Emme.

CHAPTER 17

*J*ust days after he'd asked the woman he loved to help him find a wife, Daniel arrived at the Royal Opera House. He spotted his companions for the evening waiting for him in the lobby, in the exact spot where Emme's handwritten note had said they'd be. Before he joined them, Daniel took a moment to become acclimated to the crush of well-dressed, perfumed, and bejeweled attendees. Despite the rebuilt structure being less than two decades old, the space was quintessential Old England, and the people who crowded into it were the epitome of British imperialism.

He would have turned tail and run if Emme hadn't caught his eye.

He didn't hold her gaze as he made his way to her side, focusing instead on uttering pleasantries as he weaved his way through the crowd. But the weight of her stare lay over him as he approached. Her mother, brother, and aunt had yet to notice him as he came upon her, giving them a moment to take in the sight of each other.

Tonight, she was wearing more bright colors, this time a gown with a light green skirt and darker green lace bodice. Her upswept auburn hair, her pale skin, her green eyes, her lips were all impossibly luminous. The world around them grew dim and muffled as he stared into her eyes and she stared back, a slight smile lifting the edges of her lips.

"Your coat," she said in a near whisper. "You wore it the night of the duke's soiree."

"Yes. The night of King's Cross Station." The night of everything that had happened after he'd found her there. Everything he'd hoped she would remember when she saw him in the tailcoat. Everything he tried to forget every night as he lay alone in his bed, knowing she would never be there with him again.

"Ah, there he is." Meriden's voice broke the spell.

He gathered his wits as quickly as he could and shook Meriden's hand, then exchanged greetings and pleasantries with Emme's mother and aunt, both of whom watched him too keenly for his liking.

When he looked at Emme again, she still smiled, but it wasn't the same. Now it was forced.

"It should be a lovely night," she told him. "So many blonde young ladies about, and more than a few have noticed you already."

"Have they?" he asked, truly surprised.

He never heard her answer, for a bell rang

announcing the impending start of the performance. Before her brother could come to claim her, Daniel held out his arm to Emme. She took it.

"You risk giving the eligible ladies the wrong impression," she said as the took their place in the long line queuing up to enter the theater.

"Do I?" He knew very well she was right, and knew he should care, but he couldn't rally the feeling just now when he had the chance to stand arm in arm with the woman he truly wanted. But so close to her, he could see her face was pale and her eyes were tired. "Are you feeling all right, my lady? You don't look quite yourself."

She cleared her throat. "Yes, I'm fine." But her voice sounded hoarse. "We've been busy, working out the details of my next venture with the Spinsters' Club. Well, not exactly with the club."

"It appears it will take a few minutes to reach our seats, and I've yet to hear about this venture, if you'd care to share it."

She didn't bounce or roll forward on her toes or beam up at him. It was quite worrying.

"It's at a bit of a standstill at the moment," she said. "I'd hoped—with Edward's help—to rent a storefront to open a mercantile to sell the goods made by some of the women with artistic skills who receive assistance from the spinsters. The club doesn't want to back such a venture. Not respectable enough, I suppose."

"Quite brilliant, though," Daniel said. He'd pieced together the gist of it from the landlord's less than flattering description of the lady's business in his shop, but it was lovely to hear it from her own lips.

"Do you think?" She brightened for the first time all evening. "Negotiations with the landlord have broken down, but we're hopeful to get it all straightened out soon."

He wanted more than anything in that moment to tell her why her negotiations had stalled, but Emme was right—there would be a stigma attached to anyone who invested in the mercantile. With his new-found respectability, he couldn't risk such notoriety. But he could anonymously buy the building and turn it over to Emme for her purposes.

"I'm sure it will all work out very soon," he told her. "Business matters can take time."

"Still, it's difficult." She smiled, making his heart flutter like a schoolboy's. "I remember you mentioning that reforms weren't being implemented in your factory as quickly as you would have liked."

"That's true," he said. His heart sank as they inched closer to the box seats and he knew he'd have to stop touching her soon. "It's still moving too slowly, but we're making progress. And I might soon have an opportunity to offer some labor improvements to our dock workers. We're considering starting a transatlantic line, which would mean more ships, more cargo, and more longshoremen."

"Oh!" Emme bounced forward on her toes for the first time all evening. "You could have a labor union organizer come speak with them."

He grinned. "Perhaps I should hire the workers before I suggest they bring in someone to help them negotiate against me."

She was about to say something, but Meriden turned back to look at them as he led them into the family's box.

"Emme, you'll sit beside Mother," her brother told her.

In short order, it became clear that Meriden planned to keep Emme and Daniel as far as possible from each other, with Emme beside her mother, who sat beside her aunt. Meriden sat beside his aunt, with Daniel flanking the party on the side opposite Emme. The Radcliffes would entertain him in their box, but if anyone had mistakenly assumed he was courting Lady Emmeline, their seating arrangement would do much to quell the notion. The arrangement made sense for advertising his availability to other marriageable ladies and their chaperones, but still it stung. He remained an outsider among them, relegated to the shadows in the corner.

After the house lights dimmed, his seat did offer one great advantage: his ability to watch Emme out of the corner of his eye without being detected. If she felt his gaze on her, she hid it well. She focused on the performers, clapped enthusiastically at the end of each aria, and nodded her agreement each time her mother whispered something to her.

At least, Daniel had thought his vantage point a blessing, until he realized each minute spent so close to her, while unable to touch or hear or speak to her, felt like an hour. The singers might have been quite pleasing, but their voices scraped along his raw nerve endings and left him with a raging headache before they were even halfway to the interval. When that blissful break arrived and the house lights came up, the brightness stabbed his sensitive eyes. But he smiled through the pain because, just as Emme had predicted, every important member of the *ton* was in attendance, and most of their eyes were upon him, the imposter in their midst.

Emme's aunt chose to stay in the box during the interval, so Meriden offered his arm to Emme—once again preempting any rumors of Daniel courting her—and the countess took Daniel's proffered arm. Back in the lobby and once more caught in the crushing crowd, his fear of being ostracized was quickly allayed. The irreproachable countess and her charming children drew an endless stream of admirers, each introduced to Daniel, none audacious enough to so much as glance sidelong at him while he was in the Radcliffes' care.

The family was so solicitous, it was possible the seating arrangement had been a coincidence, or a means of ensuring Daniel appeared to be the available bachelor he was. Being in the midst of their camaraderie and standing close enough to Emme to hear her voice as she chatted, eased the tension in his head. He was almost comfortable here among the peers.

A movement to his left caught his attention. As he glanced at a woman who looked familiar and a younger

264 | NANCY YEAGER

one who did not, both of whom were making their way toward his small group, Emme took a step closer to him.

"Countess Bower," she said softly.

"Now I recall her," he said. "She was a friend of my mother's. A very nice lady."

"Matriarch of a very upstanding family," Emme said. "And if I'm not mistaken, the pretty blonde with her is Lady Anastasia, her daughter who just returned from a long visit in Vienna."

"Lady Ana?" Daniel widened his eyes.

The last time he'd seen the girl, she truly had been just a girl. She hadn't even had her debut yet. Now she was tall and shapely, with a pretty smile that she flashed at him when she caught his eye, followed by a blush.

The young lady and her mother were on a mission, and unless he was more out of practice with the machinations of British society than he thought, he was their quest.

*E*mme's jaw ached from maintaining her forced smile through this disastrous evening. But that didn't begin to touch the pain in her head from the dreadful day she'd had. After learning the Billings girl and Carter boys had taken ill during her visit with their mothers that morning, dealing with one of Edward's rare foul moods that afternoon, and being in excruciating close proximity to her former lover all evening, she was exhausted.

And now the kind Countess Bower and her lovely daughter Lady Anastasia had made a beeline for the man Emme loved. Used to love. Would probably always love but could never have. If she had been capable of it, she would have burst into tears.

After introductions, which included Daniel holding the young lady's gloved hand for longer than Emme thought appropriate, Lady Anastasia touched Emme's shoulder.

"Mother's been meaning to host a tea since I returned home weeks ago," the girl said. "You simply must come. It will be this Saturday."

"In two days?" Emme panicked. Her palms sweated and her mouth filled with sawdust. This could be the woman Daniel ended up courting. Or worse. Emme could barely survive this conversation, no less an entire afternoon with the young lady. "I'm afraid we have a previous engagement. Involving my great-aunt."

Emme's mother shot her a withering look, but Emme would deal with the consequences of upsetting her later.

"One day next week, then," Countess Bower said.

"That would be lovely," her mother answered before Emme could protest.

"And you, Mr. Hallsworth," the countess continued, "are you available Saturday afternoon? Will you join the earl and our daughter and I for tea?"

Daniel remained silent for several heartbeats, and

Emme wanted to kiss him for it. When Edward nudged his shoulder, he finally spoke.

"Yes, my lady, I'm available. I would be honored to attend."

He may as well have announced their engagement.

This is how it would start. If afternoon tea went well, Daniel and Lady Anastasia would begin a brief but respectable courtship. That in and of itself would please the Committee for Privileges immensely. Then would come their short but proper engagement, culminating in—as the Duchess of Wrexham had wished—Daniel's celebrated and auspicious marriage to the lovely and virginal young lady by midsummer. Reinstatement of his marquessate couldn't be far behind.

It was what was meant to happen, what *had* to happen so they could each get on with their own lives. But right now, it only made Emme's headache intensify and travel down into her neck and shoulders.

The conversation around her continued.

"Oh, no, he sees far too much of me as it is." Edward was speaking to Countess Bower.

"You don't mind, Lady Limely?" the countess asked.

"Of course not," Emme's mother replied. "Please, all of you, enjoy the rest of the performance."

As the countess and her daughter walked away from them, Daniel said goodnight to the Radcliffes, then followed Countess Bower and Lady Anastasia. It was then Emme realized they'd invited him to spend the rest of the evening in their box. Her time with him

—for the evening, and possibly for the rest of their lives—had unceremoniously ended. Again.

"Emmeline, you don't look well." Her mother's warm hand gripped her own ice-cold fingers. "You're shivering."

"Am I?" All Emme knew was that her head pounded and her body hurt and Daniel was gone from her life.

Edward and Mother exchanged some words, then his hand was on her elbow as he led her toward the exit.

"Mother will join Aunt Juliana while I get you home, and I'll come back for them later," her brother told her.

She meant to shake her head to protest, to insist they keep up appearances and stay for the duration of the evening, but she needed every bit of her strength to keep walking. When they stepped outside to wait for their carriage, Emme shivered. Edward pulled off his tailcoat and wrapped it around her shoulders.

"Thank you," she said. "There's suddenly a chill in the air."

Edward frowned. "Actually, it's quite stifling this evening. I'm afraid you've come down with some malady."

He didn't lecture her on the time she'd been spending with Mrs. Billings and Mrs. Carter and their children in their rundown neighborhood, and for that she was grateful. But that, and the sour expression he'd worn for hours, weren't like him.

When they were finally settled in their carriage and

Emme no longer had to expend so much energy to stand on her own two feet, she observed her brother more closely.

"Something's the matter," she said. "Tell me."

He scrubbed his hand over his face. "It's been a difficult evening for all of us."

"Yes, it has. But you had this look about you when you arrived home this afternoon."

He stared out the carriage window, refusing to meet her eye. "In anticipation of this difficult evening."

"Edward, please."

She reached out her hand to him. His hand was warm when it closed around hers.

"There is something, but it can wait until tomorrow, when you feel better."

"No, I need to hear it now. I need to hear all the bad news there is to know tonight." She leaned back against the seat cushions and waited, trying very hard to ignore the fact that the bouncing carriage was exacerbating her splitting headache.

With a shake of his head, he conceded. "It's about the Bond Street property. The landlord sent word this afternoon that he won't be leasing it to us, as he's selling the building. He received an offer he couldn't refuse, so he didn't."

"But..." She gripped the side of the carriage for purchase. Nothing in her world made sense anymore. Everything she loved, everything she needed in her life, was slipping away from her.

"How can he do this? Our contract."

"It wasn't finalized yet." Edward leaned forward to take her hand again. "I don't want you to worry about this. I'm looking into it. We should know something in a few days. Perhaps the new landlord will lease the space to us, or will decide not purchase the building after all, or we'll find something even better."

That was doubtful at best, and they both knew it. There were few options available, even fewer that were in areas safe enough for both the women who would work in the store and the ladies who would shop there.

"Perhaps," she said, because he meant well.

"I'm sorry, Emme. If it were a year from now, I'd have my trust and this would already be taken care of. As it is," he closed his eyes, "I'll do everything I can."

Edward, ever true to his word, would do everything he could for her, but it might not be enough. Besides, she couldn't expect him to take care of her forever. There was one last possible solution to her problem. She'd been avoiding it for more than a year, but now she'd run out of options and needed money, and there was only one way for her to get her hands on such funds. It was time to convince Father that his only daughter must remain a spinster.

CHAPTER 18

*A*fter a day in bed with a fever and another day
recovering her strength, Emme finally felt like
herself again. But losing that time left her in an even
more precarious position. The building on Bond Street
might already be in the hands of its new owner. If not,
she might still be able to purchase it with her brother's
help, but they'd have to move fast and have funds at the
ready.

She stopped outside her father's study to gather her
courage as much as her strength, reminding herself
that it wasn't just her chance at redemption at stake.
The hopes of the craftswomen she'd met and the future
of their children mattered more than she did. They had
suffered and sacrificed so much, the least she could do
was endure the brief discomfort of begging her father's
indulgence.

He sat alone in his study, behind his heavy, carved
walnut desk with his reading glasses perched on the

end of his nose. He pored over the household ledgers. It didn't escape her that the household accounts used to be one of her mother's responsibilities, and she wondered which of them had wished to alter the arrangement. Perhaps they'd soon wish to return to their former routine, once Emme no longer posed a problem. Once she'd settled into her role as a respectable patron of young women in need.

Butterflies fluttered in her stomach. This moment had been so long in coming, and she'd hoped she'd have more to show her father in the way of accomplishments before asking for her dowry to use for her cause, but circumstances had forced her hand. Still, she was strong and capable. Nothing would break her. She'd let Daniel go, forever this time. If she could still stand upright with that gaping, unhealed wound in her heart, she could accomplish anything.

She screwed up her courage and knocked on the partially opened door. Upon Father's invitation, she stepped into the study and closed the door behind her.

He pulled off his readers and observed her as she sat in the upholstered chair opposite him. "You still don't look well, Emmeline."

"I'm fine, sir. Much recovered." She forced a smile to prove it, but couldn't hold it for long. "I've come to discuss something of utmost importance with you."

"Oh?" He leaned forward. "What matter is that?"

Her hands shook with nerves. She clasped them tightly in her lap and steadied herself with a breath.

"The matter of suitors, of doing things differently. I've been discussing it with Mother and Edward."

He set down his glasses on the ledger. "Edward has been bending my ear on your behalf. Something about spinsterhood."

Her stomach flipped over itself. She slid to the edge of her seat. "And?"

He sighed and shook his head. "Emmeline, I don't know where you get these silly notions. At your age, your sister could think of nothing but her imminent wedding and the future children she would have."

And at the same age, she'd drowned, taking with her all their parents' hopes and dreams.

"I'm not Eleanor."

"That much I know."

There was no warmth in his eyes when he said it. Had there ever been, when he'd looked at her, or had all his sentimentality been reserved for her older sister? At the moment, she truly could not recall.

She wrapped her arms around herself. "Please, Father, don't ask me to take up her life where she left it."

He jumped to his feet and leaned forward over his desk, fisted hands pressed into it. "Don't you ever speak to me that way, Emmeline. I've tolerated your selfish wallowing long enough, and your childish recklessness even longer. You're an adult, a grown woman, and it's time for you to take your place in the world."

"My place in the world?" She rose to her feet, her legs wobbling. "A wife has no place in the world, only in her husband's home. A wife is chattel, a thing to be bargained over by a father and a suitor. For most men, a wife is worth less than the animals housed in his stable, and treated more poorly."

Her father rose to his full height and walked slowly around his desk. Emme's instinct told her to run, but fear rooted her to the spot. He stopped just inches from her. He moved his right hand and she flinched.

"I should." His voice was a low growl. "I should spank you into submission. It might be the only thing to cure you of this delusion that's had you in its grip since Eleanor's death. No daughter of mine will be a spinster, an object of gossip, a spot on the family name. Do you understand me?"

Her legs shook so hard, she had to lower herself back into her chair. Her plan for her own future was the one thing in the world that was hers, the one balm that might soothe the slightest bit of the pain of losing Daniel. No matter what her father said, no matter what he did, she had to win his support. "Please, Father, hear my side of it."

Face red, fists clenched at his sides, he shook his head.

She laid a shaking hand on his arm. "Please, sir, I beg you. My only intention is to do good works, to be a better person, to make up for all the awful sins of my past."

He turned his back and walked away from her, putting space between them. She slipped out of her chair and crossed the room to stand beside the empty fire grate. She laid one hand over her churning belly and reached out with the other to grip the cold marble mantel. How she longed for a roaring fire in the hearth to spread warmth through her ice-cold limbs. Perhaps she wasn't as recovered as she thought. Or perhaps it wasn't her malady at all, but the dawning realization that Father might be immovable.

He stepped closer to the hearth. "You've begged my indulgence. Now I'm granting it. I'm listening, Emmeline. What awful sins have you committed?"

She stepped away from the hearth and perched on the edge of the blue silk-covered divan, a long-ago gift from her mother to her father, from a time when they'd all been happy. "First, there was Eleanor's death."

"No." He crossed his arms over his chest. "I will not allow you to think such nonsense for one more minute. You did not cause your sister's death."

She nodded. "I've begun to see that, I truly have. But it was an argument with me—over my childish recklessness, as you so succinctly put it—that drove her from the house in anger that day she fell into the lake. And after that, my behavior…"

She stared down at her hands, knowing what she must do, wishing for lightening to strike her or the earth to open up and swallow her whole before she could choke out the words. Heaven and earth both failed her as her father stood in silence, waiting for her confession.

"I made a foolish decision, inviting Mr. Sanderson to court me."

"Yes, I remember Sanderson. I ended that courtship for your own protection."

"I know that now. But at the time..." She glanced at him, standing so still, his gaze fixed on her face. "I kept up the courtship in secret."

He scowled. "You defied me. I assume Edward knew or learned of it, which was why he argued so hard for your year abroad."

"None of it was Edward's fault. In fact, he saved me, the night I made the worst decision of all." She stared at the fireless hearth, finding no solace there. "I led you and Mother to believe I'd stayed with a friend."

When she saw her father shift his stance back to anger, with clenched fists and a puffed chest, she knew her words had connected. "Of all the selfish, reckless, *foolish* things to do!"

"I'm sorry, Father, I truly am. I don't know how to justify it."

"There *is* no justification for it! If anyone were to learn you spent time alone with that man, the Radcliffe name would be sullied beyond repair. You'd never find a respectable husband. Even Edward's chances might be ruined."

Her father shook with rage, making Emme shake with fear. Once again, she wanted nothing more than to run from the room and hide, like a scared, feral kitten. And once again, she stayed rooted to the spot, ready to endure the worst he had to give if it meant she'd get what she needed to establish her ladies' cooperative.

"If I devote myself to good causes and don't attempt to make a match, no one will have reason to care. There'll be no wedding night to reveal my shame to an unwitting husband."

Time stopped while Emme waited for the sign that the underlying meaning of those words had connected with her father as well. She knew it had happened when he reached out one hand and grasped the mantle so tightly, his knuckles turned white.

"Leave." His voice was quiet, so quiet. Barely above a whisper.

"Father, I—"

"Leave my presence. Get out of my sight. Get out of my house."

She jumped to her feet and backed toward the study door. "Father, please—"

He slammed his fist down on the mantel so hard, she was sure the house shook around her.

"Do not call me that." His voice was calm now, steady and low. "You are no daughter of mine. Understand that. Understand I would put you out on the street today, this very minute, if it weren't for the scandal it would bring down on all our heads, when only one of us is deserving of scorn."

She pressed her hand to her belly, sure she was about to vomit, to collapse, to make everything worse than it already was.

"I'll find you a husband."

Emme froze with one hand pressed over her mouth to keep from gagging.

"The vicar we knew when the twins died is a good man. Kind, understanding, imminently forgiving. He helped us tremendously in our hour of need. He's since moved to Staveley, but last I knew, he had an unmarried son."

Emme dropped her hand from her mouth. "The vicar's son? He must be at least thirty-five."

"Closer to forty. But beggars can't be choosers, Emmeline. I'm offering you a way out of ruination."

"I've never even heard of Stavely."

"It's quite a bit north of Nottingham."

"North of Nottingham?"

He might as well banish her to the ends of the earth.

She twisted her hands together. "How will I see Mother? And Edward." And her friends. And at least a glimpse of Daniel from across a crowded room.

"You won't, at least not often, I'd presume."

She didn't even bother to ask about him. He would marry her off with as little pomp and circumstance as he could, then would go about his life as though his only daughter had died two years ago. But her mother wouldn't forget her only living daughter. She'd grieve for Emme every day. The guilt crushed the breath from her chest. She stumbled to the door, not knowing what to do other than escape her father's presence.

"I'll send word to the vicar tomorrow, explaining our need for his assistance, and will ask that he reply by the end of the week. After that, it will take some time to prepare for the wedding. No Radcliffe will embarrass the family name by getting married with a special license."

Emme pressed one shaking hand to her breast and the other to the door, praying for the moment she could turn the knob and run from the room. But still her father continued.

"In the meantime, you will be on your best behavior. To that end, you're not to leave this house without your brother chaperoning you. Is that clear?"

The volume and brashness of his voice startled her. He hated her. In every word he uttered, she could hear it. Her own father hated her. She had no doubt that if she didn't marry the vicar's son and move to the country, she'd be exiled to some other dreary, distant corner of England, possibly with nothing more than the clothes on her back. He'd do it because he couldn't stand the sight of her.

Something fragile that had been stretched taut in her chest for the years since her sister's death snapped. She slumped against the door. "Please, don't do this. I swear, I won't do a single thing wrong for the rest of my life. I'll use every penny of my dowry to help others, and I'll even stay out of London if—"

"*Your* dowry? It was never yours. And now it'll be needed as further enticement for the vicar and his son. After all, they're getting damaged goods."

The punch of his vitriol landed in her gut. She gathered every last bit of strength she had and yanked open the study door. She lifted her skirt and half-ran, half-stumbled to the staircase and up the stairs, tumbling once and nearly falling backwards. The noise drew the attention of a footman, whom she motioned away with flailing arms as she struggled to her feet and flew the rest of the way to her room. Her room for the moment, perhaps even a for a month, while her father made the arrangements to marry her off. But after that, she'd never be welcome here again.

For the past year, she'd a plan, and with it, a future. And always, woven into the fabric of her life, she'd had her family.

Now all those things were gone.

Every dream and scheme she'd carried in her heart for so long had evaporated during those brief, terrible minutes in her father's study. And like her dreams, soon everyone she loved would be taken from her, too.

Sorrow bent her in two. She wrapped her arms over her belly and crumpled to the floor in the middle of the room. Finally, tears came, tears that had been pent up for two long, lonely years. She lay on the floor sobbing. No one came to hold her. She watched dusk rise outside her window, then witnessed its disappearance into the dark of night. No one was there to share her grief.

No one came to see her, to comfort her, to so much as acknowledge her existence. As she'd feared would happen since the day of Eleanor's death, she was now utterly alone in the world.

*D*ays after the dreadful evening at the opera, Daniel sat uncomfortably in the leather chair behind his father's desk in the Hallsworth London townhouse. He finished reading the paperwork Granston had brought for him to review, regarding the used ocean-liner they'd just added to the fleet, now the largest ship they owned, and the first one capable of transatlantic voyages. It would be the last deal he would complete on English soil.

He'd spent enough time trying to convince himself he wanted all of this—his parents' country properties, the London townhouse, the study that used to belong to the marquess—and that the restoration of his title and redemption of the Hallsworth name would make him into a proper English peer. Securing a respectable marriage to one of England's better families to do it, a family like that of Lady Anastasia, would have been the jewel in the crown of his accomplishments.

Unfortunately, he'd made quite the cock-up of that two days earlier, informing her after just one visit with her family that he was leaving England after all. He'd finish his redemptive journey, receive the title from the Committee, and leave behind a well-managed estate, as well as an endowment for charitable causes. But he wouldn't stay here and play lord of the manor. Now he only need break it to Granston and Swimmer, who sat across from each other at the gaming table Daniel had bought for future evenings they'd spend together, evenings that would never materialize now.

"Is there a problem?" Granston asked.

Daniel shook his head. "No. The accountants have done a thorough job. I am wondering why you're joining us in this purchase, though," he said to Swimmer.

"Always looking for good investment opportunities," Swimmer said.

The man could spend the rest of his life making terrible investments and the dukedom would still be worth a fortune. Quite a large fortune. Daniel quirked an eyebrow.

"I suggested it," Granston said. "There's something I want to discuss with the two of you. Once the ocean liner up to Grayhall standards, I plan to take her to Argentina."

He didn't finish, as he was interrupted by a knock at the study door.

"Yes, Keats."

The butler opened the door and bowed in Daniel's direction. "Viscount Meriden to see you, sir."

"Show him in." As he steeled himself to deal with whatever threats Meriden had determined should be delivered in person, Daniel tossed back a slug of cognac and set it down on the desk.

"You're a bastard, Hallsworth," Meriden announced as he stalked into the room.

Daniel waved his hand to dismiss the butler, who closed the door behind him.

"Hell of a way to speak to a man in his own home," Swimmer said.

282 | NANCY YEAGER

Meriden turned toward Granston and Swimmer, surprise showing on his face.

"Go on," Granston told him.

Meriden shook his head. "This is between Hallsworth and me."

Granston and Swimmer looked at Daniel, waiting to follow his cue. He glanced at the glass doors leading to the back garden.

"The rain has stopped," he said to his friends. "It might be a good time for you to get a breath of fresh air."

Granston glanced at his shiny black shoes. "But I just had these—"

Swimmer glared at Granston as he walked past him.

"Fine." Granston scowled, but followed Swimmer outside.

The two men didn't go far, keeping Daniel in their sightline. They didn't trust Meriden, and neither did he. In all the years of being friends and foes, Daniel had never seen such a look of blind rage on the man's face as he saw now.

He circled around to the front of his desk. If he was going to take a punch, he'd damn well do it standing up. "Is Emme all right?"

"No, she is not all right. She will never be all right again."

Was it true, was she destroyed by their night together, by what he'd done to her? They'd both faced that morning heartbroken, but she'd seemed to move on. She was finding peace. She'd found her purpose, and before Daniel left for Spain, he'd give her a gift that would support that purpose for the rest of her life.

"Are you trying to destroy my sister's life because my father refused to accept you all those years ago?" Meriden asked. "Or is *she* your enemy because she turned down your marriage proposal, despite your nearly reclaimed title?"

"You don't know anything about why she refused me. And I'm not trying to destroy her. I'd never hurt her. I'm doing everything in my power to protect her, to give her the life she wants, a life that doesn't include me."

"Then explain this." He drew papers out his pocket and threw them in Daniel's face.

As he unfolded the pages, he recognized his own seal. "The paperwork for my purchase of the building on Bond Street. This was to be kept private. How did you get this?"

"The owner sent it to my solicitor." Meriden began pacing. "In case I saw fit to best your offer."

"That bloody cheat. And after I offered him top dollar." He had also demanded the scoundrel's utmost discretion. Were word to get out that Daniel was behind the trust that would own the mercantile run by fallen women, his shiny new reputation would be tarnished once more.

"So you admit it! You admit you stole my sister's dream out from under her, putting her in such a state that she..."

Cold dread settled in Daniel's belly. "She what?"

284 | NANCY YEAGER

Meriden didn't answer. Just paced. And shook. And paced some more.

"Meriden, what did you mean about me destroying your family? What do they have to do with any of this?"

"On the day of the opera, I learned the building owner wouldn't lease the storefront to us." Meriden scrubbed his hand over his eyes. "Emme knew I couldn't secure the funds to buy the building, so she decided she'd do it. She asked my father for her dowry, and when he insisted she marry and forget about the Spinsters' Club, she told him she couldn't marry and why. Told him she'd made a terrible decision, and what it was."

"No. Dear God, no." Daniel leaned forward and propped his head in his hands until the nausea passed. "She should have come to me. Or laid it all at my feet. She should have sent her father here to call me out, not take the blame herself."

"You?" Meriden went still. "What are you blathering on about? She told him about Sanderson."

At the instant Daniel wished he could snatch back his words, their meaning dawned on Meriden, and his face went from red to purple.

"You really are a bastard, aren't you? In every sense of the word."

And there it was, what his former best friend truly thought of him. What he would always think of him. "Watch yourself, Meriden."

The fist to his jaw came so fast, Daniel teetered backwards before his mind even registered the attack.

"Bloody hell." He pulled his kerchief from his pocket and blotted blood from the corner of his mouth.

The garden doors swung open and Granston and Swimmer dashed back into the room.

Granston scowled as he looked at Daniel's face. "Really, Meriden, I know he's an ass, but was that necessary?"

Swimmer angled himself between the men.

"I'm not planning to hit him again." Meriden gripped his right fist in his left hand. "I think I might have broken a bone."

"Come on." Swimmer took Meriden by the shoulder and pulled him toward the garden. "There's a fountain of cold water that'll feel like heaven on that."

"Is he really more concerned about that son-of-a-bitch's hand than he is about my face?" Daniel asked as Swimmer led Meriden to the garden.

Granston rolled his eyes. "We're all duly worried about your pretty face, Hallsy, but you've been goading him since you set foot back in the country. And while I'm not sure exactly what else you've done to raise his hackles, I can hazard a few guesses. I'd do the same if you had designs on one of my sisters."

"Designs? More like dreams." Daniel dropped into the leather chair behind the desk. "Dreams you'd think I would have relinquished in the past five years."

"So, it was the dream of Lady Emme that brought you home. Not your parents' dream for you after all."

Daniel nodded slowly. "I suppose that's the best way

to put it. I didn't know it yet when I was hanging off that sail rigging over the Bay of Biscay."

Granston shook his head. "I had visions of me explaining to your solicitors that they'd worked so hard all those years to restore your title, only to have the future marquess end himself and his lineage with one stupid plunge into the sea, from a docked ship no less."

"I seem to recall you said the fall wouldn't kill me."

Granston shrugged. "It could have gone either way. I wasn't about to tell *you* that."

"But you understand, don't you? Without Emme, there's nothing left for me here. Maybe someday I'll half-heartedly marry and produce an heir for my mother's sake, and send him back to England when he's old enough for Harrow."

"Heaven help him."

"Speaking of help, it turns out you were right all along—I'll need yours." Admitting that to Granston hurt Daniel more than his throbbing lip. "And Swimmer's."

Granston frowned. "What can Swimmer do for you that I can't?"

"Call the Committee for Privileges to a meeting at his club," Daniel answered. "I've had enough of their games. It's time they reinstate my title."

Then he could tell the solicitors to stop dallying about setting up an anonymous trust and just buy the storefront for the women's mercantile outright. Emme's dire circumstances meant he no longer had the luxury of hiding behind anonymity to keep his name separate from the fallen women the shop would employ. But to hell with it. If England mattered little to him with Emme no longer in his life, his reputation mattered even less.

Granston clapped him on the back. "It's about bloody time you stood up for yourself." Granston poured a cognac for each of them and lifted his glass. "To the marquess. And to the duke, for helping him."

Daniel sipped his drink and grimaced when the alcohol stung his split lip. "Speaking of the duke, why did you ask Swimmer to invest in a transatlantic shipping line with us? Grayhall has the assets to make the purchase without him."

Granston took a swig of his own drink. "I thought it would do him good, that we'd be a positive influence on him. Though given your recent behavior, I might have misjudged it."

"I'm afraid I'll have to leave him in your hands now, Granston, God help the man. But perhaps you should stay in London a bit longer, keep an eye on him."

Granston cocked an eyebrow. "And if I happen to see Steady Eddie's sister about town and send you regular missives about her, that would suit your purposes as well, I suppose."

"It's a thought."

"Not a bloody good one," Granston said. "I didn't talk you and Swimmer into buying that gorgeous bit of American engineering so I could turn her over to another man. As I said earlier, I plan to take her to Argentina as soon as she is ready to go."

Remembering how leaving on an adventure to Spain had saved him five years earlier, Daniel was seized by nostalgia. "Perhaps I'll join you. How long will it take to get her up to Grayhall standards?"

"A few months." Granston pursed his lips as he pondered the idea. "Now *that* thought is not a half-bad one, Hallsy. Settle your affairs here and in Spain, then we'll be off to conquer the New World, like explorers of old." He frowned. "But when our little adventure ends, promise me you'll come back to England and give your life here another go."

If five years hadn't made England feel like home, another five months—or ten years—wouldn't do the trick, either. "That's a promise I can't make. I don't think I'll ever be able to keep it."

Voices in the garden made both of them glance at the back door.

"Now, for what I need to ask of you," Daniel said.

Granston raised his eyes to the ceiling and sighed. "A captain's work is never done, is it?"

"Yes, woe is you. But seriously, do you recall mentioning that I might someday need Steady Eddie's help? Turns out, I need Steady Eddie's help."

"I warned you. Now that you're acting less like an ass and he's had the opportunity to punch you in the face, I think Swimmer and I can convince him to be of assistance."

For at least the thousandth time in his life, Daniel

wondered what he'd done to deserve friends like his, who—despite their many, many flaws—were some of the best men he'd ever known. "Thank you, mate."

Granston tossed back the rest of his drink and set his empty glass on the desk. "But I'll warn you now, I won't give up trying to convince you to return here someday. You might not believe this now, Hallsy, but Mother England always finds a way to bring her native sons home."

CHAPTER 19

*I*n the days since her father had disowned her and vowed to marry her off to a country vicar's son nearly twice her age, Emme had gotten her emotions in check and her affairs in order. Now she stood in the bedroom that would be hers for only a few more hours, surrounded by trunks and valises.

She brushed down the front of her buttercup yellow skirt, which might not suit for the traveling she'd do this evening, but would be perfect for the last things she had to do in London before she left the city for good. She'd begun the day in one of her comforting gray mourning dresses, but when she'd looked at herself in the glass while the maid had buttoned it for her, she hadn't see Eleanor's sister. For the first time in a very long time, she'd seen only Emme, and dark gray didn't suit Emme.

Standing beside her, Aunt Juliana took Emme's hand. They'd seen each other every day for more than a year, and as hard as it would be to say goodbye to her mother, it would be nearly as difficult to part ways with her great-aunt.

"You're sure there's nothing else to be done for it?" Aunt Juliana asked.

"I'm sure. Even Edward says it's for the best, and you know he's the last person who wants me to leave again." Emme squeezed her aunt's hand. "I worry, though, about what my father will say when he learns I won't marry the vicar's son and have run off to your house in Cambridge."

"Let him say anything he wishes, the old windbag. And if he sees fit to put me out on the street as well, I'll join you there, drafts or no drafts."

Emme hoped it wouldn't come to that. Her aunt's old bones might do fine in the dilapidated old house during the summer months, but once the cold, damp winter set in, she'd be twisted up with joint pain. For the thousandth time, Emme wished Aunt Juliana and she had never returned from Spain, that Mother and Edward and her two best friends had moved to the sunny seaside town with them. There she went again, being a foolish child, the very thing her father always accused her of being.

She blinked fast to stave off the tears. She'd become pathetic. How had it come to this? She'd once had hopes, dreams, a future, no matter how lonely it might have been. Even without the companionship of a husband, she'd expected to spend the rest of her days surrounded by love. Maybe her father had never been able to love her the way he'd loved Eleanor, but her mother, brother, and aunt had loved her just as much, she was sure of that.

And Daniel...Why had she doubted him? Why had she thought he'd wanted to leave her five years ago? Why hadn't she found some way to see him, to run away with him instead of Sanderson? And how would she ever survive this punishment for her cardinal sin?

Tomorrow would be the day the punishment became truly real. Tomorrow, she would begin her new life, exiled and alone.

A knock at the bedroom door startled both her and Aunt Juliana both out of quiet reveries. A footman announced that the carriage was ready, and Emme prepared herself for the final thing she would do before leaving London for good. With one last hug and a kiss to the cheek, she bid her aunt adieu.

"Remember to give Mother my letter when Edward arrives home without me." She gave Aunt Juliana one last hug and a kiss on the cheek, then bid her adieu.

Coward that she was, Emme couldn't bear to look her mother in the eye as she broke her heart. They'd see each other from time to time, of course, but if her father had his way, it wouldn't be soon and it wouldn't be often.

She joined her brother in the carriage, on her way to the last meeting of the Spinsters' Club she would ever attend. She carried her new parasol, which was edged with Mrs. Carter's exquisite needlepoint. It was a gift of thanks for a promise Emme would have to break, now that she wouldn't be joining the Spinsters' Club or establishing the cooperative.

Edward reached across the cab and squeezed her hand. "I'll do what I can for Mrs. Billings and Mrs. Carter."

"Thank you."

She knew he would, but it wasn't just about those two women and their children. There were dozens of women she'd already met whose handiwork she'd hoped to sell in the storefront. There were hundreds, perhaps thousands more, she'd dreamed of helping in the years to come. Now she'd sit in Cambridge and write polite letters and less-than-polite treatises and, in the end, she'd help absolutely no one.

By the time they arrived at the London Library on St. James Square, they may as well have been arriving at a funeral, given the melancholy hanging over them. When they stepped into the building, though, she breathed deeply and inhaled the calming scent of books and bindings. She tried to pretend they were just on a pleasant, late-morning outing, and not preparing to separate again. Edward would visit her as often as he could in the countryside, but he could hardly come frequently. And one day, he'd settle down and marry and have children of his own to raise, and the crazy aunt who'd run off to Cambridge would be just another nursery story to them.

Emme and Edward stopped outside the meeting room. It was a cozy, wood-paneled space with tall windows illuminated by spring sunshine and soaring rafters arching into a pointed ceiling. Twelve chairs were arranged in a semi-circle in the middle of the room. The members of the Spinsters' Club were already there, milling about and chatting like the old friends they were. She had never gotten to know them the way they knew each other, and now she never would.

She squeezed Edward's arm, then released it. "I suppose it's time. I can't delay the inevitable any longer."

As she stepped away from him, Edward caught her hand. "Emme, wait."

She saw such sadness on his face, it frightened her. "Edward, what is it?"

"I just want you to know, I need you to know, I love you. I always will. Nothing you've done or ever could do will change that. Mother, too, and Aunt Juliana, and your friends. We know you're a good person, Emme."

In the days since her father had renounced her, the rest of her family and her two best friends had done everything they could to show her their love and support. In her heart, she knew they believed in her goodness, and they wanted her to believe it, too. Still, hearing it from Edward meant the world.

"Thank you for saying that." She rose on her tiptoes and kissed his cheek.

Edward tightened his grip on her hand to keep her there. "There's one more thing. Hallsworth." With his free hand, Edward pinched the bridge of his nose. "Now Edensbridge."

Emme froze on the spot. No one had mentioned him in her presence since the night of the opera. She never would have guessed how deeply the sound of his name would cut. "That's good news. He's reclaimed the title. He promised his mother, and..." She couldn't think of what else she could say that wouldn't make her burst into tears.

"Despite what I think of him, what we think of each other, he has one redeeming quality. He loves you."

Emme took an unsteady breath. "Yes, I think he does." *It's not enough*, she wanted to tell her brother, but there was no point in discussing Daniel. Not with Edward, not with anyone.

"He's not courting Lady Anastasia. He's given up courting." Her brother frowned and looked away from her. "I thought you should know."

"I don't understand. Why are you telling me this?"

Edward hesitated, then shook his head. Dropping her hand, her ever-steady brother, her rock, her protector, took up his post on an ornately carved walnut bench a few feet from the meeting room door. Emme was relieved to let the subject of Daniel drop, but she couldn't help thinking there was something more she needed to understand. However, the moment had passed, and inside the room, the spinsters had taken their seats. There was no more time to dwell on it.

Emme smoothed down the front of her skirt and adjusted her jacket, then stepped into the meeting room. As Lady Abigail stepped out from behind the lectern several feet in front of the chairs, Emme slid into one of only two empty seats, nodding and smiling at the other women. They were all dressed in finery, with sumptuously feathered hats and starched white gloves. It appeared the spinsters maintained a certain standard for their monthly meetings, and if Emme had thought she had any hope of joining them, she would have regretted the underwhelming impression made by her buttercup yellow suit and crisp white blouse, much as she loved them.

Lady Rachel stood, remaining in front of her chair. "Shall I read the minutes of our last meeting now, Lady Abigail?"

"I think I should like to break protocol and begin with our second order of business today." Lady Abigail beamed.

Emme couldn't remember ever seeing anything close to such excitement in the elder stateswoman of the club.

Lady Rachel clapped her hands together and shot a quick glance at Emme.

Lady Abigail waved Emme forward. "Lady Emme-line, would you join me, please?"

Emme pressed her trembling hands to her belly as she stood and stepped toward Lady Abigail. This was the moment of reckoning, the moment when her dream of committing herself to cause greater than her sad, small life disappeared in a puff of smoke. The time had come to say goodbye the ladies of the Spin-ster's Club, and to the hope she'd once had of redeeming herself in the eyes of her parents and the world.

Lady Abigail turned to Lady Rachel, who opened a leather-bound tome and drew out a loose leaf of paper. Lady Abigail took it gently and ceremoniously, then turned to Emme.

"Lady Emmeline Radcliffe, it is my great honor to bestow upon you this certificate of membership in the London Spinsters' Club. You have proven yourself worthy and devoted to our cause of seeing to the welfare of women of lesser means, helping impover-ished families, and contributing to the greater good of England under her Royal Majesty, Queen Victoria."

"God save the Queen!" said Lady Rachel.

"God save the Queen!" echoed the rest of the club.

"I don't understand. I didn't secure the necessary funds to join you, and by tomorrow, I won't even be living in London." Emme's voice cracked on the last word. She reached for the certificate, but stopped short of taking it in her hands.

Lady Rachel handed Lady Abigail a few more papers, and Lady Abigail held those out to Emme as well. "This, Lady Emmeline, is the deed to a property on Bond Street, and this is the summary of a trust that has been set up with you as steward, with enough funding to keep up your cooperative and the women working there for years to come."

"This makes no sense. Who would do this."

Her mind swirled with possibilities. Edward had been unable to do this for her. Perhaps her father...she shook her head. As much as some aching part of her heart wished it would be so, she knew with every fiber of her being that he had not changed his mind about her. Perhaps the duchess, although she supported multiple charities through the duke's own trust.

Even as her mind sifted through the facts, trying to make sense of what was happening, her heart knew. Edward's words, the ones said and unsaid, suddenly made sense. And her muddled mind caught up with her sure heart.

Emme took the certificate from Lady Abigail and balanced it delicately on her gloved fingertips. She surveyed the roomful of smiling faces, a room full of pious women, where dear Eleanor herself might have felt at home. How proud her sister would be that Emme had finally found her place, her own pious, purposeful place.

But it was a lie.

Emme's vision blurred and she blinked to hold back the tears. It wouldn't work. Drop after drop fell onto the certificate so that the ink smeared on the proclamation in Lady Rachel's finely-drawn hand. For all her belief in the cause, she wouldn't thrive here. She would wither and die like a garden without sun, as she'd been doing since Eleanor's death, save for her too few stolen hours with Daniel.

Daniel. This was his last gift to her, his final act of acceptance of the life she'd chosen. It was always Daniel, supporting her even when she'd refused to let him stand by her side. Daniel, believing in her innate goodness and ability to make a difference in the world, even as her father's damnation made her doubt it herself. Daniel, offering her unconditional love even if it meant abandoning his dream of marrying her to protect her secret.

She'd been afraid of the truth all along. It had made her unable to overlook his split-second hesitation, to take him at his word that he would marry her despite the danger it posed to him. And because of her fear, he was gone from her life forever.

Over her dead body. And she was pleased to assess she still had life in said body and breath in her lungs. With those came the opportunity to set things to rights.

She wiped away the last stubborn tears. "Thank you, Lady Abigail, ladies. But I can't." She handed the certificate back to Lady Abigail. "I truly hope I can use my new trust to continue to work with the club, but I can't join your organization, as I'm soon to be betrothed. *Happily* betrothed."

Several of the spinsters gasped. Lady Abigail placed her hand over her heart. Lady Rachel smiled at Emme.

Emme returned Lady Rachel's smile, then fled the room. She found Edward still on the bench where she'd left him.

He jumped to his feet when he saw her. "What's the matter?"

She grabbed his hand and pulled him with her toward the front entrance of the library. "I need your help to put my plan in motion."

He tugged her hand to stop her beside him. "Not another of your plans, Emme, please. They'll be the death of me."

"Not to worry, brother, this is a very good plan. I've come to realize I can help women in need, oversee the trust Daniel has put in my name, *and* be a happy wife."

Edward's eyes widened as her meaning dawned on him. But he didn't look happy.

"I know you've had your differences with him, Edward. But you're the one who reminded me how much he loves me. Surely you can—"

"It's not that, Emmeline. Hallsworth is leaving."

"Leaving what?"

"Leaving England," he said. "At the end of the week. He's going back to Spain."

"Spain! Wherever did he get such a ridiculous idea?"

Her brother pressed his lips together and let out a deep sigh. "He realized Lady Anastasia, and every other lady of the *ton*, would never make him happy, so he decided he couldn't stay here any longer. I might have encouraged his decision. Quite strongly."

"Oh, Edward, really. Sometimes I think I need to watch over the two of you like children." Emme focused on the next step of her new plan. She wasn't about to allow such a small problem as an exodus from the country dissuade her. "It seems we might have a bit more work to do, then. You'll have to arrange for me to see him."

"I already have."

"And you'll have to—What did you say?"

"The duchess's garden party," Edward answered. "He'll be there. He made me promise to bring you there so he can say a proper goodbye this time."

"Hm." She gave one curt nod. "It seems at least one of you is thinking like an adult, then. But we have to go now." She tugged on his hand again. "I'll need Luci's advice on my hair. Oh, and I'll need a prettier dress than this, although I probably don't have a decent thing to wear."

"No need to run." Edward took her arm and escorted her out of the library at a respectable pace. "And don't you have several perfectly lovely new dresses mother just bought you?"

"Yes, but none of them are the *right* dress. How often does a woman get proposed to, after all, by the man she loves?"

Thrice, to be exact. But the last two times she hadn't been wearing any clothes. She wouldn't mention that to her brother, though, as for the first time in weeks, he didn't seem hell-bent on pummeling the man she intended to marry.

CHAPTER 20

*E*mme rested her hand in the crook of Edward's arm as they stepped onto the veranda at the back of the duke's London house. In the wide expanse of lawn before them, there were tables nearly overflowing with finger foods and delicacies, bowls of punch, and bottles of wine, each sheltered by its own large, blue-and-white-striped umbrella. Beyond the lawn and the dozens of guests milling about among the tables, the early roses were blooming in a riotous garden bursting with pink, yellow, and red flowers. Off to each side of the lawn were copses of tall oak trees strung with faerie lights that glowed under the slightly overcast mid-afternoon sky, looking even more beautiful than they would have on a gloriously sunny day.

"Oh, the garden is lovelier than ever today, isn't it, Edward?" Emme said.

She glanced to her right, where her mother and

aunt sat on lawn chairs under the oaks with the duchess and the two society mavens who had attended the duchess's tea on the day that Daniel had announced he should like to marry a blonde. Emme smiled. Today would be the day she foiled that ridiculous plan for good. But her own plan wasn't without risk. What if she were wrong about Daniel, about what he truly wanted?

"Do you suppose the duchess ordered the clouds just so her faerie lights could sparkle that way?" she asked, trying to keep her tone light to obscure her apprehension.

"I wouldn't put it past her, Lady Emmeline," said a man from behind them.

Emme turned to see Lord Fairbank, with Luci on his arm. Luci gave Emme a quick hug. Then she stepped back and surveyed her handiwork, as she was the one who had insisted Emme wear the bright green silk with voluminous folds and layers lace over multiple petticoats.

"Oh, you look ravishing, Emme! Doesn't she look ravishing, Papa?"

Emme had thought the outfit too much when her mother had insisted they buy it, and again yesterday when Luci and Tessa had suggested she wear it for this momentous occasion, but even the normally stoic Lord Fairbank gave a slight nod and tip of his hat.

"You do look particularly lovely today, Lady Emmeline."

As the Alcotts joined them, Tessa caught both Luci

and Emme in a quick hug. "Oh, she's right, Emme. You look positively aglow!"

Luci reached behind Emme to pick up the tail of the green ribbon in Emme's hat. "I added the matching ribbon. I have quite a talent, if I do say so myself."

Tessa fluttered her fan and sighed. Luci's father frowned. But Edward grinned. And if Emme wasn't mistaken, his cheeks colored the slightest bit.

She had no more time to ponder it, as the duke joined them on the stone terrace, with Captain Granston just behind him. And there, too, was the man who, unbeknownst to himself, was about to propose to her for the third time. Daniel wore fashionable tan trousers with dark brown stripes that matched the color of his waistcoat and frock, and he looked a bit pale, which only served to make his blue eyes more striking.

The duke approached them. "Meriden, you've arrived. Good to see all my fellow reprobates here." He bowed in the direction of Emme and her friends. "Ladies, you look lovely, as always. Fairbank, good to see you."

Fairbank greeted the duke, then shook Daniel's hand. "Congratulations to the Marquess of Edensbridge."

The greetings continued all around her, but Emme was dumbstruck. She couldn't tear her gaze away from the newly restored marquess, who was able to go through all the motions of polite sociability while making her feel as though he never quite took his eyes off her.

The duke cleared his throat, breaking the spell that had kept her attention riveted on Daniel.

"Fairbank, I'd hoped to discuss something with you." The duke laid his hand over his heart. "Ladies, please forgive me. It's a political matter of some urgency. Perhaps these fine gentlemen would escort you to greet my mother."

Lord Fairbank's face darkened for a moment. "These fine gentlemen would be the reprobates you just mentioned?"

But even Lord Fairbank couldn't refuse a private audience with the duke. As they stepped away, Mr. Alcott held out his arm to his wife and Edward held out his arm to Luci. The four of ambled onto the well-manicured lawn.

Now Emme and Daniel were left alone. With Captain Granston. Who glanced between them as though he had something desperately important to tell them.

Daniel looked at his friend. "Granston, were you about to greet our hostess, as well?"

The captain sighed. "Damn it, Hallsy, why don't you just…" He shook his head and looked at Emme. "Lady Emme, can't you see…" The captain sighed again, quite dramatically.

"Is he all right?" she whispered to Daniel.

"No," the captain answered. "I'm not sure I am." He turned on his heel and followed behind the Alcotts.

Emme looked at Daniel. "What was that about?"

Daniel didn't answer for a few heartbeats, instead holding her gaze. Then he shook his head. "I can't say for sure, but I suspect it has something to do with his true nature. Granston has a secret, you see." He dropped his voice, as they always did when they shared confidences. "Deep down, underneath all that flirtatious, obnoxious bluster, he's a hopeless romantic. I think he had quite high hopes for a romance."

"I see. And you've disappointed him." She glanced at the crowd milling about on the lawn and tsked. "And nary an unmarried blonde of marriageable age to be had today. I fear you'll disappoint him yet again."

"Well, with the lawn safely free of blondes, might I interest you in a walk about the grounds? Otherwise, I'm afraid we'll make a spectacle of ourselves, standing up here alone for all the duchess's guests to see."

Emme nodded and opened her new parasol, then stepped onto the grass beside him. "Does this mean you've given up your quest to take to wife a bonny English lass with golden locks?"

He glanced at her. "It does, though that's no reflection on your efforts in the matter. I've decided that perhaps the timing is wrong, after all. Or perhaps it's just England. You know, I once considered throwing myself into the Bay of Biscay just to avoid returning. Perhaps I made a mistake in deciding against it."

"I had quite the same thought as my aunt and I waited for the wayward captain to escort us onto the

SS *Lizette*. I'm sorry to hear of your aversion to English life, though. It must be difficult."

They'd stopped by a table laden with wine and glasses. Emme shook her head at the servant who offered her some.

Daniel took a deep breath and stared out at the rose garden. "Difficult enough to lead me to a difficult decision." He turned to face her. "I'm leaving, Emme. I've retrieved my late father's title, worked morning to night getting the affairs of the estate in order, appointed executors to oversee that the improvements in my factories continue in my absence. I'm putting off the pursuit of a wife and leaving England."

"I see," she said again. She twirled her parasol and glanced sideways at him. "Off to take up with more harem girls, I suppose."

He grinned. The sight of it delighted her.

"At this point, I'm quite ruined for both blondes and harem girls. And for England. Unless..."

Her heart tripped. She hoped that meant what she hoped. "Unless?"

He shrugged but didn't answer her.

"As Lord Fairbank said, congratulations to the Marquess of Edensbridge are in order," she said. "And a thank you, as well. Don't try to deny it. I know very well who established the trust so I can continue my work. Truly, Daniel, that's the most wonderful, thoughtful thing you ever could have done for me."

"It lightens my heart to hear it. I didn't do it for the recognition, or in lieu of an apology, which is something I owe you. I should have told you I'd bought the storefront building and why." He stared down at their feet, seeming to take in the distance between them.

Emme could have told him the measure was too great.

"And I'm sorry for that moment of panic when you told me the rest of your secret," he continued. "It was ridiculous of me. It's just that I'd spent so many years with my mother's voice in my head, with—"

She touched his hand. "There's no need to explain. All I ask is that you tell me why you gave me the money to run my cooperative, if not for the recognition or by way of an apology."

He raised his eyebrows. "To see you happy, of course. And to give you what you've wanted most— your freedom. Your chance to live your life as you see fit, as a spinster."

She smiled and twirled her parasol again. "That's just as I thought. It's so kind of you. Thank you." She forced a grave look onto her face. "I must tell you, though, I've changed my mind about that. I'm not going to remain a spinster, after all."

He took a step back. "You're going to marry the vicar's son? Oh, Emme—"

She shook her head. "Never. He's a bit too… hmm…*pious* for my tastes. I prefer someone who's more of a—what was the word the duke used?—a reprobate. That was it. And not just any reprobate. I think I shall look for one with a title."

Daniel stood frozen. Just the reaction she'd hoped to see.

He finally found his voice. "A reprobate. With a title. I see. And what would one do to make himself a reprobate suitable to your cause?"

Emme rolled forward on her toes. "Oh, something disreputable, no doubt. It could be any number of things. I'm sure the reprobate—whomever he might be —will think of something." She hesitated. This was the one part of her plan that worried her. "There is always the possibility that in marrying me, the reprobate could sully the reputation he just restored."

"That would be a shame, *if* that were important to said reprobate," he said. "But if he has half a brain in his head, I trust he'll make the right choice."

The tight knot in her belly untied. She glanced past his shoulder at the small gathering of her family and friends chatting under the oak trees hung with faerie lights. It was a place where magic could happen.

"If you'll, excuse me, Lord Edensbridge, I'm being summoned by the duchess. I'm sure she wants to admire my dress."

"Yes, of course." He hardly seemed to be listening. "It is such a lovely, lovely dress. Brings out your eyes."

Emme dropped the slightest curtsey. "Thank you. And do be sure not to leave without saying goodbye one last time."

She twirled her new parasol again as she stepped past him, and wondered if she'd be able to count much past ten before he followed.

aniel took a steadying breath and silently counted to ten to stop himself from running after Emme. Had she really just told him she was prepared to marry him? Weeks after thinking his cause lost and just a day after handing her the key to her freedom, he could hardly believe it to be true.

But she wanted to marry him now, that was clear.

His spirits rallied instantly. Suddenly the endless and unendurably cloudy sky took on the glow of shining silver. He had a taste on his lips for all things English, none more than the kiss of his auburn-haired English lady. His lady, and as soon as he could manage it, his marchioness.

Throwing back his shoulders, he strode across the lawn. Though silent, his progress drew the attention of each cluster of the duchess's guests as he passed them. Let them stare. Let them all bear witness to him becoming the reprobate, the cad, the disreputable Marquess of Edensbridge the lady desired.

As he moved across the lawn, Swimmer and Fairbank started toward the duchess and her court, picking up their pace as they watched him. Fairbank looked horrified—could the man now read minds, too?—but Swimmer gave a nod of approval. Granston grinned. Even Meriden looked resigned.

Emme had her back to Daniel as she stood speaking to the duchess. He touched her shoulder and she whirled around to face him. They stood just inches apart while he paid his respects to the ladies. Even a reprobate had need of manners, after all.

"Your Grace, as always, it's an honor." He inclined his head to the gray-haired mavens and Emme's aunt. "Ladies, I bid you good afternoon." He then bowed to Emme's mother. "Countess, I beg your forgiveness."

He turned back to Emme, laid a hand on each side of her face, and kissed her as though he might never have the chance to kiss her again. Hell, if he didn't get this right, he might not. He poured his heart and hopes and pent-up longing from the weeks spent away from her into that kiss. As her lips pressed back into his, her parasol clattered to the ground and she slid her hands up his arms and grasped his shoulders.

He forgot the existence of everyone else on the planet for some amount of time, but when he ended the kiss and stepped back from Emme, the gasps from the ladies reminded him of their audience.

"Not to worry, ladies," he said without breaking Emme's gaze, "I'm going to marry this stubborn woman the minute I can lay my hands on a special license."

That drew a gasp from Fairbank and Meriden. But it drew a raucous cheer from his other old friends who were there to witness the decline of his barely-restored reputation.

"That is, if she'll have me this time." He dropped to one knee, realizing that for all the audacity of this proposal, it was by far the most respectable one he'd made so far. "Lady Emmeline Radcliffe, for the third time, will you please do me the great honor of being my love, my challenge, my wife."

She grinned at him. "Well, of course!"

He jumped to his feet and kissed her again. This time, their more modest exhibition drew applause from the crowd that had gathered around them.

"I thought you'd never ask," Emme whispered to him. "I'd counted to fifteen by the time you followed me."

"Then you counted too fast. And didn't I make it up to you by suggesting the special license?" He picked up her parasol and handed it to her.

She chastely laid her hand in the crook of his elbow, but even that caused a spark to travel up his spine. "Yes, that was a nice touch. The *ton* will be still be gossiping about it a week from now."

"Given the kiss that preceded it, I fully expect we'll still be the talk of the town when we return from our honeymoon." He sighed, but couldn't make it sound as though he were the least bit disappointed.

As they walked toward the veranda, she leaned close to him. "Once we're wed, it will be much more difficult to find ways sully our reputations."

The now reprobate marquess grinned as the fickle English sun shone through the silver clouds. He was thankful he'd abandoned his plan to plunge into the Bay of Biscay and had returned home after all.

"I'm sure we'll think of something, kitten. We always do."

20 May, in the Year of Our Lord 1870

To Daniel Hallsworth, the Marquess of Edensbridge:

At our meeting on 10 May 1870, at which time the Committee granted your petition to reinstate the Marquessate of Edensbridge, with all the rights and privileges accorded thereof, the honorable members of the Committee shared their displeasure at your purchase of a mercantile shop for women of questionable character. They impressed upon you the importance of taking more care with your reputation.

Since that time, it has come to the attention of the Committee that you have engaged in more activities unbecoming a peer, including: Engaging in lewd behavior with the daughter of the Earl of Limely in front of dozens of peers and several impressionable young ladies; procuring a special license to marry Lady Emmeline Radcliffe without a suitable courting period; and allowing union organizers to speak to the longshoremen employed by Grayhall Shipping at the Royal Victoria Dock. This is hardly the behavior the Committee for Privileges anticipated when they agreed to restore to you the title of Marquess of Edensbridge.

It is the sincere hope of the Committee that you will remember the responsibility that comes with being a peer of the realm and you will modify your future behavior accordingly.

Respectfully yours,

The Hon. Mr. Charles Alby
Clerk of the Committee for Privileges
House of Lords
London, England

P.S. Speaking for myself and expressly not for the Committee for Privileges, allow me to say it has been a pleasure watching your auspicious return from distant shores and your contributions to improving the lot of your countrymen. I congratulate you on your recent marriage and wish you and the new Marchioness of Edensbridge every happiness.

Yours,

Charles Alby

WHAT TO READ NEXT

NEXT BOOK IN SERIES: TWO SCANDALS ARE BETTER THAN ONE

Two old friends meet in London's seedy underworld...

After years of holding his crumbling family together, upstanding Lord Edward Radcliffe is desperate for one illicit adventure. The only woman in a family of men whispered to be spies, Miss Lucinda Fairbank is drawn into a dangerous world in search of her father. Edward and Luci agree to keep each other's secrets that could end in scandal while threats assail them from all sides. But the biggest threat of all might be their irresistible passion.

Read *Two Scandals Are Better Than One* today!

Nancy's News

For sample book chapters, hero introductions, and an
exclusive author Q&A, sign up for Nancy's News at
nancyyeagerbooks.com/newsletter
to receive your free copy of
Harrow's Finest Five Sneak Peeks.

TWO SCANDALS ARE BETTER THAN ONE SNEAK PEEK

CHAPTER 1

London, May 1870

*E*dward Radcliffe, Viscount Meriden, the right and proper son of the Earl of Limely, adjusted his velvet face mask and looked out over the debauched scene in front of him. From the outside, this had appeared to be a perfectly respectable house in the slightly less-than-reputable Elephant and Castle district of London. But here in the great room, half-undressed women sprawled across the laps of shirtless men on sagging sofas of indeterminate color. Heavy cigar smoke tinged with something sweeter hung in the air. The wooden floor planks were slick and sticky by turns from spilled spirits. And three different high-stakes card games were underway in this room alone.

Edward glanced at his friend Swimmer, otherwise

known as Simon Wellesley, Duke of Wrexham. Tonight, behind his own black mask, Swimmer was just another anonymous stranger to the rest of the revelers. That was the primary rule here. Neither recognize nor be recognized.

"Are you sure you wouldn't prefer a gaming hell or a reputable brothel for your one and only foray into London's seedy underbelly?" Swimmer asked quietly.

"It's just this once, as you said. No point doing it in half measures." Edward pulled out his silver flask, having taken seriously Swimmer's warning about the swill served at such house parties, took a long draw of cognac, and tucked the flagon back in his breast pocket.

"Ah, gentlemen!" A short, paunchy man stripped to his waistcoat approached them. He wore a bright red mask with one white feather attached at the left side. It identified him as one of the event's hosts. "Crisp shirts. Straight spines." The man grinned. "You must be new arrivals."

Swimmer nodded.

"Do allow me to give you a brief tour."

Edward prepared to follow the man, but the host stood his ground and opened his arms wide. "As you can see, this is our main hall, a common area, if you will. If you need more privacy at some point in the night, there are unoccupied rooms on this level. Your entrance fee entitles you to full run of the ground floor." He inclined his head toward a laughing red-head whose dressed had just slipped down to expose a very round, very creamy breast. "And access to any of the ladies here. Peccadillos to be negotiated according to your needs, of course, but no haggling." He winked. "These are whores of the first water. Worth every shilling."

Edward blinked quickly, truly out of his element but doing his best to look unfazed. He wished he'd kept his flask in hand.

"The most entertaining pursuits can be found upstairs. There's an additional charge for access. Opium rooms are in the back. Group rooms are in the front."

Edward looked at the man. "Group rooms?"

The host grinned, making him quite resemble a jackal. "He's green as grass, isn't he?" he asked Swimmer.

Swimmer sighed. "The rooms where groups gather for orgies."

No amount of fast blinking could stave off the heat that gathered at the base of Edward's throat and spread up his face.

Swimmer, ever a friend, angled himself slightly in front of Edward to block the host's direct view of a grown man blushing. "I think we'll ease into things, stay down here for now."

The man gave a slight bow, and Swimmer stiffened, causing Edward to do the same. But if the man had recognized him as the Duke, he covered it well. *Neither recognize nor be recognized.*

"Just a few more rules while you're here," their host

continued. "Do not start any brawls. Do not get caught cheating at cards. And do not lay a finger on any of the *ladies* wearing masks." He winked from behind his own mask. "Unless you have their permission, of course. They've paid their own entrance fee to pursue their own amusements, not to entertain yours." He followed the line of Edward's gaze, which kept returning to the maskless, bare-breasted red head. "Good choice. Wendy gets invited to every party. She's one of our most accommodating girls."

Swimmer patted the man's shoulder none too gently. "I think we can take it from here."

"All right. You lads enjoy yourselves, then." The host inclined his head toward the ceiling. "And if you change your minds later, just find any one of us with a red mask and we'll give you the *grand* tour."

With a parting leer, the man turned on his heel and disappeared into another room. Edward was glad to see him go, although now he might need a long soak in a hot bath to feel cleansed of the illustrious host. He bent his head from side to side to stretch his neck and realign his thoughts. Steady Eddie, as his Harrow friends had dubbed him, would need a hot bath after such an encounter. But tonight, anonymous Edward would bathe in depravity, and he would relish it.

"Shall we start with a game of cards, then?" he asked Swimmer.

His friend nodded. "But first…"

Edward followed his friend to the bar that was lined up against the back wall. There was no bartender, just rows and rows of bottles, each more questionable than the last. Swimmer propped his arms against the scarred mahogany, and Edward did the same. Swimmer fished something out of his pocket and held it out to Edward. It was a stack of cards—aces and kings.

Edward didn't take them. "The man said no cheating at cards."

"The man said don't get *caught* cheating at cards." Swimmer pushed the stack closer to Edward. "The stakes are high enough, so don't be drawn into some kind of drunk pissing contest where you gamble away the country estate or some such nonsense. Don't scowl. It's happened, as you know very well."

That sent a shiver down Steady Eddie's spine. Their most raucous schoolmate, now Captain Lord Granston, but just Percy to the five friends, had left Harrow at age 16, the year he'd lost his father, gained his title, and inherited a pile of family debt. It hadn't happened in a gaming hell, even one of the more disreputable ones. It had happened at a gentleman's house party like this one.

"I'll be damned. I hadn't thought of that. Fine, then." Edward took the cards. He slid the kings up his left sleeve and the aces up his right.

They turned around to face the room again. The drunk men on the sofa were laughing louder, and the women with them were wearing fewer clothes. Those at the card tables spent as much time watching the amorous displays happening on the edges of the room as they did watching their own cards and each other.

Edward saw two different men at two different tables swap out cards from their own sleeves.

"If I play while I'm still sober, I might win a small fortune," he said.

"If you stay sober too long, they'll call you out for cheating on that alone," Swimmer countered. "Look, two seats are open at the far table. I'll join you for one hand."

Edward cocked an eyebrow. "Oh? Big plans after that?"

"Oh, yes." Swimmer scowled. "I'm headed home. The Duchess will be waiting up."

Edward stifled a laugh, as his friend seemed anything but amused to have his mother staying with him. Again. "I thought she'd just moved back to her own house, now that every inch of it has repainted and repapered."

"She had." Swimmer pulled out his flask and took a large swig. "Now she claims the workers were careless and let in mice. She saw two different mice last week. As if one could tell mice apart! She's staying with me until the servants can get the situation sorted."

Now Edward did laugh. "Your mother never struck me as the type to be afraid of a mouse, or even two."

"Nor I, seeing as my brother and I spent a disproportionate amount of our early years slipping all manner of furry, scaly, and slimy creatures into her housecoat pockets, and never elicited so much as a squeak out of her."

"It's a sad day when our aging parents develop new fears," Edward said.

They both knew he was lying. Swimmer's mother, the duchess, was relatively young, quite beautiful, and still unquestionably fearless. Which meant that she, like everyone else who cared deeply for Swimmer, was still worried about his state of mind, even if he had significantly cut back on drink. He'd lost his father a year and a half ago to a swift and brutal bout of pneumonia, and his own duchess a few short months later to a tragedy. Come to think of it, a debauched house party on the edge of town was probably the last place the still grieving duke should be.

"If you don't mind me saying, old man, you're bound to be recognized as Your Grace any minute now."

Swimmer took another swig and tucked his flask back into his pocket. "Probably already have been, judging from our hosts' sidelong glances." His voice held no hint of fear, or even concern. Such was the luxury of a man born to such a high rank and to parents with reasonable expectations.

"Still, it will be impossible for me to wallow with the other riffraff if they recognize my companion and start bowing and scraping all over the damn place," Edward said.

A hint of a grin lifted the corners of Swimmers lips. "Fine. They'll kick you out at dawn and load you onto one of the hired hackneys with any number of your new friends. My man Hareford will be waiting for you at the drop-off point half a mile down the road. If you don't spot him, he'll know to look for you among the pile of unconscious revelers."

Swimmer took one last look around the room, at the games and drinks and available women. "Sad, really, to pay ten pounds and stay less than an hour." He quaffed Edward on the back. "You'll have to get both our money's worth."

Edward grinned and slapped his shoulder. "I'll consider it my personal mission tonight."

Swimmer turned to go, then paused. "Really, Eddie, do be careful. More than half these easy-going drunks are armed."

He nodded and mumbled assurances to ease Swimmer's mind, but as his friend left, Edward's eye was drawn to the opposite side of the room. A wave of energy rippled through the air and caught several of the men and the handful of hired women in its wake. There in the archway, framed by the gas lanterns in front of her and the flicker of candles in sconces from the hall behind her, stood the most glorious creature Edward had ever seen.

The lady—for her bearing screamed lady, making her appearance so unexpected and mesmerizing in this foul place—took the measure of the room and each of its occupants. Her gaze finally rested on him, lingering a bit longer than on anyone else, or so he liked to think. From half a room away, he couldn't see the color of her eyes, but the weight of her scrutiny pinned him to his spot.

He returned the impolite stare, taking in her long black hair pulled away from her face and tumbling in waves down her back. While the butterfly-shaped black mask embedded with jewels hid most of her face, the alabaster skin of her chin and throat and décolleté was spectacularly displayed above the tight-bodiced, full-skirted black gown she wore. And the curves shown by that gown made him temporarily forget where he was, why he was there, and perhaps even his own name. *This woman*, something inside him growled, *this woman is what I want*. Not one night of drink and cards and whores, but night after night with the mysterious beauty whose very existence sent dangerous excitement thrumming through his veins.

She was on the tall side for a woman, and she moved with the grace of a cat. A silky black cat who would purr in his lap. Her glide across the room stirred a hint of familiarity. It was as if he'd known her all his life, or perhaps he'd just been fated all his life to meet her. She moved in his direction, although no longer looking at him, focused instead on one of the two empty seats at the nearby card table. He moved in tandem with her, getting there seconds before her, just in time to pull out the chair for his heart-stopping mystery woman.

Edward could hardly believe his luck as he slid into the seat beside her. Everything he'd dreamed of each time he'd pined for an escape from his dull, prescribed life was personified in the mysterious woman sitting next to him.

◈

*M*iss Lucinda Wagner could not believe her ill luck. Lord Edward Radcliffe was here, at the most notorious house party in all of England. Fine, pious Edward, whose propriety was only outshone by that of his pompous father. Her best friend Emme's father. A father who had disowned his only daughter. And now his son sat at a card table in a place of such ill repute, the Radcliffe name would never recover from the scandal should it get out.

But of course it wouldn't get out. Most of the men here were peers. All of them were wealthy. And as long as they protected each other, all of them were safe. Except, perhaps, Luci's father, if he was to be found here after all.

Two days ago, with her father already three days overdue from his trip, she'd broken into his office in search of an explanation. In his desk, she'd found the address of the house party she was now attending, as well as a name written in her father's steady hand. With one of her brothers off somewhere in the north of England and the other on yet another trip to France, she'd been home alone with servants, the only other witnesses to her ever-punctual father's delay. No letter. No note. No words to explain it. Which left it to Luci to devise a way to find him.

This was so like her, to be found out, to spoil a secret and ruin a plan. And there'd never been a more important one. This was possibly life or death, *her father's* life or death, and she was about to fail him. The shame of her own incompetence burned in her belly.

"Well, well, well." The large man directly across from her leaned forward and propped his elbows on the table.

At least her reason for being here seemed unaware of her intentions. With his height, girth, and tell-tale green waistcoat, the large man across the table from her wasn't anonymous to her. It was Sly Hombrage, real name unknown. But it was that fake name that she'd found in her father's study. If Hombrage knew she meant to get him drunk—or drunker, as would be the case—and question him, he'd have her thrown out on her ear. Or more likely, would do it himself.

"What do we have here?" The man's Cockney accent was faint, nearly undetectable. But his slurred words belied just how much he'd had to drink, and the drink was returning him to his roots. The man glanced at Edward. "You two together, then?"

"No, sir." Even here, Edwards impeccable manners and unerring speech remained with him. "Much to my chagrin."

His boldness shocked Luci and she glanced at him to find him staring back at her. This was new. This was nothing like Steady Eddie, whom she'd known since childhood and had even fawned over in her adolescence, before she'd realized what a stick-in-the-mud he truly was. Now she observed him carefully. Not only did his stare reveal rudeness; it conveyed true naiveté, as if he didn't recognize her. Perhaps her luck wasn't as bad as she'd feared. Perhaps she hadn't ruined everything after all.

Hombrage slammed his hand on the table, disrupting her thoughts and making her and the other three men at the table jump. "You in, or you going to find your own whore?" He addressed a man who'd been so distracted by the amorous couple on a nearby sofa, he now seemed surprised to see Luci at the table.

"I uh...I'm headed upstairs." The man slid back his chair and stalked out of the room.

Luci did her level best not to blush. The wealthy, wicked widow she was playing would not be abashed by thoughts of what was going on in the rooms upstairs, the details of which had been described to her by the host whose sharp-toothed grin had made her think of a cornered fox.

Hombrage elbowed the man beside him, who had recovered from the earlier table pounding and slipped right back into slumber. The man snorted and snored in reply. Hombrage scowled. "Too much time in the opium room. Looks like it's just the three of us. We'll keep the stakes low for now. Two-pound buy in. Lady's choice of game."

Yes, good luck was with her. It smiled on her again when one of the hosts stopped at the table and offered her a drink. She declined, but Hombrage nodded, and the host handed the already drunk man an oversize portion of what smelled, even from a distance, like whisky.

"Five-card draw," she said. She silently blessed

Captain Granston for teaching her the newfangled American card game. She'd had an inkling that card gamesmanship would be a useful skill to learn, but no idea how soon or how desperately she'd need to use her newfound abilities.

"I'm in," Edward said beside her. He no longer openly stared at her, but he did glance at her frequently.

They each placed their buy-in chips on the table. She'd had to use far more of the emergency cash her father kept in the house to gain entrée to this party and purchase a reasonable amount of poker chips than she'd hoped, but he'd forgive her extravagance if she rescued him. *When* she rescued him.

The game went smoothly and Luci won, but it ended too quickly. Hombrage had gulped down the entire whisky by the end of it. Still, Luci worried over how many more hands and drinks it would take to make him loquacious. With the new twist of Edward's presence, she didn't know how she'd get Hombrage alone when it was time. And even when she did get the opportunity, she could hardly cut straight to the chase. She'd have to make her questions seem like a natural outgrowth of conversation. Meaning she had to lay the groundwork here in front of Edward.

"Tell me, Mr...uh...sir, what line of business are you in?" She batted her lashes as she said it.

"Tsk, tsk. No questions about life outside these walls, Missy. House rules." Hombrage dealt out the next hand.

"I apologize. I was merely trying to make conversation." Luci glanced at Edward, who'd gone rigid beside her.

After a few more hands, none of them won by Hombrage, the thoroughly slurring man came up with the solution of privacy for her. "How about the lady and me play one hand, just the two of us, hmm?"

"That hardly seems sporting." Edward's words were light, but his tone cut with an edge of steel.

Hombrage gave Edward a hard look. "Stakes'll be too high for you."

Edward held the man's gaze and leaned forward. "I doubt it."

Luci got a small thrill from seeing him take such a brave, albeit foolish stand.

"Think again." Hombrage grinned. "If the lady wins, I'll tell her anything she wants to know about my business."

Luci's mouth went dry. It was too much to hope for. Too good to be true.

"And if you win?" she asked.

"You show me everything I want to know about what's under your dress."

Edward flattened his palms on the table. "No touching a masked lady." His voice a low growl, and Luci wondered anew whether he'd recognized her as his sister's friend after all and thought her in need of protection.

Hombrage locked eyes with Edward. "No touching a masked lady *without her permission*. Agreeing to the bet would be granting permission." Hombrage turned his head slowly to look at her.

Channeling the wealthy, wicked widow, whom she now hurriedly named Madam X, Luci gave him a fake smile. "I'm afraid those stakes hardly sound even, sir."

Hombrage raised an eyebrow. "That's because you still haven't heard about my business." He sighed and reached into his pocket. "But to sweeten the pot," he dropped an exquisitely detailed, gem-studded gold pocket watch onto the table, "I'll up the ante. That's worth three times what the best whore here'll take home with her in the morning, after fucking god knows how many men in god knows how many ways tonight."

His assessment was probably true, but it sickened and humiliated Luci, not only for the women working here tonight so they could feed themselves and their children this week, but also for herself, having just been reduced to something to be weighed against a hunk of metal and stone.

She swallowed the bile that threatened to gag her. Taking offense would get her nowhere, and Hombrage had just put in reach the one thing she'd come here to get. Even if she lost the hand, she'd have him alone and drunk and could press him for answers. In fact, perhaps she'd be better positioned if she lost the hand. She'd need to get away from Edward to ask Hombrage very pointed questions without rousing Edward's suspicions about her father's disappearance. Luci was absolutely forbidden from discussing the family's business with anyone, despite not actually knowing what that business was. She couldn't risk Edward learning the reason she'd come here.

"Well?" Hombrage pressed.

"Yes." It only came out as a whisper. She cleared her throat. "Yes, I'm in."

"Then so am I." Edward reached into his waistcoat and pulled out a silver flask, encrusted on one side with small diamonds in the shape of an E.

Luci gasped. She recognized that flask. It had been a gift for Edward's twentieth birthday, from his and Emme's sister, who had died three years after giving him that gift.

"It's worth more than the pocket watch, I assure you."

Luci nodded her agreement. It hardly mattered. She intended to lose this hand and Hombrage intended to win it, no doubt nefariously if it came to that. She couldn't play the complete fool, though, or he might suspect her ulterior motive.

"Deal the cards, then, sir," she told Hombrage. "And do me the courtesy of keeping your hands in plain sight at all times."

He laughed as he dealt, then they all picked up their cards. Luci held up three fingers and laid down three cards. Hombrage slid three replacement cards in her direction. Edward took two cards and Hombrage took one, then called the hand.

Luci's hand shook as she laid down her hand, a pair

of sevens over a pair of fours, along with a worthless two of hearts.

"The lady has two pairs, sevens high." Hombrage turned to Edward. "Young man?"

Edward flipped over his cards. "A full house, aces high."

Hombrage threw down his cards, a mixed-suit flush. A vein in his neck bulged and his face reddened. "Cheater," he mumbled at Edward.

For his part, Edward had gone pale and was taking deep breaths. "For a minute, I was worried I'd lost," he whispered so only Luci heard it.

Hombrage jumped to his feet and tossed the undealt deck in Edward's face. "On your feet, you scrawny bastard. We're taking this outside."

Four red-masked hosts surrounded Hombrage. "Sir, some of the guests are becoming...agitated," one of them said.

Hombrage pointed at Edward. "He cheated."

Edward held up his hands in front of him. "I won the hand. I did not cheat."

All four hosts turned to look at Luci. She could say it was a misunderstanding and that she thought Hombrage had probably won, after all. That would get her alone with him. But it might also get Edward taken outside and beaten, if not worse. She thought of the words told to her by Miss Temple, the former prostitute who'd provided Luci with most of her information about this house party: *The hosts take card cheating very seriously. And they all carry guns.*

Luci nodded her head toward Hombrage. "I'm afraid he's mistaken. No one cheated. This gentleman simply won the hand." She smiled at Edward. "And now if you'll excuse us."

She stood and sidled away from the table, toward the back hallway that led to the private rooms, each with its own bed and a choice of body oils, as the cornered fox had gleefully told her. Edward stayed a mere foot behind her the entire way.

When they reached the hallway, he angled in front of her and found the first room with an open door. He peered inside to make sure it was empty and not merely occupied by exhibitionists before waving Luci inside. He closed and locked the door behind them. They both breathed a sigh of relief.

With a smile, Luci prepared herself for his questions. *What are you doing here, Miss Luci? Where's your father? Where are your brothers? Do you know what my sister will do when she finds out I met you at a den of iniquities and didn't immediately drag you out of it?*

But Edward wasn't asking. He wasn't speaking at all. He was staring at her again, as he'd done when they'd spotted each other across the room, like he'd done again when he'd sat down beside her. He had the look of a man who'd just woken from the most pleasant dream, but was still half in it. And for the life of her, she swore he hadn't recognized her, that he still didn't recognize her.

He slowly looked her up and down, his gaze lingering over every exposed inch of skin—and there were more than was decent—and every curve exhibited by the expertly fitted costume that had been sewn by Mrs. Billings, Miss Temple's neighbor. "Do you have any idea how beautiful you are?" His look was feral and possessive, but his voice was silky smooth and calming.

She'd known this man since she'd been five and he'd been Emme's protective ten-year-old brother. When she'd been twelve, she'd said more prayers than she cared to admit that her best friend's seventeen-year-old brother would be moved to kiss her, knowing a young man of such integrity never would. She'd rolled her eyes when she'd been seventeen herself and learned he'd taken a lovely but boring widow as his mistress, something she'd never have known if it hadn't been for Captain Granston's love of gossip, because Edward himself was the epitome of discretion. But in fifteen years of knowing him, he'd never aroused such a shock of awareness in her.

The man looking at her right now, the man who'd come to this depraved party for a purpose she couldn't fathom, had no thought for protection or integrity or discretion. The man ravishing her with his gaze still didn't realize who she was.

"I'm sorry for what that horrible man said to you. And I have no expectation..." He shook his head. "That's not true. Perhaps I did have an expectation, or at least a hope."

He stepped close to her and slowly raised his hand toward her face, stopping just inches from touching her. Luci didn't know whether her heart pounded most from the worry he might pull off her mask, the hope he might kiss her, or the fear he wouldn't.

"I won't touch you if you don't wish it."

She shouldn't be in this house. It had been foolish to come looking for Hombrage, as her father and brothers would tell her if they were here, but they weren't. Their absence was at the root of all of this. But Edward had kept her safe. Whomever he was trying to be right now, whatever role he was playing, for reasons she didn't understand, Steady Eddie was still at the center of this man. He was a good man. A fierce protector. And whether it was fear, adrenaline, or sheer attraction, she desperately wanted him to kiss her.

"The lady gives her permission for a kiss. Just a kiss."

He brushed his fingertips along her jawline. "It's more than I could have hoped for when this evening started." He bent his head toward hers.

She'd been kissed before, exactly twice, by two different suitors. One had been a long, wet kiss on the cheek. The other had been a quick, dry peck on the lips. As Edward's mouth brushed softly against hers, then lingered and pressed more firmly, she knew she'd never really been kissed until now. And when his tongue flicked against her lips and teased them open, she wasn't sure what she did and didn't know anymore. She vaguely remembered that something about this was wrong, or so she'd been told. But everything about it felt right.

Luci laid her hands against the smooth material of

his evening jacket, meaning to gently put space between them. Instead, she slid her hands higher until she grasped his shoulders. He cupped her jaw in one hand and slid his arm around her waist, pressing his other hand into the small of her back. Instinctively, she arched toward him, and every nerve ending in her body sparked to life.

When he ended the kiss, they breathlessly clung to each other. He slid his hand up her face, running one finger under her mask. This was it. He would reveal her. And she would allow it. She would show him her face, confess her mission. After that life-altering kiss, she would tell him everything.

"They're in one of the rooms!" It was Hombrage, out in the hallway, muffled, still a bit of a distance away, but not for long. "And when we find them, you're going to let *me* shoot that cheating bastard."

Luci pulled away from Edward and grabbed his hand. "We have to get out of here before they kill us both!"

Read the rest of *Two Scandals Are Better Than One* today!

ACKNOWLEDGMENTS

Thank you for spending time with Daniel and Emme, the reunited lovers in *One Kiss from Ruin*. A writer only begins a story. A reader completes it by bringing her unique perspective to it, so thank you for helping me complete this book.

Special thanks to my many writing tribes, including my real-life besties, the Eight Ladies Writing, and my Author Accelerator family. You each teach me new things about story, the writing life, and life beyond writing (yes, there is such a thing!) every day. I am forever in your debt. And once again, thank you to my editors, Mary Theresa Hussey and Justine Covington.

And as always, all my love and gratitude to my wonderful family. You make it all worthwhile.

ABOUT THE AUTHOR

Nancy spent her early years longing to be an English countryside vet thanks to James Herriot's All Creatures Great and Small series, and dreaming of being an adventurist archaeologist like George Lucas's Indiana Jones character. After studying veterinary pre-med and earning an anthropology degree, she realized her true passion is story in all its forms.

When Nancy's not writing, reading, or binge-watching story, she's often pursuing a physical challenge like studying Krav Maga or aspiring to achieve the perfect crow pose. She also spends her time drinking too much coffee, not enough red wine, and just the right amount of Bourbon. She lives in Maryland with her fabulous family, which includes some very spoiled rescue cats.

To learn more about Nancy, the Harrow's Finest Five series, and other upcoming books, stop by her website at nancyyeagerbooks.com.